Crackpots

Ruby Reese's Family Tree

Evans

(m.1864)
Marietta Anna Jones (Maryann) Ø Thomas Asa Evans, Jr. (Asa)
(1845–1932)   (1840–1881)

— Isadora (Aunt Dorrie)
   (1865–1957)

— Thomas Ansel (Ansel)
   (1867–1871)

— Asa Owen
   (1870–1871)

                         (m.1894)   (m.1902)
— Isabella Anna (Aunt Izzy) Ø Harlan Söderberg Ø William Wise
   (1871–1959)   (1860–1898)   (1842–1903)
                       └ Nelson Harley (1896–1903)

— Francis Fielding (Frank)
   (1874–1890)

The Dogs

Tom Thumb (Edgar Albert & Eleanor Opal's
white terrier, circa 1900)

Go-Jeff (Reese family wire-haired terrier, ?–1957)

Flo (Tony Fellini's cocker spaniel, circa 1950s)

Tippy (Mr. Kepler's toy poodle, circa 1950s)

Roo (Ruby's first black Lab, ?–1973)

Shorty-Long (Gladys Tupper's dachshund, circa 1975–?)

Phineas T. Gooddog ("Phinny")
(Ruby's second black Lab, 1975–1990)

Igor (Moster Fritjof's bulldog, circa 1990)

Walter Cronkite (1992–, Ruby's third black Lab)

Bonnard (Walter Cronkite's brother, Ruby's friend
Bobbie's dog, 1992–)

Benny Goodman
(Aunt Frannie Linn's parrot)
(circa 1940–1984)

The Birds

The Cats

Sassafras   Princess   Archimedes
(Ruby and Eva's cat)   (Miles's cat)   (Ruby's cat)
(?–1967)   (circa 1970s)   (1981–2001)

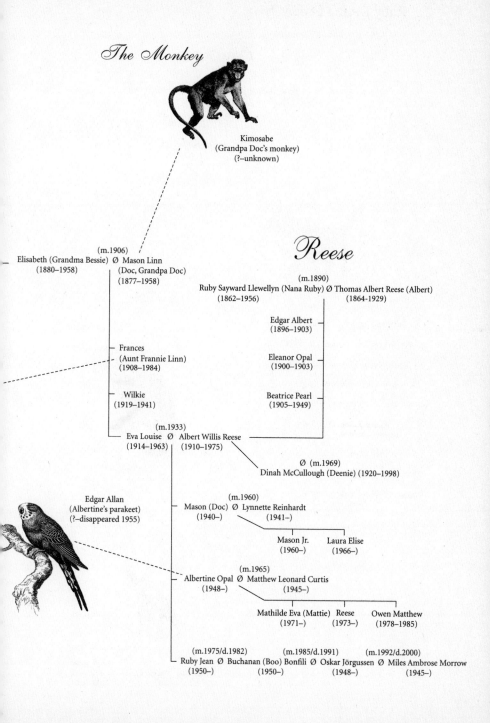

The Monkey

Kimosabe
(Grandpa Doc's monkey)
(?–unknown)

Reese

Elisabeth (Grandma Bessie) Ø Mason Linn
(1880–1958)

(m.1906)

(Doc, Grandpa Doc)
(1877–1958)

(m.1890)
Ruby Sayward Llewellyn (Nana Ruby) Ø Thomas Albert Reese (Albert)
(1862–1956)   (1864-1929)

Edgar Albert
(1896–1903)

Frances
(Aunt Frannie Linn)
(1908–1984)

Eleanor Opal
(1900–1903)

Wilkie
(1919–1941)

Beatrice Pearl
(1905–1949)

(m.1933)
Eva Louise Ø Albert Willis Reese
(1914–1963)   (1910–1975)

Ø (m.1969)
Dinah McCullough (Deenie) (1920–1998)

Edgar Allan
(Albertine's parakeet)
(?–disappeared 1955)

(m.1960)
Mason (Doc) Ø Lynnette Reinhardt
(1940–)   (1941–)

Mason Jr.   Laura Elise
(1960–)   (1966–)

(m.1965)
Albertine Opal Ø Matthew Leonard Curtis
(1948–)   (1945–)

Mathilde Eva (Mattie)   Reese   Owen Matthew
(1971–)   (1973–)   (1978–1985)

(m.1975/d.1982)   (m.1985/d.1991)   (m.1992/d.2000)
Ruby Jean Ø Buchanan (Boo) Bonfili Ø Oskar Jörgussen Ø Miles Ambrose Morrow
(1950–)   (1950–)   (1948–)   (1945–)

Crackpots

Sara Pritchard

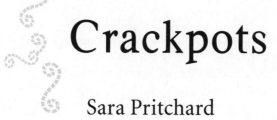

A MARINER ORIGINAL

Houghton Mifflin Company

Boston · New York ·

For information about permission to reproduce selections from this book, write to Permissions, Houghton Mifflin Company, 215 Park Avenue South, New York, New York 10003.

Visit our Web site: www.houghtonmifflinbooks.com.

Library of Congress Cataloging-in-Publication Data
Pritchard, Sara.
 Crackpots / Sara Pritchard.
 p. cm.
 "A Mariner original."
 ISBN 0-618-30245-X
 1. Women — Fiction. 2. Divorced women — Fiction. 3. Re-
married people — Fiction. 4. Pennsylvania — Fiction. 5. Outer
Banks (N.C.) — Fiction. I. Title.
 PS3616.R575C73 2003
 813'.6 — dc21 2003047898

Some parts of this book have been published under the pseudo-nym Delta B. Horne and in slightly different form in the following journals: *Antietam Review:* "Shuffle Off to Buffalo"; *Bellingham Review:* "Postcards from Portland"; *Chattahoochee Review:* "The Blue Hat" (under the title "The Shape of Things to Come"); *Louisville Review:* "Isotopes"; and *Northwest Review:* "Statues." "Stardust" was published as "The Piano" under the name Sara Pritchard in *Mid-American Review.* Permissions appear on page 189.

Crackpots is a work of fiction. Places, events, and characters in *Crackpots* should not be confused with real-life places, incidents, people, or animals, especially dogs.

Design by Melissa Lotfy

Printed in the United States of America

QUM 10 9 8 7 6 5 4 3

For Kevin, Janie, and Worty

and in remembrance of
Mary Jane Kehler Pritchard
Roland W. Pritchard
David Evan Moore

Anything can happen. Anything is possible.
Time and space do not exist. On a flimsy ground of reality,
Imagination spins out and weaves its own pattern.

—AUGUST STRINDBERG, *A Dream Play*

FOREWORD

I feel honored to introduce this passionate and absorbing novel to you. From the beginning of *Crackpots,* I was drawn into Sara Pritchard's lyrical prose, her stunning vision. And I began to learn from her when she showed me the face of a woman in a way I'd never seen a face before: "Covering her face are thousands of tiny scars, no bigger than eyelashes, and whiter still. They give her face a kind of woven look, a thread count."

Sara Pritchard has a gift for creating complex and believable characters. By choosing pivotal moments in their lives that are masked as normal but are actually odd, she takes us right up against the edge and challenges us to contemplate our own oddness.

With wisdom and wit, she pulls us into the lives of her characters so deeply that we identify with them. She juxtaposes vivid scenes that shift and rub against each other, collide, and in doing so create dramatic tension.

Her treatment of time is sophisticated. Not tied to conventional restrictions of time, *Crackpots* moves freely through layers of time, seeking out the emotional connections between the characters' present, past, and future. One of these connections spans more than a century in just a few words. In 2002, Ruby remembers kissing her Nana Ruby, who arrived on Ellis Island in 1865. "And then to think, whose cheek had Nana Ruby perhaps kissed? and where had that person been? and what had he or she seen? . . . all this succession and passing . . . this turning, bending, kissing . . . down through time."

I believe that as soon as we commit something to memory it becomes distorted. Each time we encounter that memory, it will be different, depending on where we are with our emotions and thoughts at that moment in our lives. "Memory is an odd fellow," Sara Pritchard tells us in the first line of *Crackpots,* inviting us to consider the story behind the story, the many angles from which each moment can be seen and revisited—not just what happened in that particular moment, but also what could have happened. As with Etienne, who once loved Ruby, and whose letter she reads every day, "with the same regularity as a nun saying her prayers: without fail. Night after night, year after year, after all the blue lines had faded, and the penciled words, too, were gone, and there was nothing at all left except two tiny incisions forming a cross in the centerfold where the letter had been folded and unfolded thousands of times."

This weave of memory, reality, and imagination is absolutely fascinating. Funny, at times. A cat follows Ruby home from school. It's true. Well, almost true. Depending on our definition of what the word "follow" can mean. "With very little coaxing and carrying, and only minor scratches, a big orange cat follows you . . . home from school." There's an entire story in that sentence, not just about the cat and about the scratches, but also about Ruby's way of seeing, of balancing herself on that intricate border between inner and outer reality. She has an imaginary friend, Blinker, who lives out her mischievous side and "comes up with the concept of butter writing," which "progresses to Crisco writing and escalates to Crisco erasing."

Sara Pritchard dares to be serious and irreverent all at once. She tells Ruby's story from different perspectives, going from second person to third person, first person to an omniscient voice:

"It's dawn, and the water dream, the dream of drowning, has had its little say in the dream of the dog, but the water dream isn't satisfied, and so it walks over to the man who is sleeping next to the empty space in the bed, the space still warm with the troubled dreams of the woman sitting under the table with the dog."

In her retakes of previous scenes, Sara Pritchard mirrors experiences, tilting the mirror in such a way that it reflects something new and revises our perceptions. She has a unique understanding of love that's revisited, of the inevitable discrepancy between the experience of love and the memory of that love as it recasts itself in different shapes.

She takes the ordinary and makes it totally unique. I found myself shifting to her way of seeing, expecting it from her. And yet, again and again, I felt surprised, stunned. I touched hands that were "hard and cold like Lawn Jesus." Saw radiators that looked "like dirty sheep grazing underneath the windows."

URSULA HEGI
Bakeless fiction judge, 2002

Crackpots

Prologue

Memory is an odd fellow. Say you are retelling a story you have told many times before, the story about how your grandparents met in 1902. Say your grandfather, Mason Linn, was a train conductor who played the trombone and dreamed of being in vaudeville, and your grandmother, a young woman who played the violin, a young woman named Bess, with heavy dark hair, rode the train every day from Downingtown to downtown Philadelphia, where she worked as a salesgirl in Ladies' Hats in Wannamaker's department store.

Say this time, though, while you're telling this familiar story about your grandparents' courtship, Imagination clears her throat and pipes in with something about a hat, a truly magnificent hat that this young woman who will become your grandmother is wearing on the train to Philadelphia—a big, black, fur-felted hat with velvet trim, a small paper bird, and a pink ostrich plume—a hat far too magnificent for Bess's worsted coat.

And as the story moves forward, Memory relaxes, takes a seat by the window, orders a double Dewar's straight up and stares, mesmerized, at his double-exposure reflection in the passing landscape. Meanwhile, his traveling companion, Imagination, takes up the story about your grandparents and weaves it into something so *other*, and in the end—according to Imagination —the woman in the beautiful hat dies in the diphtheria epidemic of 1903, single and childless, and the train conductor— who has, of course, fallen in love with her—becomes a professional musician, playing in P.T. Barnum's circus band and, eventually, with Tommy and Jimmy Dorsey.

Say he—Mason Linn—this Hungarian man whom everyone calls Doc, this man who may have been your grandfather, never marries. Time passes and he joins the army and fights in the Great War overseas. He returns home, grows old, chews Mail Pouch tobacco, spits in a can, and lives in a damp combination basement/garage, drinking Mogen David wine, sleeping in the back seat of a 1939 Plymouth sedan, and, in the evenings, sitting in a lumpy mohair chair the color of an old teddy bear. And in his ribbed, sleeveless T-shirt and baggy trousers, with his ear against the huge illuminated dial of a Motorola radio, days and years roll by, and his hair and mustache turn snowy white.

Now it's 1950, and Mason Linn no longer has the breath to play his silver-plated trombone. To get by, he's working as an organ grinder—with a little monkey in a red jacket, a monkey named Kimosabe—in front of Wannamaker's department store, and one day a young, beautiful woman with heavy dark hair walks through the revolving doors, and from where the old organ grinder is playing under the flapping maroon awning, he sees the woman reflected, spinning in the glass wedges of the revolving door, and for a moment his heart does a fantastic leap and he is young again, punching tickets on a Chessie train to Philadelphia and whistling Scott Joplin, and a beautiful woman in a large black hat with a fluttering ostrich plume, a woman carrying a violin case, is walking toward him in slow motion, and the train is rumbling and rocking, and the flat ginger-brown fields of Chester County, powdered with a confection of snow, are flicking by like postcards framed in the train windows, like celluloid pictures in a View-Master disc, and all of this is, in some respects, quite preposterous, in other respects, true.

Sisters: A Dog Story

1951 — I did not come here kicking and screaming like Albertine. I did not resist. I counted the days carefully on my fingers and toes and then left quickly, arriving easily and a tad bit early, entirely of my own volition. Feet first, I made my entrance, like someone arriving at a party on a luge. There were minor complications, but they were quickly taken care of. Everything went smoothly. And then I slept a long time, sucking heartily on my thumb.

Albertine, she came here two years earlier, but late. They yanked her out with forceps, and as they pulled, her soft head stretched like Silly Putty. They showed her to our mother, and she screamed. That was why I chose the feet-first entry — an invention all my own — to prevent that terrible screaming.

I don't recall any of this, of course. What I do recall is the kitchen. Its dark blue sea of linoleum. Our mother in her print apron with the red rickrack. The big white stove. Its blue flames and silver knobs. Albertine in her high chair and I in mine. Her white, hard shoes and shiny oatmeal bowl. Our father in his undershirt and braces, singing,

> *So take care! Beware!*
> *Of the green-eyed dragon with the thirteen tails!*

He feeds! with greed!
On little girls, puppy dogs, and
BIG FAT SNAILS!

The quick little terrier, Go-Jeff, his tiny pink tongue and stinky doggie breath, looking up at us from in between our chairs. His coal-lump nose, pointed ears, their tufts of wiry hair! The sunny-side-up egg leaving my plate, sailing to the floor. Go-Jeff's scrambled-lightning reflex. Albertine leaning over her tray and I over mine. The toppled milk, the spinning bowl, the flying cornmeal mush, Albertine's curly hair, the great commotion, our glee! Our Grandma Bessie tapping on her cup with a silver spoon, tapping like a wedding guest calling for a kiss.

"Order in the courtroom!" she cried out. *Ting-ting! Ting-ting!* "Order in the courtroom! Let the monkey speak!"

Crackpots

Summer 1957—"Wake up, Nelthin, ith time," my Great-Auntie Isabella whispers, poking the bedcovers with the rubber tip of her cane.

I climb out of bed in my Hopalong Cassidy shirt and red shorts and crawl under the bed—where there are dust balls the size of tumbleweed—to drag out the strongbox.

Auntie Izzy is already all ready. I'm supposed to call her Mother. She has twisted her hair into two long and skinny yellow braids and wrapped them around above her ears like cinnamon buns. Over her nightie she wears a funny little black jacket, buttoned all crooked, with big shredded sleeves, a pin called a cameo, and a long, long black skirt. Along with her cane, Auntie Izzy carries a tiny, coiled whip and a torn and ruffled parasol. I love the whip. I want the little whip and plan to ask Santa for one for Christmas. Auntie Izzy looks a lot like Grandpa Doc's monkey, Kimosabe. She has only three teeth, but all of them are real gold.

The strongbox is heavy, and I hoist it up onto the bed. Auntie Izzy unlocks it with the key she wears around her neck and takes out the little velvet pouch with the gold coins. The coins rode on

5

a stagecoach that was held up by bandits, but the bandits didn't get away because the Cisco Kid came along and killed them dead. Auntie Izzy puts the pouch of coins on her head, then pins a tiny black hat with a veil over it. The hat fits Kimosabe, too. The hatpin is very long and rusty and sharp and has a pearl on it, just like the saber the Incredible Shrinking Man used to fight the Fly.

It's just getting light. I pull on my red cowboy boots and buckle my holster. We do this early every morning. I love my guns and the way they smell. They're silver with pearly white handles and rolls of red caps. I put on my Dale Evans watch and my new Dale Evans hat, red with a string and a wooden bead. You can wear it on your head or let it hang down your back like Annie Oakley.

I pick up the pretend suitcase, the little black leather doctor's bag with the ear horn inside. Auntie Izzy lifts up her skirt and pees in the china pot in the corner, and then down the crooked attic stairs we go.

In this movie, my name is Nelson, and I am the dear little boy who will die in the diphtheria epidemic of 1903. Auntie Izzy is my mother, and I am her only little boy, and she is a young, lonely widow and we are eloping. A man named Dr. William Wise, with a white handlebar mustache, is supposed to come with a carriage to pick us up. We wait on the porch and listen for the *clomp clomp clomp* of horses' hooves. When the carriage comes, Dr. William Wise will get out and walk under the elm trees, swinging a walking stick like Bat Masterson's, and at the corner of the house he will stop and whistle, probably like Benny Goodman or Woody Woodpecker. Then Auntie Izzy and Dr. William Wise will kiss and we will all run away and then I will die. My job is to make sure Auntie Izzy doesn't fall down the steps or wander off the porch. I do this for a nickel.

I have another job, too, which also pays a nickel. In the daytime, I follow my Grandpa Doc when he leaves the basement and goes out walking with Kimosabe, but I don't let them see me. In that movie, I wear my silver badge and my Lone Ranger mask.

In this movie, I walk in front of Auntie Izzy, carrying the doctor's bag with the ear horn inside, and Auntie Izzy walks behind with her hand on my shoulder. At the bottom of the stairs, I kick the door open with my boot. Straight ahead is my Grandma Bessie's bedroom, where my sister Albertine and Grandma Bessie sleep. Under the bed is some dried-up monkey poop and boxes of brown and yellow postcards with stamps like Lilliputian paintings. I see Albertine's arm hanging out of the bed and beside her the big lump like Gulliver that is my grandmother snoring. Albertine and I are here this summer because our mother is tired and needs a rest. Her nerves are bad.

In the next room, our Aunt Frannie Linn snores with pin curls in her hair. On her bureau a big black fan buzzes, jerking its head this way and that. Inside her bedroom, Aunt Frannie Linn has taught Albertine and me how to play gin rummy and how to do the Charleston, the shimmy, and the hoochie-coo. Under her bed is a bottle with a picture of a boat called a clipper ship on it. Aunt Frannie Linn gives Albertine and me manicures and paints our nails and lets us light her Lucky Strikes. The next time our mother goes away to get her nerves fixed, Aunt Frannie Linn is going to cut off our braids and give us Tonies.

In the hall outside Aunt Frannie Linn's door sits Benny Goodman, the parrot. "Here, Kimosabe," Benny Goodman cocks his head and calls. "Pretty Boy, Kimosabe. Kimosabe want a peanut?" Benny Goodman can whistle, too.

In the next room sleeps my Great-Auntie Isadora, who is thousands of years old and could be dead. Under Auntie Dorrie's bed there is only dust and dirt and a stinky, sticky pan. Albertine's job is to check all the time to see if Auntie Dorrie is dead yet. To do this, Albertine must put her ear down on Auntie Dorrie's bony chest. Tickling doesn't work. This job pays a dime. With our nickels and dimes, Albertine and I go to the drugstore next to Aunt Frannie Linn's beauty parlor and buy vanilla Cokes or lime rickeys and look at movie magazines. Albertine is in love with Eddie Fisher.

Here's a joke Albertine and I made up on the long ride to Philadelphia:

"Isabella necessary on a door?" Albertine says to me, and I say, "Isadora necessary on a bathroom?" We can barely say this without cracking up completely. Aunt Frannie Linn says we're naughty, but she blows a smoke ring while she's driving and cracks up, too.

The longest stairs are the stairs to downstairs, and I long to slide down the banister, but I must walk along slowly, doing the wedding march like Aunt Frannie Linn taught me, Auntie Izzy's bony hand clamped on my shoulder like Benny Goodman's claw foot on his bar.

Out on the porch, we sit on a wicker settee facing the street, waiting for Dr. William Wise. Auntie Izzy listens with the ear horn to her ear. It's very quiet and foggy and, as Grandma Bessie says, "close." Across the street is where my new friend, Neddy Turner, lives. Neddy has two of everything. Two bows and arrows, two lariats, two Lone Ranger masks and Davy Crockett hats. On his porch are two big bouncy horses, the likes of which I've never seen. Neddy rides Trigger and I ride Buttermilk because I'm really a girl. My name is Ruby Jean. We gallop along, side by side, shooting Indians who are attacking our fort: the brick walls of Neddy Turner's porch.

"Your family's a buncha crackpots," Neddy says to me, practicing his draw. "Watch this," he says. "Bam-bam-bam," he says, firing his guns, twirling them like Maverick, and blowing across their barrels.

Auntie Izzy keeps touching her hat. To pass the time before Dr. William Wise's carriage comes, we count in Roman numerals or recite the books of the Holy Bible or say our Psalms.

"Eye," Auntie Izzy says, "Eye-Eye."

"Eye-Eye-Eye!" I hop and shout. "Eye-Vee!"

"Vee. Vee-Eye."

"Vee-Eye-Eye."

We count to fifty, which is El. My favorite Roman numeral is Ex-Ex-Ex-Vee-Eye-Eye-Eye, which is thirty-eight, but Auntie Izzy gets to say it this time.

"Thalm one twenty-one," Auntie Izzy says after a while.

"I will lift up mine eyes unto the hills . . ." I stand up and shout into her ear horn. The hills I see are full of Indians crawling on their bellies, the horizon black with arrows.

". . . from wenth cometh my help," Auntie Izzy says, touching her hat.

The Very Beautiful Sad Elegy for Bambi's Dead Mother

1952—You are two years old and eating a book. Albertine is four and reading aloud, over and over: *James James Morrison Morrison Weatherby* . . . You wish that she'd shut up. The spine on your book is gold and particularly tasty. You gnaw on it with your front teeth like it's an ear of corn. *Baby's House* the book says on its chipboard cover. *This is baby's house* . . . the Little Golden Book begins, the text running underneath a bright illustration of a white clapboard house with a red roof.

This is baby's living room . . . the next page continues, on and on—a real page-turner—through the traditional American home of the Truman and Eisenhower years: baby's dining room, baby's kitchen, up the stairs to baby's parents' room (twin beds), baby's brother's room, baby's bedroom . . . but your favorite room is baby's bathroom. In baby's bathroom, baby stands on a bright red bench beside a big clawfoot bathtub and brushes her teeth in front of a medicine cabinet mirror.

This is *your* bathroom, too. You also have a big clawfoot bath-tub—big enough for your mother, your sister Albertine, and you to fit in all together—and a bench painted bright red, a brown door with a ceramic doorknob and a shiny silver lock that goes *click-click click-click*—like your brother Mason's pocket cricket —when you turn it back and forth, back and forth, back and forth, back and forth . . .

1955—The bathroom of the house at 41 Cherry Street in Ashport, Pennsylvania, has great acoustics: a high ceiling with a light you turn on and off by pulling a long string with a crocheted tassel, and a checkerboard floor of black and white tiles. There's a tiny window with frosted glass that pushes out and affords an excellent bird's-eye view of the alley, Go-Jeff's doghouse, the cherry tree decorated with its white caterpillar tents, and the clothesline with its chorus line of laundry. There's a radiator, too, for help climbing from the stool onto the sink, and above the sink a medicine cabinet with a mirror and chock-full of salves, Band-Aids, various cold and upset-stomach remedies, *plus* iodine and Mercurochrome in tiny brown bottles with glass sticks. There's also a tall metal locker painted white, which smells inside of Cashmere Bouquet and has two shelves of scratchy towels, *plus*—to your five-year-old wonder—magnificent and curious things in the bottom like a toilet plunger, which is really a combination pogo stick, wall sucker, and marching hat; a box of some kind of mattresses for the beds in a mouse hospital; a black rubber pear with a hole in one end and a little snoot, which is for puffing dead flies off the windowsill; a big vitamin-colored rubber bag with a long, black rubber straw, which can glug up toilet water and other things; and—on the door—A LOCK!

Locked in the bathroom at 41 Cherry Street after morning half-day kindergarten, while your father is out working for Atlas Powder Company, your sister Albertine and your brother Mason at school, and your mother doing laundry or teaching piano lessons downstairs, you spend many happy hours laying crayons out on the radiator and watching them melt, tap dancing on the tile floor while singing the McGuire Sisters' "Sugartime" or Burl Ives's "Big Rock Candy Mountain," playing Albertine's flutophone (which she keeps hidden in a Buster Brown shoebox under the bed and that you are forbidden to touch), eating Vicks VapoRub out of the jar with your finger, sipping Cheracol cough syrup, watching St. Joseph's aspirin for children dissolve on your tongue, taking your clothes off and examining every square inch of your body with your mother's hand mirror, shaving the hair off your arms with your father's Gillette razor, or standing on the bright red bench, staring into the medicine cabinet mirror on the opposite wall and repeating endlessly your favorite phrase in many different voices, pronunciations, variations, accents, and volumes:

Yellow Velvet.

YEL-LOH VEL-VET!

yel-LOW vel-VET.

YEL-low VEL-vet.

YEL-low vel-VET

VELVET YELLOW

Vellow Yelvet

VellowyYellowysmellowyVELVET

yellowvelvetyellowvelvetyellowvelvet.

YALLLLLOUH VALL-VETTTT!

Now you're a little older and learning to read and write. There are many wonderful words to say and write and spell, but the most glorious, wonderful word of all is SQUIRREL. SQUIRREL, with its big, squirrelly-tail S, its magnificent squirrelly-footed Q, its dog-barking *R-R*. SQUIRREL is a word to be written in the dirt in the alley with a stick, to be written with your finger on the side of your father's DeSoto and on steamed-up windows in the kitchen and in the dust on the coffee table and the television screen. With one of your father's mechanical pencils, SQUIRREL can be written very small on the wallpaper going up the stairs or low to the floor, just above the molding, or longwise, marching up the corner of Mason's room.

In blue ballpoint pen, SQUIRREL can be printed in Mason's Latin book, on your Aunt Frannie Linn's playing cards, on dollar bills in your mother's wallet, and inside Albertine's Buster Brown shoes. With the mechanical pencil point, the word SQUIRREL can be scratched into the back of wooden doors and on bureaus underneath doilies, and on the headboard of your bed. One night in bed you think of SQUIRREL backwards, and the magical word LERRIUQS, pronounced Larry Ukus (the Mighty Mouse of squirrels), appears in blue ink on your sheets. Brushing your teeth one morning and looking in the mirror, the even *more* magical word lɘɿɿiυpƨ appears on one of the white horizontal stripes on your pajama top where the word squirrel had once been.

Life is beautiful.

But briefly. You are no longer allowed to have a pencil, a pen, a crayon, a piece of chalk, nor any other writing instrument on your person without supervision. For one hour—Dale Evans time—you must sit quietly in your room and think about what you have done, and it is during this very thoughtful, quiet period that Blinker comes up with the idea of invisible writing: writing with water. Blinker is the person who fed Betsy Wetsy a bottle of real milk and then put her to bed without making her pee, and a rank odor began to spread from your side of the bedroom. Blinker is the person who drank the entire bottle of Cheracol and then threw up in the hall. It's a damn good thing he threw up, too, or he could be dead or in St. Vincent's getting his stomach pumped. Blinker is the person whose breath smells like Vicks VapoRub. Blinker is the person responsible for the fact that the cricket lock on the bathroom door is now rusting in a Chase & Sanborn can in the basement.

After this quiet, thoughtful hour is up, Blinker must go to the bathroom. There, Blinker experiments on a very small scale with the first invisible water writing, and it is quite successful, but Blinker can't leave well enough alone. During dinner that evening, eating corn on the cob, Blinker comes up with the concept of butter writing. Butter writing is a kind of shiny water writing. After dinner, with a purloined stick of Land O'Lakes, Blinker writes the word SQUIRREL on the wallpaper behind the davenport and then gives the remainder of the stick of butter to Go-Jeff, who gulps it down whole, paper and all. The next day while your mother is doing laundry, butter writing progresses to Crisco writing and escalates to Crisco erasing, which involves using big globs of Crisco to erase or blend together shiny spots on the wallpaper, leaving the can of Crisco full of dust and dog hair and big patches of the wallpaper a dark pee-colored yellow.

Blinker has really done it this time. You fear for your life, so you go upstairs and get in your bed and pull the covers up over your head. Downstairs, your mother comes in the back door with a laundry basket. She walks into the living room and sets the basket on the davenport.

"What's this?" she says, but you cannot hear her because you're taking a nap, you're sound asleep. Because you're sick. Because you have a terrible stomachache. Because you're dying. You are sound asleep and dying at the same time. You're snoring loudly, as only dying people with stomachaches can: *Ckckcooonkckck. Ckckcooooooonkckck.*

Your mother is coming up the stairs calling your name. "Ruby!" she calls. "Ruby Jean Reese!"

Should you add the whistling exhale like in the Bugs Bunny cartoons, or would that be too much?

Ckcknnkckck. Pfffffwwwwww. Ckckcnnnkckck. Pfffffwwwwwww.

a few days later

You're sitting on the davenport with your bride doll on your lap, your brother Mason beside you. You're watching *Mighty Mouse,* and Mason says to you, without turning his head:

"So did you hear about that buddy of yours, that, er — Blinker, is it? — fella, Blinker, the famous Crisco painter?"

"What about Blinker?" you ask.

"He bought the ranch," Mason says.

"What ranch?"

"He turned up dead, stupid."

"Did not."

"Did."

"Did not."

"It was on the radio . . . last night . . . while you were asleep. Blinker was run over by a truck and decapitated."

"Well, maybe he got run over by a truck and he was declumpertated, but he's OK," you insist. (Blinker had been hit by a car on another occasion, but it turned out to have been a mistake. It was somebody else.)

"He got his stomach pumped and now he's OK," you elaborate. "Dr. Elsworth said Blinker's OK."

"Yeah, he's OK, all right. He's just fine without a head!" Your brother Mason starts laughing hysterically and beating on one of the davenport's fat arms. "Yeah," he says, laughing, "he's just gotta big canna Crisco where his head used to be! Ha ha! Ha ha! Ha ha ha ha ha! Ha ha! Ha ha! Ha ha ha ha ha!"

"Whaddaya mean, without a head? Blinker's got a head. He does too got a head!"

"No, stupid, he's been DE-CAP-I-TATED. You don't even know what DE-CAP-I-TATED means. It's too big a word for you."

"Shut up. I do, too, know what D-coppertated means."

"D-coppertated! Ha ha ha! Ha ha he he ha ha! You can't even pronounce it! Ha ha ha! Ha ha ha! Ha ha he he! So what does D-coppertated mean, smartypants?"

Silence.

"DE-CAP-I-TATED means he got his head cut off!" Mason says. "Blinker got his head cut off. Just picture Blinker's head rolling down the street like a bowling ball. Ha ha ha ha! Ho ho ho ho! He he he he he!"

"Don't tell her a thing like that!" your mother scolds. She's passing by the living room and has overheard Mason's remark. She walks around the corner and swats your brother on the back of his head with a tea towel and then leaves.

You watch some more *Mighty Mouse,* and then it's over. *Sky King* comes on, then *Sergeant Preston of the Yukon.*

"Mason, how do you spell that clumpertated word?" you turn and ask your brother.

"I believe in the holey ghost, the holey Christian church, the communion of saints, the forgiveness of sins, the resurrection of the body, and the life everlasting, hey men!" you say to yourself, bouncing a ball, walking Go-Jeff on a make-believe leash, jumping rope, hopping on one foot, skipping to school, whumping your Slinky down the stairs. "The life everlasting, hey men! The life everlasting, *hey men!* The holey Christian church. The holey Christian church. The holey-moley, roly-poly, holey Christian church."

Now it's Thanksgiving vespers, and after your favorite poem, the Apostles' Creed, everyone is singing one of your favorite hymns, "Bringing in the Cheese," their voices happy and cheerful, their faces kind in the yellow light. Mrs. Kline, at the pipe organ, is trying to keep up, her crow wings flapping, her feet going one direction, her hands the other.

> *Bringing in the cheese, bringing in the cheese,*
> *We shall come rejoicing, bringing in the cheese.*

You stand next to Albertine in the children's choir and sing as loud as you can, sort of shouting. You sing with your top lip curled under and your top teeth sticking out like a mouse because this is a hymn written by church mice, and you are pretending to be one of them as you sing. Gus and Jock—from *Cinderella*—probably had a part in composing this wonderful hymn. They probably know it by heart. They are probably singing it right now at the top of their lungs in one of the dark, echoing alcoves of Riverview Lutheran Church, maybe over to your right there behind the baptismal pot, standing on a big hunk of Swiss cheese.

The hymn is over. The congregation claps shut their hymnals, but everyone remains standing as Mason, an acolyte, puts out the altar candles with the big candle snuffer on a pole. Reverend Creech raises his arms like he, too, is about to fly. "Let us pray," he says, and then the beautiful words wash over you, the words you will always remember all the long days of your life and whisper to yourself when you're afraid, when you're alone, when all the sadness of being human gathers itself around you:

> *May the piece of God, which passeth all understanding,*
> *keep your hearts and minds in Christ Jesus, Amen.*

For many, many years you ponder just exactly which piece of God Reverend Creech might be referring to, but for now you forget about all that because the choir is filing out and everyone is singing your very most favorite song in the whole world, the one your mother plays for you on the piano at bedtime, and your father has taught you and Albertine to sing in two-part harmony:

> *Now the day is over, night is drawing nigh,*
> *Shadows of the evening steal across the sky.*

> *Now the darkness gathers, stars begin to peep,*
> *Birds and beasts and flowers soon will be asleep.*

> *Thru the long night watches may thine angels spread*
> *Their white wings above me watching 'round my bed.*

> *Grant to little children visions bright of Thee*
> *Guard the sailors tossing on the deep blue sea.*

> *Comfort every sufferer watching late in pain*
> *Those who plan some evil, from their sin restrain.*

> *Jesus, give the weary calm and sweet repose*
> *With thy tenderest blessing may my eyelids close.*

1957—With very little coaxing and carrying, and only minor scratches, a big orange cat follows you and Albertine home from school. A big orange cat with silky fur and a big round pumpkin head. An orange cat who walks around the house rubbing her head on the legs of everything, including you. She walks in and out your legs, in and out, and her tail goes up your dress and makes you giggle.

"Our cat must have a very beautiful name," Albertine announces. "Princess!" she exclaims. "Here, Princess! Here pretty Princess Kitty!"

"Kyrie Eleison!" you call, after the beautiful and mysterious words of the Kyrie sung in church. "Here, Kyrie," you call, crawling across the carpet toward your cat. "Here Kyrie! Kyrie Eleison!"

"Daisy," Albertine says resolutely. "DAISY BUTTERCUP."

"Here Dona, here Dona," you persist. "Here Dona Nobis Pacem!" and Albertine rolls her eyes so far back into her head they disappear completely. Only the whites—like Orphan Annie's—show.

"Panis Angelicus?" You pout and beg. "Adeste Fideles? Agnus Dei?"

For many hours that night, you lie awake, wandering through the enchanted forest of all words you know, bumping into trunks and branches, tripping over roots and stumps, searching for the perfect name for your beautiful orange cat: *mimosa, marmalade, gladiola, peony, poppycock, forsythia, taffeta, pinochle, piano forte, aspen, pumpkinseed, Leviticus Numbers, lickety-split, fiddlesticks, Worcestershire, nincompoop, whippoorwill, whippersnapper, Fridgedaire, DeSoto, squirrel, pollywollydoodle all the day* . . . and on and on. And then . . . you find it! There it is, lying on its back, humming "Row, Row, Row Your Boat," kicking its feet, and doing the backstroke around your brain: the perfect name for your cat. So you can go to sleep now. But come morning, you wake up in a panic because the perfect name you've now forgotten! You should have written it down! Your heart is racing: *mimosa, gladiola, peony, forsythia, taffeta, squirrel* . . . Oh, praise the Lord, there it is! You run downstairs, but . . .

Your cat is gone.

"He wanted out," Mason mumbles, dripping a big, sloppy serving spoonful of Wheaties up to his mouth and never looking up from the cereal box he's reading.

Other than the time Mr. Rossi crawled out on his roof and hollered for everyone to turn themselves into little children and the time Mrs. Wagner's pressure cooker exploded split pea soup, there is not much excitement in Ashport. Except on Saturday. Every Saturday, you and Albertine walk to the Strand theater on Center Avenue. Matinees start at noon with double features that last until four o'clock. Every single kid in Ashport is there, it seems. Ushers dressed like Johnny Philip Morris unhook the velvet sausages, and you pour in like lava, hundreds of you racing down the aisles and up the steps to the balconies, you and Albertine running, too, holding hands. The ushers close the doors and slouch around the lobby, smoking Old Golds, reading magazines, and playing cards, betting pennies, never paying you any mind until they open the doors hours later. Until then, behind the closed doors, it's mayhem, a zoo. The Strand has two balconies; a gilded, domed ceiling; and tiered side boxes like the ones in Ford's Theatre where Lincoln was shot — two- and four-seaters with heavy maroon curtains. Kids are everywhere, screaming, running, hanging off the balconies like apes, choking on popcorn, losing their fillings and swallowing their teeth along with Jujubes, throwing wads of Bazooka bubble gum at the screen, and making elephant noises with empty Good & Plenty boxes.

You'll watch *A Light in the Forest* and *Johnny Tremain; Westward Ho! the Wagons; 20,000 Leagues Under the Sea;* and *Tarzan, the Ape Man,* and it's at the Strand that you'll see *Old Yeller.* There won't be a peep out of anyone when Travis discovers Old Yeller has rabies. Everyone knows what Travis must do. All the children at the Strand will be sniffling, boo-hooing, wiping their snotty noses on their sleeves as Travis raises his twenty-two.

Shortly after *Old Yeller,* Walt Disney's *Bambi* will come to the Strand, and around the same time, your father will begin reading you and Albertine *The Yearling.* Next will follow a book about an orphaned bear cub named Wob. Quickly and wholeheartedly you will begin to embrace the morose romanticism of female pubescence, priming yourself for the death of Beth in *Little Women,* a passage that Albertine reads to you every night in bed.

The Saturday you see *Bambi,* though, you will begin your life's work as a writer and editor, an epic poem entitled "The Very Beautiful Sad Elegy for Bambi's Dead Mother." That is your poem's final title, but it will go through literally hundreds of titles and revisions as you work on it over the next two years. "The Very Beautiful Sad Elegy for Bambi's Dead Mother" isn't just any old elegy. It is a very special genre: an illustrated elegy. Crying fawns standing on their hind legs and wiping their eyes with floral handkerchiefs crowd the side margins. Stiff dead deer with their legs sticking up in the air like upside-down coffee tables adorn the bottom. And, throughout, there is a lot of corn—corn on the cob and the Jolly Green Giant canned variety, too—because you know deer like corn, and for some reason you feel the poem should have both visual and taste appeal for deer. With confidence, your "Very Beautiful Sad Elegy for Bambi's Dead Mother" could masquerade today as a long-lost collaborative effort of Rod McKuen, Andy Warhol, and Betty Crocker.

Here's the first stanza of the final version of your poem, "The Very Beautiful Sad Elegy for Bambi's Dead Mother":

> *In the meadow still and calm,*
> *Lays the lovely stag.*
> *Never will she run again,*
> *Nor never leap the crag.*

You know the word *elegy* because it's the name of a song you learned to play on your Grandpa Doc's trombone. At first you played it as fast as possible, like you play everything else, but when your mother told you to slow down, it was supposed to be sad because somebody had died, everything seemed to miraculously come together—music, art, movies, fairy tales, poetry—like the missing piece of a puzzle showing up at the bottom of a shoebox full of broken crayons.

You decide on the synonym *stag* for deer after casually asking everyone you know: "Excuse me, excuse me, excuse me, what's another word for 'deer'?" Your brother Mason offers you *stag,* a wonderful word, a great gift. Likewise, *crag* would be found by asking people the meaning of every possible word you can come up with that rhymes with *stag*, as in, "Excuse me, is 'klag' a word?"

In fact, the whole poem will be written pretty much that way. You have never heard of a thesaurus, although you are learning to use your father's *Webster's* dictionary.

You repeat this poem to yourself all the time and work on it every day after school in a very ritualistic fashion. You keep it rolled up, with a rubber band around it, in a black metal miner's lunch pail that your father has given you, along with some broken crayons, a mechanical pencil your brother Mason has been looking for for some time, a beautiful fountain pen on loan from your mother, a jar of Schaeffer's blue ink, a candle stub, and some books of matches from the Knotty Pine. The fountain pen is a dark, marbled blue, with a little metal lever on the side that lets the pen suck up ink like an elephant's trunk. "The Very Beautiful Sad Elegy for Bambi's Dead Mother" is written on very thin graph paper (also from your father) with a pale blue grid.

You keep the lunch pail under your bed. Every day after school, you crawl under the bed, retrieve the lunch pail, and take it up into the attic, where you light the candle and work on your chef-d'oeuvre. It's all very difficult — the writing and drawing on the uneven, splintery floor boards, the curling paper, the fountain pen and all — but this is the path you've chosen.

The only person you ever show your poem to is your mother, to whom you read it many, many times, every revision. Every time you sit on your mother's lap and read her "The Very Beautiful Sad Elegy for Bambi's Dead Mother," she hugs you and then puts her hand over her heart and says, "Sweetheart, that's really, really beautiful. I know you'll be a famous poet someday, Ruby Jean."

When you are nine, though, in September 1959, you start fourth grade with a young, pretty teacher, Miss Barrett. Miss Barrett is just out of state teacher's college. She's very stylish in a Thalia Menninger kind of way, with fawn-colored hair. Miss Barrett wears muted cashmere twinset sweaters and a single strand of pearls with a big gold clip. You've always been quite shy, but you trust Miss Barrett, with her fawn-colored hair and fawn-colored camel's hair coat, her fawn-colored sweaters and white pearls, and you really want her to like you. After much deliberation, one fall Friday when school is over and Miss Barrett is in the front of the room erasing the blackboards, you tiptoe up to her desk and place "The Very Beautiful Sad Elegy for Bambi's Dead Mother" on it, rolled up and tied with a hair ribbon, and tiptoe away. All weekend you daydream about Miss Barrett reading your poem, imagining that she will love your poem, love you, praise you. She'll probably come to school on Monday, you speculate, with her eyes all red and puffy from crying.

On Monday morning, you put on your favorite dress—black watch plaid with a big white Pilgrim collar and a black velvet bow —and your patent-leather Mary Janes. Miss Barrett is wearing her tan cashmere sweater, her white pearls, and her camel's hair skirt—her most fawnlike ensemble. She's walking up and down the aisles, calling names, taking roll, something in her hand with a rib—... *Could it* ...

When she calls your name, Miss Barrett places "The Very Beautiful Sad Elegy for Bambi's Dead Mother" on your desk— without a word, in front of the whole class—and pats you on the head. Embarrassed, you stuff it quickly into your plaid bookbag.

All day you feel sick.

After school, you run home and race upstairs to the attic stairwell, throw open the door, heart pounding, and click it shut. Unbuckle your bookbag and unroll "The Very Beautiful Sad Elegy for Bambi's Dead Mother."

On the first page in red ink, Miss Barrett has printed in her big, neat handwriting: *A stag is a <u>male</u> deer!!!* Three exclamation marks and a thick red underline like a bad cut.

A little ways down the page and running right over a particularly poignant fawn (possibly even Bambi herself) in the margin, Miss Barrett has drawn a thick red circle around the word *lay* and written: <u>*Only chickens lay!!!*</u> Three more big red exclamation marks like war paint and, again, the thick red underscore like an open wound.

You are overcome with shame and humiliation and tears. Into your room you run, banging the door, and under the bed you scramble and grab the black miner's pail. Up the attic stairs you fly with your pail and your stupid elegy poem, your Mary Janes flashing, and into the attic closet, where you kick the door again and again and strike the matches and set that stupid poem that goddamn stupid holey shit Christian goddamn very beautiful sad piss-on-it damn elegy on fire.

Stardust

I. Stardust, One

When my brother, Mason, was a freshman in high school, he started hanging out with Chantz Phillips, who was two years older, two years behind in school, and a hood. Before that, Mason spent most of his time in his room, reading J. D. Salinger and listening to 78s of George Shearing, Erroll Garner, Art Tatum, Bill Evans, and Dave Brubeck. When he was twelve, Mason won a national jazz piano competition. That was in 1952 — two years after I was born — and Mason played "Stardust." One day my mother would say the piano was what saved him, but she was wrong. Back when he was just a kid, Mason wanted to play piano in a jazz trio when he grew up or be an escape artist like Harry Houdini, but somehow he became a pharmacist instead.

After he started hanging out with Chantz Phillips, Mason got into some kind of trouble and was sent away to a Quaker school outside of Philadelphia. Chantz was sent to a reformatory. The night Mason and Chantz were arrested, three police cars came to our house in the middle of the night with their gumball-machine lights spinning, and a policeman called out through a bullhorn,

"Mason Reese, we have the house surrounded. Do not flee."

Albertine and I got out of bed and looked out the window. My father and Mason left the house with the policemen. My father had his trousers on over his pajamas. Albertine went back to bed, and my mother and I sat in the dark, me on my mother's lap, rocking in the gooseneck rocker by the front window.

A couple times after that night, I asked my mother what had happened when the policeman called out for Mason, but each time I asked, she said, "Nothing, sweetheart, that was a bad dream." Shortly after that night, the warts appeared between my fingers, and a few years later I heard someone say that the incident that landed Chantz Phillips in a reformatory involved a fourteen-year-old girl.

The year Mason went away to live at the Friends school was 1955. I didn't see much of him after that, because after high school he went away to college and then to pharmacy school, and during that time, too, he got married.

II. Song to Celia

She's new out on the Jackson Tract, your new next-door neighbor. She's renting the Tuppers' old house, she and her little boy, Cloud. What a strange name, you think . . . but after all, it's 1978, and someone you went to graduate school with recently changed his name from Todd to Shamu, and then there are the vegans who live a few houses away: Happy and Sky Blue.

Pink Floyd. Happy. Sky Blue. Shamu. Cloud . . . oh, whatever!

Cloud's skin is white, and so is his mother's: white as the refrigerator, the cupboards, the sugar in the sugar bowl, the gas stove. Covering her face are thousands of tiny scars, no bigger than eyelashes, and whiter still. They give her face a kind of woven look, a thread count, as if she's wearing a white buckram mask, pink rabbit eyes staring out like carnival glass beads. She blinks rapidly, incessantly. After she leaves, you try this and find that everything's like the flickering of an old movie reel about to break, or a room trembling from a fluorescent light fixture's broken ballast. It makes you sick. But you can't stop doing it. For now, her looks, her blinking, make you nervous and you don't want to stare, so you choose to sit awry in your pressed-back chair, at an angle to the kitchen table, your back against the window, your profile to her full white blinking face.

Through the French doors, a slab of morning light stretches out on the blond floor, and there Cloud plays, throwing a penny into the mullioned squares, muttering, and hopping on one foot. The boy is also albino, but there's something wrong with him. His face is too long, too flat, too narrow—like a thumb puppet —his fingers webbed and splayed.

Her real name comes, she tells you, from a poem written by the seventeenth-century wit Ben Jonson. (You wish she would leave now so you can practice your piano lesson.) *Drink to me only with thine eyes, and I will pledge with mine,* it goes, she says. (You don't know at this point she's always lying.)

"Um . . . Celia?" you guess, your mind straining back to English 320: Seventeenth-Century British Poetry.

"*Song* to Celia," she corrects you. "Do you know it? Can you play it on that grand piano?"

So you get up and go to the piano bench and find the song she means in the old torn book, *Songs You Love to Sing.* It's one of the few pieces you can play; so simple—like a hymn. Your favorite key: three flats. You play it mechanically, and from somewhere comes a strange high-pitched sound like a theremin. Things in the curved glass china cabinet begin to chatter and walk like windup false teeth. It's the boy—Cloud—singing, transfixed in the ephemeral hopscotch board made of light and dust motes in the hall, still holding up one blackened sole against his bottom.

III. Beautiful Dreamer, One

When you were five your mother took you to the gypsy. "Don't tell anyone," your mother said, examining the warts between your fingers, "and I'll take you to see the gypsy who lives by the bridge on Buck Run."

Everyone knows the gypsy's house. It's a shack practically right in the road. It's the place to duck down in the car when your father drives by and to peep out with just your forehead and half your eyes showing out the rear window, peep out through the dust cloud once you're safely past. If she catches your eye, she'll cast a spell on you. Obediah had looked and stuck out his tongue and then had fallen from the garage loft.

You're pigeon-toed, your hair is dull and thin, and there are tiny warts in between your fingers. It's early morning, and you walk to the end of Elysian Avenue and out Buck Run Road, along a steep bank where a stream trickles and two deer leap across then disappear into the mountain laurel. Your mother carries a basket with teaberries, two Dutch cakes, a smoked mackerel, a can of Bugler tobacco, Zig Zag cigarette papers, and three fresh brown eggs. You helped arrange all this in the basket early in the morning and cover it with a dish towel that is also a calendar. The gypsy is old and as brown as a paper bag. She wears a dirty babushka and men's shoes. The thick black stockings rolled down around her ankles look like part of your game called ring toss.

"Eva!" the gypsy calls to your mother from the rickety porch. "I've been expecting you, Eva . . . and this must be your precious little Ruby!"

You never look up but keep your eyes on your shoes. Oxblood, they're called, with laces striped dark yellow and tied in double knots. The gypsy cuts off a hank of your hair and counts the warts between your fingers. Her hands are as hard and cold as Lawn Jesus, and her chin is covered with stiff bristles like a hairbrush. She pulls up your shirt and pokes your belly. Just beyond the porch, a black snake is sunning itself on a rock. The gypsy goes inside and comes back out and gives your mother something wrapped in a page from the funny papers with Dagwood and Blondie on it.

"Put this in her shoe," she tells your mother.

The gypsy goes back inside. Your mother unwraps the funny paper and tells you to sit on the step. The black snake is still sunning itself on a rock. Your mother unties your shoe and pulls it off. Inside the paper is a slice of soggy bread that makes a mushy, creepy feeling when you put your foot back inside your shoe. "Ugh," you say. There's something else in a rag that is to be buried at night in the road. Your mother puts this in the basket.

You start back up the road with the terrible squishy feeling in your shoe. At the top of the hill, at the crossroads, your mother squats down and puts her hands on your shoulders. "Where are you going to say we went today?" she asks you.

You make the sock-monkey face: eyes wide open and a closed-lip smile, and pretend to slowly zip your mouth shut.

Your mother smiles and hugs you. At home you eat bow-tie noodles with Worcestershire sauce, and before your nap your mother plays your favorite song on the piano; you stand by the piano bench and sing,

> *Beautiful Dreamer, wake unto me*
> *Starlight and moonlight are waiting for thee.*

IV. Suzanne, One

I'm a sophomore in college. May 1970. Mid-morning. Chilly. I'm lying on my bed in my fringed buckskin jacket and my red cowboy boots, leaning back against a big green corduroy pillow, smoking a Kool and eating a York peppermint patty. Listening to the same song— "Suzanne" by Leonard Cohen—over and over, trying to burn it into my brain, driving my roommate, Phyllis, crazy with this obsessive repetition.

I don't really understand the lyrics, but it doesn't matter; something about the rise and fall of Judy Collins's voice makes the incomprehensibility of the words inconsequential. I just want the song to become part of me because it reminds me of my mother and of a sick girl I knew a long time ago, a girl named Etherine who lived along the Susquehanna River.

I have about fifteen minutes until my Shakespeare class when I see this silver bathtub Porsche pull up in front of my dorm. It's my brother, Mason. Everybody calls him Doc. He's a pharmacist in a town right next to our hometown, about a half-hour away, where my father still lives—in the suburbs now—with his new wife, Deenie. Two years ago, my father helped Mason and his wife, Lynnette, buy a nice brick house that belonged to a pharmacist who was retiring. The pharmacist—a Mr. Schaeffer—had converted the attached garage into a small pharmacy, a quaint little store with a wooden sign, a red door, a picture window, and a window box with red geraniums. Schaeffer's Pharmacy was an established business that had been operating for thirty-some years in a nice neighborhood, just two blocks from downtown. An ideal situation for Mason, everyone said.

Last Thanksgiving, my father and I went over to Mason's for dinner. Lynnette had cooked a turkey and made cranberry-orange relish, creamed onions, mashed potatoes, pumpkin and mincemeat pies, the whole bit, and the kids were all dressed up, but Mason never showed. Lynnette said she hadn't seen him since Tuesday night. My father went out and drove around for a couple hours, looking for him, but came back alone, shaking his head. The kids watched television, never saying anything unless spoken to. Mason Jr., the nine-year-old, got up and played the piano once. He played Dave Brubeck's "Take Five."

"Where'd you learn that?" my dad asked Little Mason—what we used to call Mason Jr. back then.

"Nowhere." Little Mason shrugged and went back and plopped down beside his sister, Laura, on the sofa.

Around sundown, Lynnette went into her bedroom and shut the door.

"Anybody hungry?" I said to the kids. "Come on, let's eat."

"I'm not hungry. I'm not hungry," the kids said. They were watching some Three Stooges movie on TV. Laura was sucking her thumb and rubbing the binding of an aqua blanket in a circular motion on her cheek.

By that time, I had a terrible headache from smoking too

many cigarettes. My father made Mason's kids each a plate of food and set the plates in front of them on the coffee table. He poured them each a glass of milk, and I straightened up the kitchen, put everything away. The turkey wouldn't fit in the kitchen refrigerator, so my father put it in the fridge in the hall outside the door that led to Mason's pharmacy. That fridge was full of beer and prescriptions, and my father put the beer in grocery bags and carried the bags out back to the trash cans in the alley.

Then we said goodbye to the kids and called goodbye down the hall to Lynnette and drove home. As we were leaving, my father gave Little Mason and Laura each a ten-dollar bill. My dad, he was famous for that, those ten-dollar handshakes.

V. Suzanne, Two (A Place Near the River)

Trace is the youngest. He's six. The year is 1962. Trace opens the bedroom door and takes you into their father's bedroom. "There are voices in the air conditioner," Trace tells you. "A man, a lady, a cat, and a baby."

You and Etherine lie on the unmade bed. The ceiling is stained brown, the sheets are gray and rumpled and smell like potatoes. Trace closes the door and turns on the window air conditioner. You listen closely and you hear them, too. When the cat starts its yowling, Trace screams, "The lady is choking the cat!" and Etherine begins to whimper.

In other rooms, empty rooms, the radiators look like dirty sheep grazing underneath the windows. And outside, outside there is the fog, the river fog that gives everything an underwater smell and a grainy texture like construction paper, the river fog that blurs and erases things outside the windows and blends them all together like a chalkboard smudge.

There are two other children: Ramona and Chantz. Ramona, Etherine's older sister, is the beauty, with black hair and eyes the color of Tootsie Rolls. She's married and has a little baby named

Maurice. Chantz, the oldest, is twenty-four and in prison. He wears a chain in his pocket and carries a knife. Chantz, he has the devil in him, people say. You're afraid of him, and, even though he's in prison still, the one time you get to stay overnight at the Phillipses' you ask to sleep in the middle, between Etherine and Trace, and you fall asleep keeping an eye on the door. There isn't a mother. Only a father and sometimes a woman named Maxine. Sometimes when you go there, Mr. Phillips and Maxine are sitting at the kitchen table, smoking cigarettes and drinking whiskey. Something about Maxine reminds you of Jimmy Durante, but you can't put your finger on it.

Etherine is eleven, a year younger than you. She was born with a hole in her heart, a blue baby. Her features are wide and flat like an Eskimo's, and her skin is sallow with a blue-green undertone like the belly of a frog. Her fingertips are broad, the nails flat and blue. Her lips a bluish brown, her hair straight, stringy, dull brown. She was bluer when she was a baby, before the operation to sew up the hole in her heart. If you close your eyes, you can see Etherine as a baby, a beautiful blue of blue hydrangeas baby, wrapped in a crocheted white blanket.

You love Etherine. The look of her. The yellow blue-green-ness of her. The one time you get to stay overnight with Etherine, you lie next to her in the moonlight and watch her sleep: Etherine with her dingy underpants and dingy undershirt gleaming against her beautiful blue-green skin. You hold her cool hand while she's sleeping and feel a little tingle between your legs as you gently stroke her wide, flat fingernails one by one, ever so lightly with your index finger. A train calls, rumbles and clangs along the river, rattling the windows in Etherine's room. Late that night, rain comes; it sounds like piggy banks being emptied on the tin roof. On the other side of the pillow, his face close to yours, Trace drools.

It's summer, and every morning you ride your bike out Elysian Avenue to the end of town, across the railroad tracks and the suspension bridge and out along the River Road to Etherine's house, which is the old lockkeeper's house that stood abandoned for years. From the top of the hill, you can see the railroad tracks and the river. Etherine's house is hidden by hemlock trees with ruffled arms that dangle clusters of tiny cones. The path to the house is nothing more than damp dirt covered with pine needles and the tiny cones. There's a porch with many broken windowpanes and a soggy, rolled-up rug. The house smells like gasoline and pine and another, deeper smell like red beets and the ladies toilet at the Bloomsburg Fair. You can smell the house before you can even see it.

Etherine can't play. She can't ride a bike or walk very far, even down to the river. During the school year, Etherine couldn't walk to the bus stop on River Road but had to be driven to school by her father in his beat-up station wagon. Etherine can't stand the cold. Most school days Etherine stayed at home on the living room davenport and watched television. She doesn't talk much because she gets out of breath. The days she came to school, you carried her books and her lunch tray. You like to give her things: Black Jack gum and squares of Sky Bars, your Dixie cup of rice pudding. Little treasures: a rhinestone pin your Aunt Frannie Linn gave you, a pocket cricket that was your brother's, magic paper dolls, a cameo.

"Thank you, Ruby," Etherine says so sweetly. She takes a little white Chiclet between her blue fingers, lowers her head, and smiles.

The Saturday afternoon after you spend the night at Etherine's, you are riding your bike home, and when you get near your house on Cherry Street, you see your mother throwing her hair out her bedroom window. Great hanks of her hair whip around the corner of the house and fly up into the trees. From a few pavement squares away, before you even see your mother in the window, you see the movement of something black in the air that you can't make out, and you wonder what it is. A goblin?

Your mother has been sick with cancer, and you lied to her so you could stay at Etherine's. You said you were staying overnight with Pauline Witherspoon, the undertaker's daughter who lives two streets away. It's easy to lie to your mother, because no matter what you say, she believes you.

"Have a good time, sweetheart," she called to you weakly as you walked out the door.

You don't go upstairs for a long time, but when you do, your mother is sitting on your parents' bed in front of the window, the window screen lying on the bed. She doesn't turn around, but you see her face reflected in the vanity's mirror. She looks to you then like the beautiful Madame Alexander doll you have, the one your Aunt Frannie Linn gave you for Christmas, the doll whose hair you yanked out, tuft by tuft, just for the fun of it and because once you started doing it, you couldn't stop, and then in shame and horror you stuffed it, with its soft body and hard, shiny head, behind your bed. You stand in the doorway, but your mother doesn't move.

"What would you like for dinner, sweetheart?" she asks you after a few moments, still not turning, her voice so flat and far away. "Fish sticks? Pierogies? Bow-tie noodles?"

Soon after that, Etherine is sent to live with her grandmother in Minneapolis, Minnesota, and the next spring your mother dies from breast cancer. She is buried in Riverview Lutheran Cemetery along the Susquehanna River, near Etherine's father's house out on the River Road, and everyone joins hands and sings, *Shall we gather by the river, the beautiful, beautiful river?* The next October, the Susquehanna River floods and washes away all the graves in the Lutheran cemetery and Etherine's house, too, with Mr. Phillips, Trace, and Maxine in it.

You write Etherine two letters, but she never writes back. One letter is not really a letter but a card—a large valentine with real satin ribbon and a puffy satin heart. Inside the card is a diamond ring wrapped in Kleenex.

VI. Hello, Everybody, I'm a Dead Man

It's almost time for my Shakespeare class, and here comes Mason. I stub out my Kool, stick my head out the dorm window, and call, "Hey, Mason!"

"Hey, Ruby," Mason calls. *"Ruby, Ruby, when will you be mine?"* he sings, snapping his fingers in time. "Howzit goin'? Come on down, Ruby. Come on down and go for a ride!"

I know I'm not supposed to leave campus without signing out. My school's a small Lutheran university in a rural setting, a school far removed from the noise and haste, a safe and secluded school with high academic standards, a school that watches over its female students like a shepherd over his flock. Coeds must report to a central office and sign out before they leave campus, indicating where they are going and with whom and at what time they will return. Women have a ten P.M. curfew on weeknights, midnight on weekends. We attend mandatory chapel every morning and vespers every evening. We eat dinner off of gold-rimmed china plates on linen tablecloths set with lots of heavy silverware. In unison, we mumble the chaplain's graces: *Heavenly Father, what we have comes from Thee / Accept our thanks and bless us . . .* We daren't smoke or wear blue jeans in public.

I know Mason is trouble, but I don't care. Besides, he's my brother, and it's almost the end of the semester. What difference would it make now if I skip a class? I've hardly missed any! Mason puts the top down on the Porsche and I blow off my Shakespeare class and the whole Reformation thing and get in.

As soon as we get out of town, we stop at a bar for a beer. I'm underage and have been in only a few bars. I don't even like beer, but I drink half of a Yuengling anyway. Then we both have a shot of Dewar's. Now, that I like! I take a big swallow and it slides down my throat like a blade of fire. I have another Dewar's on ice and Mason has two more double Dewar's straight up. We drive along the back roads at high speed, passing Amish buggies, passing everybody. The sky is as blue as delphiniums, and I feel good. I just lean way back and close my eyes and stick my arm out, catching the wind, then letting it go again. Catch. Release. Catch. Release . . .

We stop at another roadhouse. Mason has a couple beers and orders us both a shot of Dewar's. We split a hoagie, and then we end up at Angela Park. It's the first day of the season. *Hooray!* we

say and race to the roller coaster, the Hurricane. We're the only riders.

"Pick your seat," Mason says.

He takes the front car, and just for the heck of it, I take the back. We ride three times and then head on out. I'm beginning to regret skipping my class and want to get back to school. I'm feeling sick and dizzy. "Thanks, Mason," I say anyway, "that was really great."

We leave the park. I have a terrible headache, and I need to write a paper on *Typee*. We drive about a half-hour back toward my college and Mason pulls into a gravel parking lot by a dive called the Rainbow, about five miles outside our hometown, Ashport. I've seen this place a million times but would never think of stopping here. It's got a rough reputation. Boarded-up windows. I'm really tired. I want to get back to school. "Mason," I say, "please . . ."

"Come on, Ruby," Mason pleads, "just one more drink. Come on!"

"I'm going to miss dinner and vespers, and somebody will report me missing," I whine.

"Big fuckin' deal," Mason says, and we both laugh.

There's one other car in the parking lot, a beat-up Corvair convertible, and Mason pulls up right beside it. A man in a motorcycle jacket and black wraparound sunglasses gets out of the Corvair, walks around behind it and over to our car, smoking a cigarette, and I see a chain on his belt, disappearing into his black jeans pocket.

"Howzit goin'?" he leans on the car door and says to Mason. I recognize him now; it's Chantz Phillips.

I don't want to get out of the car. All I want is to be back at school, but Mason insists we'll only be a minute. Chantz is already at the Rainbow's door.

"Come on, Ruby," Mason says. "Chantz isn't a bad guy. Really. That's all in the past. He's been rehabilitated. Forgive and forget."

Reluctantly, I get out.

"Ruby Baby, when will you be mine?" Chantz croons to me,

holding the door. I don't say anything. He gooses me as I pass and I jump. I want to scream and slap him, but I also want to get away from him, so I just go on in. The blast of late-afternoon sunlight from the open door fills the smoky room, then it's dark again, and the beer signs come out like stars: Schlitz. Yuengling. Budweiser. Carling's Black Label.

"Here comes trouble," the barkeep says to us. "Howzit goin', Doc? Howzit goin', Chantz?"

"Goin' real good," says Mason. "This is my baby sister, Ruby Jean," he says. "She's at school down in Selinsgrove."

"Whaddaya studying?" the barkeep asks me.

"English," I say, and he raises his eyebrows and turns down his mouth and nods.

Mason and Chantz go over to a pay phone and Chantz makes a call. "Listen, Ruby," Mason comes back and says to me, jiggling the change in his pocket, "Chantz has got this friend who's having a little car trouble. Let me just run up there with him and see if I can help. Why don't you order a pizza or something? I'll be right back."

He gives me a twenty-dollar bill, and he and Chantz are gone, and I'm really mad. I think about trying to hitchhike back to school or calling my father to come get me, but I don't want to worry our dad, so I give in and order a double shot of Dewar's on the rocks and play the jukebox and just go lie down in one of the wooden booths. My head is spinning, and I have to keep the toe of one boot on the sticky floor to stop the bench from going into orbit.

Finally, hours later, Mason comes and slides in the other side of the booth.

"Listen, Ruby," he says, "I'm sorry. Here." I sit up and Mason hands me a shot of Dewar's. The Budweiser clock says 9:10. Mason looks really wasted. He blinks his eyes real slowly, and his head wobbles like it's on a spring.

"Let's go," he says.

We get out to the car. "You drive, Ruby," Mason mumbles. "I'm too fucked up."

I'm feeling pretty woozy myself and don't really want to drive. I've never had so much to drink, but I take the keys. Mason taught Albertine and me how to drive in 1963, the summer after our mother died, when I was thirteen and Albertine was fifteen. He had an old black 1952 Jaguar XK120 that reminded me of a big ant. He and my dad had worked on weekends rebuilding the engine in it that summer, and Mason taught us how to drive, how to keep our arms straight, and how to double-clutch, downshifting up hills so as not to lose speed. Over the next few years, whenever he came home from pharmacy school to visit, with Lynnette and Little Mason, he'd let Albertine and me drive around town in broad daylight. That was seven years ago. I've never driven the Porsche, though.

We put the top up. The latches are a pain. The car is all wet inside because it's been drizzling and Mason left the top down.

I get in and run through the gears. Start the car. Fumble around for the lights. Mason is slumped in the passenger seat, leaning against the window. I pull out of the gravel parking lot onto the highway, grind the gears from first to second, start up Buck Mountain, faster and faster. The car feels too wide, too heavy, too tight, too fast. The road's black, shiny, hard to see. Curves, twisting, winding. Try to keep my eyes on the road. Car skids. Spins. Bam! Hits a guardrail. Bam! And then we're flying. Everything slows down. A song comes into my head so clearly; I see all the notes in every chord like arpeggios. *Hello, everybody,* the song goes, *I'm a dead man, but I ain't even six feet underground.* Asleep at the Wheel is the group. Funny, I think: Asleep at the Wheel, and I laugh out loud.

We're flying for what seems like an eternity. Everything's so quiet except for the smashing of branches like a stampede, an elephant crashing through the jungle in a Tarzan movie, and then we're going down down down with nothing underneath us. The Great Wallendas. I let go of the wheel, and Mason and I turn to each other. We join hands like we're getting married. Mason smiles at me, the sweetest smile, and blinks real slowly like a baby doll. And then there's this huge crash, tumbling, sliding. We're all twisted up on top of each other, glass everywhere. I don't know which way is up or which way is down. All I hear is a sizzling sound and the tinkling rain of glass, then Mason's voice, "Ruby? . . . Ruby? . . . Ruby, you OK?"

Somehow, we crawl out. I try to stand up but fall over. I've lost a boot. Instinctively, we crawl away from the car. When we look back, the car looks prehistoric, a mangled heap of steaming silver, a wounded, snorting rhinoceros, a slain dragon in the pale moonlight.

"Wait," Mason says, "I gotta get my . . . I gotta get something outta the glove box!" He tries to crawl back.

"Mason, don't," I plead. "Don't, Mason!" I'm holding on to his pant leg, and the car explodes. Mason collapses on top of me, and we just lie there on the muddy bank, gasping and coughing, black poisonous smoke swirling all around us. The only other sound's the river's slap, the whap and sizzle, the hoarse roar of flames.

A woman is standing by the burning car. Where did she come from? She's too close! Get back! Wait. It's our mother in her recital gown, her braids undone. I try to call to her, but I have no voice, no breath, no words. I reach out my hand, but she just stares. That's right, she probably cannot see us here in the darkness, in the night, behind this black veil. She turns slowly and walks into the river, holding a small boy's hand. Flames adorn her hair like satin ribbons. Her gown blossoms like a parasol opening on the water. The boy's head has already disappeared.

VII. The Bach Four-Part Inventions, One

A woman is playing the piano but not very well. She plays the same piece — one of Bach's four-part inventions — over and over again. The first few measures she plays perfectly and then she makes a little boo-boo. She cringes and keeps going. There are more mistakes and then it's out of control. She has fucked it all up. She bangs on the keys a few times like a chimpanzee, lights a cigarette, gets up, walks around the piano, and then stubs out the cigarette, sits down, takes a deep breath and blows it out like she's blowing out the candles on a birthday cake, and starts over.

The first few measures she plays perfectly and then she makes a little boo-boo. She gets up again and goes into the kitchen, opens the cupboard under the sink, moves a gallon jug of Clorox, and pulls out a fifth of Dewar's scotch from behind it. She takes a big swig and another, then puts the bottle back, goes back to the piano, sits down, and tries again. The first few measures she plays perfectly and then she makes a little boo-boo. She keeps going. There are more mistakes and then it is out of control. She's fucked it all up again.

Directly above the room where the woman is playing the same Bach four-part invention over and over again, a man is putting on a roof. The hammering is what's messing up the woman's concentration. Sort of. Not really. There are picture windows on each side of the room and a long hall that goes from the back of the house up to the front, to this room with the French doors and the grand piano. Beyond the door is a deck without a railing and eight feet below that a yard that is nothing but white beach sand.

The rooms in the back have only studs for walls and patches here and there of pink insulation like cotton candy. There are places without insulation where you can walk through the walls like a ghost. The house is a work in progress. For four years, the man on the roof and the woman playing the piano lived in a circus tent while they saved money for building materials and worked little by little on this house, which they have both grown to hate. The woman calls the house Mephistopheles.

The woman playing the piano is taking piano lessons. She's taken lessons before, quite a few times. Every time the woman begins taking piano lessons, she starts out with the John Schaum violet book: "Deep River," "Tales of Hoffman," *"Für Elise," "Kinderszenen."* These she can play well. In no time she's progressed to the Clementi sonatinas, and everything's hunky-dory. Inevitably, though, one day she'll go to her lesson, ready for a new piece, and the teacher will pull out a book of Bach inventions. Her heart will race. The party's over.

The Bach inventions are what she's been dreading, waiting for. The Bach inventions are the edge of the plateau she's been playing on. Now, she's at the precipice. She'll quit taking piano lessons, and then she'll start taking correspondence math courses. She'll stay up late at night doing quadratic equations at the kitchen table and copying them neatly onto graph paper with a mechanical pencil, then mailing them off like love letters to her teacher at the University of North Carolina. Then waiting, waiting for the answer, for the mail.

All she wants to know is this: *Is she right or is she wrong?*

The piano belongs to the woman. It once belonged to the woman's mother, who was a concert pianist before the woman was born and for many years taught piano. The woman's brother was also an accomplished pianist who won a national jazz piano competition when he was only twelve. That was twenty-nine years ago, in 1952, when the woman was only a baby. Everyone in the woman's family could play the piano, in fact, her father and her sister, Albertine, too. When the woman was a little girl, she could pick out the melody of anything on the piano, all the songs on the radio, anything she heard anybody sing. She always started on the right note, in the right key, no matter how many sharps and flats there were. But once she started taking piano lessons, the songs in her head got all confused with the black bars and fly droppings on the sheet music. Sometimes she would kick the piano. She bent the hand off the metronome and dropped it down the furnace vent. *Clink!* She banged the keys with her fists. She hated taking piano lessons, she hated the piano. Her mother said she could quit taking lessons and play the trombone instead, an instrument that played one note at a time, a note you got to make yourself and didn't have to find with keys and fingerings.

"This trombone belonged to Grandpa Doc," the little girl's mother told her. "Playing a trombone is as easy as whistling," the mother said. "Grandpa Doc played this trombone in P. T. Barnum's circus, and he played it in vaudeville, and he played it in Tommy Dorsey's band, and I bet you can play it, too, Ruby Jean! Here, sweetheart, try it!"

Ruby Jean did learn to play the trombone when she was a little girl, but when she got older, she thought maybe she could play the piano after all. She thought she could get it right, but she was wrong. Sometimes she plays now just to annoy her husband, Boo, the man on the roof, but when he's out, she plays without the music: "Take Five," "Laura," "Old Dog Tray."

Boo, the man putting on the roof, goes up and down the ladder, carrying stacks of roof shingles on his shoulder. He wears shorts and a tool belt. Red Wing work boots. A white T-shirt wrapped around his head like a turban. A hammer swings from his belt. Up and down. Up and down he goes. He doesn't look in the window at Ruby playing the piano, and Ruby doesn't look up or out . . .

The sun is just beginning to burn off the morning haze, and Ruby takes another swig of Dewar's. She lights another cigarette and takes a few drags and then sits down in front of the Bach four-part invention. The first few measures she plays perfectly and then she makes a little boo-boo. She cringes and keeps going.

Boo has had it up to here. He comes down off the ladder and kicks open the door.

"Goddammit, Ruby," he shouts, "just stop it. Do you hear me? I said stop it!"

But Ruby keeps playing, staring straight ahead, her hands shaking, playing anything at all. Playing pieces of "Chopsticks" and "Little Brown Jug." Playing "Tales of Hoffman" and *"Kinderszenen"* and more "Chopsticks" and "Heart and Soul" and *"Für Elise"* and more "Little Brown Jug" and *Mamma's little baby loves short'nin', short'nin' / Mamma's little baby loves short'nin' bread / Short'nin', short'nin', short'nin', short'nin'* . . . Louder and louder. Again and again. *Short'nin', short'nin', short'nin', short'nin'.* Playing, playing. *Short'nin' bread!*

"Goddammit, Ruby, I'm warning you," Boo shouts. "I'm sick of your fuckin' shit." He knocks Ruby off the piano bench and kicks the bench across the room.

Ruby lies on the floor, pretending she's dead.

"Get up, Ruby!" Boo shouts. "Get the fuck up! I know you're

not hurt." He kicks her once in the butt, but Ruby doesn't feel anything. She doesn't flinch. She's removed herself from her body, something she often does, and is standing in the kitchen, watching this melodrama.

"OK, Ruby, that's enough! Get up!" Boo demands. "Get up or the piano's going out the door."

Nothing.

Boo struts over and opens the French doors and pushes the piano toward the opening.

A five-pound bag of Gold Medal flour sits on the kitchen counter, watching, and Ruby imagines she picks it up and throws it at Boo. She aims for his head but misses it by at least twelve feet. The bag lands not far away from Ruby but explodes with a satisfying thud and wonderful poof, a big white cloud like a gloved magician might produce.

"Ruby," Boo says through his teeth, really losing control now. The cords in his neck stand up like stays in a corset. "Ruby, goddammit, don't make me do this . . ."

He rolls the piano right up to the threshold.

"Ruby, you're making me fuckin' do this . . . Ruby, I know you hear me, Ruby, you're the one who's doin' this. Ruby . . . for chrissake, just get up. I'm giving you one last chance to get the fuck up . . ."

Nothing.

VIII. Beautiful Dreamer, Two

"You wanna kill yourself, Mason?" my father says. "Go on, Mason. Do everybody a favor. Just kill yourself, but leave Ruby here. Leave your sister and your wife and your kids here." My father's voice is shaking. He turns around and walks out. The door slams. The house is dark except for a Mickey Mouse night light in the hall. Behind the bedroom doors are Mason's wife and kids, but not a sound, not a peep out of anybody.

"I'm sorry, Ruby," Mason says. "I'm so fuckin' sorry. Here." He reaches in his pocket and hands me a wad of money, a crumpled paper. His hand is clammy and shaky, his eyes bloodshot and rheumy, his breath sour.

"I don't need it," I say.

"Take it," Mason insists, blinking and swaying. "You can use it."

"I don't want it," I say, but I take it anyway. "Thanks, Mason. I'm sorry."

He's wobbling back and forth and I hug him. I really love him, but he's so fucked up. It's about one A.M., and I've just taken a shower at Mason's house and put on some of Lynnette's clothes from the laundry room. A pair of jeans, a gray sweatshirt, a pair of rubber flip-flops. Mason and I have been treated at Saint Vincent's emergency room for bruises and lacerations, and released.

"Let me take care of everything," Mason had said when the police came to the scene of the accident. "Don't say anything, Ruby."

Mason knew the sheriff. He managed to pull himself together and tell the sheriff some big whopper about a deer, a big buck running out in front of the car. "Yes, I was driving . . . No, no one was drinking . . . No, no one was speeding."

"Close call, there. Take it easy, Doc," the sheriff said, patting Mason on the back when he dropped us off at St. Vincent's. The sheriff's name is Jerrad and he and Mason went to grade school together. He's a total loser.

IX. The Bach Four-Part Inventions, Two

All afternoon the rubberneckers have been driving by on Jackson Circle to gawk at the busted grand piano in Boo and Ruby's yard. From the sky, Ruby imagines, the piano must look like a huge burnt pork chop on a dinner napkin, something to be taken home to a dog. Ruby's still lying on the floor, pretending to be dead, willing herself not to have to pee, not to crave a cigarette, perfecting the position she landed in when Boo knocked her off the piano bench, holding it like a child playing the game Statues, concentrating on the rigidity of every muscle, the density of each bone, the red velvet sponge cake linings of her eyelids, the sea-raucous in the chambers of her ears—the little hammers, anvils, and stirrups furiously pummeling the sound waves—the crazy buzz of atoms crooning, *Ruby, Ruby, when will you be mine?*

Ruby will not move until Boo apologizes—however long it takes—until he gets down on the floor and picks her up. Maybe someone, maybe Ruby's best friend, Vivvy, will come to the door and then Boo will have to keep her at bay so she won't see Ruby looking dead on the floor. That would serve him right. Most likely that won't happen, though. Vivvy would see the piano out front and put two and two together and stay away.

Ruby hears the cars go by slowly every now and then on Jackson Circle. She hears thunder. She hears rain.

X. Beautiful Dreamer, Three

Outside Mason's house that May night in 1970, our father sat in his car with the engine running and the window open, smoking a Kent. I got in, and he started driving home. He was only sixty years old then, when I think of it now, but he looked so old and tiny that night behind the steering wheel—like Geppetto, the puppet maker.

We drove in silence, through the town where Mason lived and out onto the highway. "He could have been anything," our father said after a while, his cigarette glowing red, the dash lights green. "He was always the brightest. He was always the smartest. Your mother used to hold him on her lap and play the piano all day. If she stopped playing, he'd scream . . . She used to sit there, nursing him, one hand playing the piano. First the treble, then the bass clef . . . He could read music before he turned four. Just put it together on his own. He could have been anything, and he's nothing but a drunk . . . and God only knows what else he's taking. They say he doesn't have any customers anymore. I've heard people talk. Lynnette's been making excuses for him, but she can't keep it up. He's not there half the time. And he's going to end up giving somebody the wrong prescription; he'll mix something wrong and kill somebody if he doesn't stop. It's just a matter of time. He'll lose his license. He'll lose his home. And his family. He'll end up killing himself if he doesn't stop. Your mother's heart would break if she could see him now. Nothin' but a . . ."

We drove a few more miles. I pressed my forehead against the window and pretended to be asleep, listening to the steady *slish* of the tires and the windshield wipers keeping time. Cold. Beautiful cold. My hand and my knee were starting to throb in spite of the Demerol and Valium. In the car window, I looked at my reflection and within it I saw my mother playing the piano, baby Mason hidden behind the veil of her long black hair. Flames with blue tips tangoed across the keyboard. *Beautiful Dreamer,* I sang to myself over and over,

> *wake unto me*
> *Starlight and dewdrops are waiting for thee*
> *Sounds of the rude world heard in the day*
> *Lull'd by the moonlight have all pass'd away.*

We were just a little ways now from the new development outside Ashport where my father and stepmother lived.

"Daddy, it was me," I said as we pulled in the driveway. "It wasn't Mason. It was me driving. Daddy, I'm the drunk driver. Not Mason."

My father didn't reply. He turned the engine off, and we got out. A big white hoop encircled the moon and one puny star as well, and Orion was balancing precariously on the chimney of my father's house, looking more like a silly jumping jack than a great warrior. The porch light was on, and from the room above the garage, Deenie, in huge pink hair rollers, was looking out the master bedroom window.

The night had turned cold. I blew a little puff of breath into the night air, but you couldn't see it. I hid my hands in Lynnette's sweatshirt and wrapped my arms around myself against the chill as we walked to the front door. I began to wonder what had happened to my buckskin jacket and my cowboy boots, and I tried to retrace the day's events—Mason coming to my dorm, Angela Park, the Rainbow and Chantz Phillips, the accident, Officer Jerrad and the squad car, St. Vincent's emergency room, Mason's house. My head was spinning.

Inside the house, my father hung his coat and hat in the closet and went upstairs. I heard him and Deenie talking. I went over to my mother's piano and opened the top, held down the soft pedal and played with one hand, picking out "Beautiful Dreamer" and then "Suzanne," wishing somehow I could put them together, play them both at the same time, not like a medley but strands of them at the same time like Mason could do. I could hear them at the same time in my head but couldn't play them together. I knew only that they were in the same key and anything in the same key could be played at the same time like a fugue, but I couldn't play them together any more than I could hum them at the same time, but still they went on that way in my head.

My father came and put his hand on my shoulder. "Go to bed now, Ruby," he said. "Please. We're all tired. It's been a long night. It's very late, and Deenie has to get up early."

XI. The Bach Four-Part Inventions, Three

The rain has stopped, the night has cleared, the moon dangles plump and bright against the night like a pearl on a fishing line. Outside the bedroom window, in the moonlight, Ruby can just make out the laundry, motionless on the line. It's been hanging there for days. A mile away at the Chicken Moon a rockabilly band is playing loudly, and the bass reverberates across the salt marsh, across the dredged-up sand flats of the Jackson Tract and right up under Ruby and Boo's bed, where it throbs like the Tell-Tale heartbeat. Every time Ruby thinks Boo is finally asleep, she tries to move a little, but he groans and tightens his grip on her wrist. Sooner or later, though, he'll fall deeply asleep—he's drunk, he'll fall asleep—and Ruby will get herself free, make her move. In the meantime, she lies there, plotting.

To pass the time, she recites silently her favorite parts of the Lutheran service and bits of *Alice in Wonderland*.

May the peace of God, which passeth all understanding, keep your hearts and minds in Christ Jesus, Amen. . . . The keys to the Beemer are in Boo's shorts pocket, on the floor by the bed. . . . *"The time has come," the Walrus said, "to talk of many things"* . . . I have to find the other set of keys . . . abscond with both sets so he can't come after me in the truck. *"Of shoes and ships and sealing wax"* . . . The big jar of tips is on the kitchen counter. *"Of cabbages and kings"* . . . My clothes are on the living room floor . . . *"And why the sea is boiling hot"* . . . I'll go out the back door where there aren't any steps yet. Jump down . . . wake up Phinny from under the deck, lead him by his collar . . .

Shaking, her teeth chattering like she's in the grip of a fever, Ruby finally gets the key in the ignition. Her left leg wobbles as she pushes in the clutch. *Reverse. . . . Reverse. . . . Where the hell is reverse? Please don't let the porch light come on.* She turns the key and breathes in a shallow, choppy breath. It must be just before dawn. She looks over her right shoulder to back out around the pickup, out onto Jackson Circle, and there's a knock on the driver's window. Her heart stops, and she's so terrified, too terrified to turn or even scream. She's paralyzed. She's shaking and crying now, and through the blur, straight ahead, a light comes on in the back of Mephistopheles, illuminating a block of white sand in the side yard, like a slice of Wonder bread. Her brain and heart are racing. She half turns toward the driver's window and with a start takes in Cloud, his long, moon-blanched face, whiter than possible, the fantastic pink eyes and silver halo of hair. The pale, loose pajamas. The open mouth. The high-pitched, frantic gibberish. The webbed fingers gesturing, pointing frantically to the shipwreck of a piano in the yard.

The year is 1981. The month is April. High above and far away, a space shuttle is just passing out of the Earth's atmosphere on its maiden voyage. From inside the spacecraft, Commander John

Young and Pilot Robert Crippen peer out in wonder at the galaxy sprinkled like dandruff on the black, vast shoulders of the universe. With a clumsy gloved finger, Commander Young points in the direction of Earth, which appears as a pale, watery blue dot, rapidly receding.

Pilot Crippen raises his hand and waves. "Bye-bye," he says. "See ya later, alligator."

"Sayonara," says Commander Young.

"Shalom."

"Ciao."

XII. Stardust, Two

The last time I saw Mason was 1986 in Philadelphia. I was attending the annual meeting of the American Society of Technical Writers, and I looked him up. Mason was living in a seedy hotel —a flophouse, I guess you could call it—in the inner city. I pulled up across the street from the hotel in my ex-husband's Beemer, the car I had stolen from him for my great escape five years earlier. There was trash everywhere around the building where Mason lived. Soggy newspapers and fast food tinfoil wrappers were clotted and glistening in the gutter. I didn't recognize Mason at first because he looked smaller and his hair was dyed black. I hadn't seen him since a few months after our father's funeral eleven years earlier. Mason's nose was purplish, and he was wearing a dingy yellow leisure suit and a maroon, pilled Banlon shirt that emphasized his belly. He stood on the corner with his hands in his pockets, jingling the loose change in his pocket.

"Howzit goin', Ruby?" Mason asked as I got out of my car. "That your car?"

"Yeah," I said. "Same old piece o' shit. A hundred and eighty thousand miles. It was Boo's . . . my ex-husband's. It was an old piece of junk when he bought it, and that was years ago. Nothing works but the gas and the brakes. Want it?"

"Nah, you keep it, Ruby." Mason laughed and coughed. "I don't drive anymore."

We walked a few doors down to a Chock Full o' Nuts coffee shop. Some desperate-looking people sat alone in separate booths. "Howzit goin'?" Mason said to each of them as we walked by. "Howzit goin', Buddy? Howzit goin', Timbo? Howzit goin', Cecil?"

"Howzit goin', Doc?" they mumbled back, as if we were walking through an echo chamber.

Mason and I each ordered a cup of coffee and just sat looking at each other, smiling nervously. I didn't know what to say.

The waitress brought our order. "Do you ever play the piano anymore?" I asked Mason after a while.

He just laughed. He took his right hand out of his pocket and brought it up to his coffee cup. His hand shook so badly the coffee sloshed out over the saucer and the table. He mopped up the spilled coffee with wads of tiny, inadequate napkins from the chrome dispenser, his hand seeming to enjoy the circular motion. He put his head down to the thick china cup and slurped up some coffee. A gray, crooked stripe ran down the crown of Mason's head.

"You still got that old silver-plated trombone of Grandpa Doc's?" Mason asked me. "Now there was a buncha crackpots for ya!" he added, laughing and coughing.

"Nah, that's long gone," I said, and we both laughed.

"You got Mother's piano, didn't you," Mason asked me, "after Daddy died and Deenie sold the house? That Kurtzmann," he said, coughing into his hand, "now that's one beautiful piano."

Before I could answer, Mason started coughing again. He coughed and coughed, and the coughing turned into a coughing fit. He couldn't stop coughing. He knocked over his coffee cup, and coffee dribbled off the table onto his shirt and into his lap. We both stood up, and while I was cleaning up the Formica table with wads of the teeny napkins and Mason was wiping the coffee off his pants, he turned and said to me, "Listen, Ruby, I gotta run. It was nice seein' ya, but I gotta go. I gotta . . ."

He coughed some more. "Take it easy, Ruby-Ruby, ya hear? I'll be seein' ya." He patted me on the back and leaned toward me like he would kiss me on the cheek. A warped blind of transparent

49

amber plastic, serving as a sun shield, was pulled down over the front of the Chock Full o' Nuts, and through the smudged and wavy film and the backwards letters painted in an arc on the window, I watched Mason in his stained and rumpled leisure suit disappear.

XIII. Old Dog Tray

When I think of Mason, I like to remember him as far back as I can: the big brother I adored, a boy in blue jeans with the bottoms turned up, a kid doing rope tricks, a boy about thirteen or fourteen playing the same three pieces on the piano over and over again: "Beautiful Dreamer" by Stephen Foster, Beethoven's *"Für Elise,"* and David Raksin's "Laura," the theme song from the 1944 Otto Preminger movie by the same name.

The day our dog Go-Jeff died in the summer of 1957, I woke up in the middle of the night after crying myself to sleep and heard someone playing the piano. I got out of bed and went out in the hall. Albertine was sitting on a step halfway down the stairs, looking through the railing, and I went and sat down two steps above her. The living room was dark. Mason was home from the Friends' school that summer and was seated at the piano playing "Old Dog Tray," another Stephen Foster piece, but woven all through it and wrapped all around it were the teardrops of *"Für Elise,"* and the long, ethereal strands of "Beautiful Dreamer," and the heartbreaking cadence of "Laura," like George Shearing played it, all mixed together in a syncopated, slow jazz tempo. My mother came and sat beside me in her blue robe and put her arm around me. I heard my father light a match behind us and smelled its sulfur and then the smoke from his Kent.

Earlier that day, our father had buried Go-Jeff under the cherry tree in our backyard, and I played "Elegy" on my Grandpa Doc's trombone. I had made a grave marker out of a tomato stake and a piece of cardboard from one of my father's dry-cleaned Sunday shirts. I drew a cross on the cardboard in blue crayon and Albertine wrote on it:

Go-Jeff
R.I.P.
Beloved Reese Family Dog

I added some daisies and a little brown and white dog to the cardboard marker.

That night, when Mason was done playing "Old Dog Tray," he just sat there with his hands on his knees and his head bowed over the piano keys as the last note drifted out through the open window and down Cherry Street and across Elysian Avenue, across the railroad tracks and over the old iron suspension bridge, out past Buck Run and down River Road to the Susquehanna River, where Mr. Phillips, Etherine, Trace, Ramona, and Chantz would live for a short time, and a little ways farther where the dike along Riverview Lutheran cemetery would give way, caskets sweeping all the way down into the Chesapeake Bay, where one day our mother would appear to Mason and me along the riverbank, then wade back out, indifferent, into the cold, lapping water, holding Trace's hand, and on up Buck Mountain where some years away I would total his Porsche, up over the top of the rickety wooden roller coaster, the Hurricane, at Angela Park, and off into the black and starry night sky, and we stole back to our beds—my mother, my father, Albertine, and me—without so much as a word, and outside our windows the billions of crickets and peepers sang their two-note songs.

Shuffle Off to Buffalo

1958 — Our mother couldn't sleep at night, and so she walked. She walked all night in a long blue nightgown and a blue quilted robe, up and down the hallway, playing her violin. The hall was long, with a hardwood floor and a dark, wine-colored runner. Ivy twined and dogwoods blossomed on the walls. We left our bedroom doors ajar, and it was so comforting to see our mother walking back and forth, playing whatever she was playing, especially if you were lying awake and couldn't sleep, maybe worrying about something like a recitation for school or a trombone lesson from Mr. Wallace, with his hot, stinky breath, stringy hair, and bleeding fingertips — the nails bitten down below the quick.

Sometimes I'd wave to our mother when she passed by our door. If she had her eyes open and saw me wave, she'd come into our room and stand by my side of the bed and play her violin, and I'd reach out and pet her puffy satin robe. Sometimes she'd walk over to the front window and look out across Cherry Street, toward the cemetery and Elysian Avenue, the river, and the little blue mountains. Sometimes she'd play me a sailor's hornpipe or a jig.

Our mother rarely wore shoes. Her feet were wide and flat.

The bottoms of her feet had their own brown soles like gum shoes: hard, flat, pocked a little, worn smooth. When the weather was nice, sometimes our mother would walk around outside our house at night and play her violin. We could see her out our bedroom window, walking back and forth underneath the clothesline in her bare feet, with her blue robe and her long black braids. Around and around the cherry tree she'd walk, and up and down beneath the clothesline.

Sometimes our mother would climb up on the brick coping where the ladybugs lived and walk back and forth between our house and the next double house, where the Ivkovitches and the Wagners lived. Sometimes you'd see the Ivkovitches looking out their bedroom windows, too: Mr. and Mrs. Ivkovitch in one window, Larry in the middle window, and Ruthie in the little room on the end like Albertine's and mine, their white, sleepy faces all looking down on our mother as she walked back and forth atop the coping, playing her violin. Sometimes Ruthie and I would wave to each other from our bedroom windows. Sometimes we'd hold up our Revlon dolls in their shortie pajamas and make them wave, too. After a while, we'd all—except our mother—go back to sleep.

While our mother walked at night playing her violin, our father slept in the sleigh bed in the room at the end of the hall, the door wide open. Sometimes, late at night, you could see him in there reading. When he got up in the morning to go to work, our mother put down her violin and made us tea with Carnation evaporated milk, and toast cut diagonally, with butter and Dundee orange marmalade, which we ate off of Fiestaware saucers. Sometimes we'd have cornmeal mush with milk and King syrup, and sometimes a piece of shoofly pie—my favorite!—made with Brer Rabbit molasses.

Then, when our father put on his hat and got into his fat, two-tone car and drove away, our mother went to bed. She slept in the exact same spot where our father had slept all night, a warm, nestlike place with a goose-down pillow and a yellow wool blanket, the violin on the bedspread-covered pillow beside her. Sometimes I'd stay home from school for no reason (except maybe to avoid a recitation or a dreadful trombone lesson), and then I'd scoot over the violin and its bow and pull the spread down and get in bed beside her.

Sometimes I'd sleep, and sometimes I'd read a favorite book, the same book over and over, like *Little Bear Goes to the Moon, Baby's House,* or *Mister Dog: The Dog Who Belonged to Himself.* Sometimes I'd color a little or get my black View-Master and its shoebox of picture wheels and click through spokes of strange dioramas: *Little Red Riding Hood, Peter Pan, Mary Poppins, The Big Bad Wolf,* and poor, frantic *Chicken Little*—all frozen in motion like statues—or the View-Master's fly-size picture postcards of the wonders of the world: Vesuvius, the Leaning Tower of Pisa, Pompeii. But mostly I'd just lie there next to our mother's violin and whisper made-up stories to myself, or hum my favorite tunes and pull the tufts out of the white chenille bedspread with the pink cabbage roses. Sometimes I'd just look around the room and listen to the music of the birds in the cherry tree, the bathroom's dripping faucet, the clanging radiators, Mrs. Ivkovitch's clothesline pulley, while I said my favorite words over and over to myself like a person counting sheep: RAIN-DEER, WORCESTERSHIRE, ASPEN, TAFFETA, NINCOMPOOP, SQUIRREL.

Sometimes I'd close my eyes, and big white sheep with black faces would jump across the bed, then file out the door, down the hall, and down the stairs for a cup of tea made with Carnation evaporated milk, which is milk from contented cows. When each sheep was midair across our parents' sleigh bed, it would turn its black face to me, smile or yawn, and in a gravelly, sheeplike voice mutter: RAIN-DEER, WORCESTERSHIRE, ASPEN, TAFFETA, NINCOMPOOP or SQUIRREL. There were hundreds of sheep downstairs while our mother and I slept, standing on their hind legs, sitting on the davenport, sipping tea, and making conversation, saying things to one another like:

"I had a rain-deer. I fed him Worcestershire sauce."

"He dressed in taffeta?"

"You don't say, you nincompoop!"

"Hello, my name is Aspen!"

"Look, there goes a squirrel!"

When our mother woke up in the afternoon, we'd go downstairs and make more tea with Carnation evaporated milk and have ourselves a bowl of bow-tie noodles with butter and Worcestershire sauce and lots of salt and pepper. The sheep would be gone by then, without a trace, except for here and there a sheep-shaped impression on a davenport pillow or an indentation on a footstool where a hoof had been. After lunch, I'd tie on my tap shoes, and our mother would accompany me on the piano while I rehearsed my routine for *The Ted Mack Amateur Hour*. Out in the tiled vestibule, just beyond the piano, I'd tap dance and sing:

> *Sugar in the mornin'*
> *Sugar in the evenin'*
> *Sugar at suppertime*
> *Be my little sugar, and*
> *Love me all the time.*

When our father came home from work, he'd hang his hat on the coat tree, set his lunch pail down on the cobbler's bench, take off his work boots, and say, "So, how was school today, girls?" and Albertine and I would both say "fine," pronouncing it as a long, two-syllabled word, my sister not looking up from her book.

While we were still saying *fiiiii-ne,* our mother would sneak a look at me, cover her mouth with her fingers, and wink. Albertine, who always had her nose in a book, would emit an exasperated sigh and roll her eyes, and then continue reading, rocking in the gooseneck rocker so fast, our father would have to put his foot on one of the rockers and say, "Slow down there, cowgirl!" Then Albertine would go to her room and read all evening. She'd come down for dinner—Mrs. Paul's fish sticks and Mrs. T's pierogies, or Swanson's chicken or beef potpies, or, my favorite: Dinty Moore meatball stew—but she always ate behind a book. We rarely saw my sister's face, which was very round. She had pink cheeks, skinny black braids, black eyes, and thick, pale blue glasses with diamonds on the corners.

Every Saturday night our mother and I washed our hair while

Albertine—who was allowed to wash her hair by herself in the tub—stayed upstairs and read her books. First our mother took a little tin pan and put a big lump of Crisco in it. Next, she struck a kitchen match and lit a burner on the stove. When the Crisco was melted, she let it cool a little and added some vanilla. Then we rubbed the vanilla oil into each other's braids with our fingers and wrapped our heads in old towels. Then we played a card game, either slapjack, gin rummy, or my favorite, crazy eights.

Sometimes Albertine would play cards with us, too, her book in her lap and her cards spread out in front of her face like a geisha girl's fan. Our mother was a cheater, but Albertine and I always pretended not to notice. We always let her win. Our mother was very pretty, especially when she smiled or laughed. She had a little space between her front teeth, and when she smiled, like for a picture, she always put her tongue behind the space. Her eyes sparkled and she laughed when she won at crazy eights or rummy. She'd slap her hand down on top of the cards, lean back in the kitchen chair, and say, "Better luck next time, my little chickadees!" and then Albertine would take off her glasses, and we would both laugh, too, all three of us at the table laughing, our mother and me with fraying towels wrapped around our heads, Albertine with *Little Women* or *A Boy's King Arthur* in her lap, rubbing her eyes.

Then Albertine would go back upstairs, and I would stand on a stool, and our mother and I would wash each other's hair in the kitchen sink, which had two faucets high up on the wall. We'd take turns with the plastic juice pitcher, going back and forth, back and forth, under the hot and cold spigots. Then we'd rub each other's head with towels and braid each other's hair and smooth out the stray ends—the *escapees,* our mother called them—with the remaining vanilla Crisco.

Our mother was not supposed to go out of the yard, but one night I woke up and looked out the side window to see if Ruthie Ivkovitch was looking out her window, too. She wasn't. I looked out the front window, and I saw our mother in her blue robe across the street in the Catholic cemetery, walking on the gravel path, playing her violin! I thought maybe I should wake up Albertine or our father, but then, for some reason I don't remember, I changed my mind. I pulled on my cowboy boots and zipped up my red sweatshirt with the hood over my shortie pajamas, and ran downstairs. I put on my Davy Crockett real live coonskin cap and went out the front door and crossed over to the cemetery, but when I got there, I couldn't find our mother. I ran down the path we always walked and up to the big stone angel with the poem, *For in that sleep of death what dreams may come when we have shuffled off this mortal coil?*, but our mother wasn't there.

Then, through the iron fence, I saw our mother in her blue robe and bare feet walk past the Neapolitan pizza parlor on Elysian Avenue. I ran around to the other gate and out, and waited for the traffic light to change, and then I ran across the avenue. Our mother was playing a Mario Lanza song, "Be My Love."

"Mother," I said, touching her robe, "you better come home. Daddy said you weren't supposed to go out of the yard."

"Sweetheart," she said, still playing and leaning toward me, smiling, "it's OK. I just ordered us a pizza!"

"Will it have anchovies?" I asked, jumping up and down.

"You betcha!" our mother said to me and winked, her face so white against the violin's little black chin rest.

The pizza parlor smelled so good. We hardly ever got pizza, and it sounded like such a good idea. You could see our double house with its green shingles under the streetlight on the other side of the cemetery. *Be my love . . .* went the words to the song our mother was playing. I walked back and forth in front of the pizza parlor with our mother, and sang the song. I put my hands over my heart and sang like Mario Lanza while our mother played:

> *Be my love*
> *For no one else can end this yearning*
> *This need that you and you alone create*
>
> *Just fill my arms the way you've filled my dreams*
> *The dreams that you inspire with every sweet desire . . .*

A man in a baseball jacket and a woman in a big circle skirt came out of the pizza parlor. Our mother was playing "Indian Love Call."

> *When I'm calling you Oo-oo-oo Oo-oo-oo*
> *Will you answer too Oo-oo-oo Oo-oo-oo?*

I sang. The man cupped his hands and lit a cigarette and threw the match down. He took the woman's hand and they walked away, but the woman kept looking back. I jumped up in the air and clicked my heels together and waved to her. Our mother played two more songs while we were waiting for the pizza, and I sang along: "You Belong to Me," then "Lover, Come Back to Me."

> *I remember every little thing you used to do*
> *I'm so lonely!*
> *Every road I walk along, I've walked along with you*
> *No wonder I am lonely . . .*
>
> *The sky is blue, the night is cold,*
> *the moon is new, the song is old.*
> *This aching heart of mine,*
> *this heart of mine is singing,*
> *Lover, come back to me!*

I was getting so hungry for the juicy pizza with the salty anchovies and the thick, warm fingers of crust, but suddenly the blue neon lights flicked off over the front of the Neapolitan pizza parlor, and a man in white pants with a white apron and a white T-shirt with a pack of cigarettes rolled up in the sleeve came out the door. He put his hands on our mother's shoulders and said, "Eva, please. Eva, please don't do this. Eva, listen to me. Eva, take your little girl and go on home now, or I'll have to call your husband. I'll have to call Albert again. Eva, please."

He turned around to go back inside. Our mother started to cry. She jumped in front of the pizza man and scowled and made the violin bow chop angrily across the strings: the violin was mad! the violin was screaming! the violin was swearing! The

58

pizza man went inside and slammed the glass door. A sign jumped, a little bell rang. He flipped over the sign from OPEN to CLOSED and turned out the lights.

Above the café curtains, the street lights shone in on the dark pizza parlor, and we could see the pizza man turning all the wooden chairs upside down on top of the dark tables and hear the chair legs make their sharp, scraping sound. He never turned around or looked our way.

Our mother stood there, staring in the pizza parlor window, two big white handprints on her pale blue shoulders like she would, in a second, start to polka with a ghost. She had her violin in one hand, the bow in the other, and she just stood there crying. The violin slipped from her fingers and sang a little hollow song on the sidewalk. I picked it up and took our mother's hand. The street light was buzzing, her hand was limp, my heart was pounding. I didn't know what to do or say, so I tried to say very cheerily, "Shall we shuffle off to Buffalo?" like our father always said when we were going out the door.

Out on the Jackson Tract

Land was cheap then out on the Jackson Tract—in the mid-seventies—and Boo and Ruby had a little money. Those lots on the Jackson Tract have increased in value a hundredfold, but back then in 1975 when Ruby and Boo were just out of graduate school, they had this bit of money—cash graduation gifts from family, and Ruby had sold her car for six hundred dollars, an old '62 Mercedes named Pete, who needed a new engine. And there was the small inheritance Ruby's father had left her, enough to get her through a year or so. And they had so few expenses, camping all summer as they had been. They had been living together since spring break, since soon after Ruby's father died, and after graduation, they took Ruby's new puppy, Phineas, and packed everything into Boo's VW microbus and headed east and south, toward the ocean and the sun, devoid of ambition and career goals, and full of life. They had master's degrees in English from West Virginia University, and what could they do with such degrees?

"English teacher, eh?" the career counselor had said to both of them, smiling, leaning back in his chair and petting his tie. "A dime a dozen. Try something like technical writer. Work for the big guns."

Later, walking home, Boo asked Ruby, "What the hell's a technical writer?"

"I think it has something to do with directions, writing directions maybe, like operating instructions for electric knives and stuff," Ruby replied. "What are 'big guns'?"

They shrugged their shoulders and the next night started driving. They ended up on the Outer Banks of North Carolina, working in the tourist establishments—Ruby first as a maid and then as a waitress at the Pirate's Cove, and Boo as a bartender at the Dolphin—bringing home jars overflowing with dollar bills every night. During the day they slept on the beach or made love in the dunes, and Ruby collected shells and read her nineteenth-century novels, and Boo snorkeled or bodysurfed on a yellow boogie board, or read his Stephen King, Richard Brautigan, and Kurt Vonnegut. When it rained, they stayed in their tent, reading or playing pinochle, listening to mixed tapes—Bruce Springsteen, Fairport Convention, Sandy Denny, Jackson Browne—or they moved from restaurant to restaurant with their notebooks and novels, eating baskets of greasy hushpuppies and drinking cup after cup of coffee and yaupon tea.

They'd been living in the national park campground all summer—seven dollars a week—and it was almost October. The tourists were gone for the most part, except on weekends, and before long the restaurants and inns would be closing and the stormy season would begin, driving away even the sport fishermen. Ruby and Boo had not really talked about where they would go or what they would do, and then one night Boo just up and bought a lot out on the Jackson Tract. Lot number 11. A thousand dollars cash. Just about all the cash they had. Signed the papers in the pool room in the back of the Chicken Moon while Ruby was in the can. She didn't care, though. They could work in the fish house, get paid cash all winter, he said, and collect unemployment, too. And there would always be free fish. All the fish they could ever eat. Mullet and sea trout, flounder, bass, and blues.

That was a long time ago. It's been twenty years since Ruby and Boo's divorce. They had married in the summer of 1975 on the south point of the beach, in their bare feet, wearing leis made of sand pennies and coquina shells. Then, seven years later, a nasty divorce that left a bitter taste in the mouth like a piece of pecan shell stuck to the sweet nutmeat, and they have not spoken since. There were no children and so contact could easily be severed once and for all. With children, it was different. For months after she left, though, Boo wrote to Ruby frequently, begging forgiveness for the busted piano and his indiscretions, she supposed, but Ruby never opened the letters. She was back in West Virginia, where she'd gotten a job as a technical writer with a coal fly ash research center. She lived alone then with her dog, Phinny, and when Boo's letters arrived, she wrote the word DECEASED across them in big block letters, then dropped the letters into the mailbox on the corner of Dorsey and Barrickman. That was how she felt, too, as if the person who had been married to Boo and lived out there in a circus tent on the Jackson Tract all those years and helped build that damn house, Mephistopheles, had died. Dead and buried. After a few weeks, though, unsatisfied with Boo's apparent remorse and wanting to punish him more, Ruby didn't bother to return the letters. She didn't want to give Boo the satisfaction of knowing the letters ever reached her or that she had taken the time to handle them and write on them in big angry letters and carry them however far in order to mail them. After the first few letters, Ruby placed them, unopened, in a shoebox in her closet, never once tempted to open them, keeping them only as emotional hostages.

She kept in touch, though, with her best friend, Vivvy, who had lived next door to them on the Jackson Tract. Vivvy and Ruby wrote to each other once a year — at Christmas time — for years. They had waitressed together at the Pirate's Cove, and it was Vivvy who taught Ruby how to knit and how to dye yarn with vegetable dyes, stewing the skeins in a cauldron of beets or walnuts or saffron suspended over a campfire; how to weave baskets out of cattails and sea oats; and how to make wind chimes out of driftwood and seashells, rusty bolts and nails, and pork chop bones. When she wrote, Vivvy avoided the subject of Boo and Felicia and told instead of books she'd read and things she was making and news of other people they worked with or who had lived out on the Jackson Tract: Happy and Sky, Celia and Cloud, Angeline and Hobie, and all the others.

All the years she lived there on Jackson Circle, Ruby had rarely navigated by car, just a rusty iron bicycle that she painted every year with white Rustoleum. The bicycle was heavy but simple, and in its whiteness looked more like an abstraction, more like the *idea* of a bike, she always thought, than a bike itself. After she moved back inland where the streets were steep and narrow and the white bike had been left behind to combine with the elements, the bike was what she missed the most. Not the husband. Not Boo. At night after her divorce, Ruby's legs ached like an amputee's with the phantom motion of pedaling against the offshore winds, and in her dreams she flew along Highway 12 like the witch out of *The Wizard of Oz,* her wicker basket full of books, seashells, and big balls of yellow yarn.

Hindsight. Ah, hindsight. Looking back at her marriage to Boo now, Ruby can't imagine that she'd ever really lived such a life. Had she really married Boo? Could it really be possible? There had been a great attraction, a great tumbling passion between them at first when they'd met in *Seventeenth-Century British Poetry* during their last year in graduate school, but in retrospect it was Andrew Marvell and John Donne, not Boo, whom Ruby had fallen in love with then. The semester before that she had fallen hopelessly in love with a boy in one of the English classes she taught as a graduate teaching assistant, and soon after he broke her heart, along came Boo, sashaying up to her at a department party held in a big Victorian house of one of the professors. Handsome Boo, with a big shimmering glass of scotch in each hand, reciting for her in his New Jersey accent, *"Had we but World enough, and Time . . ."* segueing into a finger-snapping, *"Ruby, Ruby, when will you be mine?"*

Although Ruby left the Banks when she found out about Boo's carryings on (from Angeline, finally) and moved more than six hundred miles away—back to West Virginia—she still dreamed about the Jackson Tract. About Jackson Circle, where they all lived. About the dunes along Highway 12, and their grasses, the sea oats especially, and the sage grass that turned gold, then purple in the fall, and the way the wind could run over the grasses like a hand over a headful of hair and lay them flat and then in the twinkling of an eye turn around and run the other way and pick them up again like the nap of a plush fabric or fur. There was a kind of sea grape, too, that grew in thick, low hedges like box huckleberries along the dunes, and the Bankers (what the natives of the Outer Banks called themselves) made a wine from it, like nothing you have ever tasted. Sometimes Ruby longed for a sip of that wine after all these years, like some excommunicated Catholic might long for holy communion.

One year, around Christmas, Vivvy up and sends Ruby a box full of assorted seashells packed in purple sea grass.

Picture a board game like Monopoly, a board game with a big oval drawn on it, labeled Jackson Circle. A cluster of houses at one end. On one side of the board is the ocean, represented by white-capped waves, shark fins and shipwrecks, and a candy cane–striped lighthouse. On the opposite side is Pamlico Sound. Solid blue. Across the sound lies the mainland. Out in the sound a big ol' dredge crouches like Captain Hook's crocodile. Gigantic bilge pipes the diameter of human bodies tentacle out into the Jackson Tract, and the dredge sits hunkered down in the bay all day and night, doing his business. After dark its spotlights glow like eyes as it sucks the sludge out of the bottom of the sound and vomits it up into the Jackson Tract. Land fill. All day and night you hear the sucking-belching sounds and the motors of the bilge pumps rumbling like a big empty stomach.

This is where Boo has bought a lot. There are forty-two lots on Jackson Circle, the only road in the Jackson Tract, but only a few of the lots have been sold. Every couple months, though, Boo buys another lot with his and Ruby's tips. The Jackson Tract lots are advertised in glossy supplements to Sunday newspapers and grocery store tabloids like the *Star* and the *National Enquirer.*

Very enticing, indeed. But these lots don't sell. Except to Boo. The Jacksons are hoping to become millionaires once the dredging operation is complete. For now, most of the lots are still swamp, but the Pamlico Sound is being dredged by the U.S. Army Corps of Engineers — in the name of commerce — a stroke of luck and at no expense to the Jacksons — or Boo — and the black bottom sludge is filling in the Jackson Tract around the clock like an evil brownie mix. Seven families live on the Jackson Tract during the time Ruby and Boo live there — in homes of varying degrees of modesty, ranging from an old circus sideshow tent with a center pole, a pointed roof, and blue and white striped sidewalls (Boo and Ruby's) to a post-and-beam showpiece meant to look like a frigate. There are no zoning laws as of yet in the Jackson Tract. Anything with a septic tank goes.

The county health inspector comes once a month from the mainland to inspect the septic tanks and sign building permits. He arrives on the morning ferry, spends half the day with Vivvy, the other half in the Chicken Moon, drinking drafts and shots of peppermint schnapps, or in the winter, the Chicken Moon's specialty — Georgia moonshine and Campbell's chicken noodle soup, served steaming hot in a mug, accompanied by a spoon — exchanging jokes and twenty-dollar bills and signing permits until the last ferry for the mainland leaves.

The showpiece home on the Jackson Tract, owned by the Jacksons themselves, flies the Jolly Roger from its bridge and has a sign on its deck that Barbara and Randall Jackson find supremely funny: THE POOP DECK, the sign says in wood-burnt sans serif.

The Jacksons are from Raleigh. They drive a silver Saab 99 and have matching candy-apple red dune buggies as well. They wear his and hers running suits, matching shorts, matching baseball caps, and matching T-shirts — all of which say I ♥ LIVING ON

THE JACKSON TRACT. Mrs. Jackson — Barbara, or *Bahbahrah,* as she pronounces it — has legs as thick and white as Ruby and Boo's center pole. Every morning, the Jacksons run around Jackson Circle, smiling and waving. Their son, Chick, an aspiring actor, runs too. But Chick runs alone, at the crack of dawn, reciting Shakespearean soliloquies as he jogs. *To be or not to be . . .* Boo and Ruby hear him every morning from their hide-a-bed. *Whether 'tis nobler to . . .*

There is also a sultry sixteen-year-old daughter, Felicia, who wears a black maillot and has had silicone, people say, injected into her lips, which are swollen to about the size of a pony's. Something about Felicia reminds Ruby of the stuffed wolverine displayed in one of the glass cases in the library on the mainland where Vivvy's sister, Moe, is assistant librarian, but Felicia's lips predominate. Behind her back, Ruby calls her Mick Jackson.

So now we have the board game — Jackson Circle — with Chick and Bahbahrah and Randall running around it, Chick reciting his soliloquies, and Felicia sulking on the Poop Deck. Now let the players pick a playing piece.

Team 1 — Boo and Ruby (lot 11). They'll take the circus elephant.

Team 2 — Gladys and Leviticus Tupper (lot 10). They pick the iron Scotty dog.

Team 3 — Washie Howard (lot 22). He's the captain of the dredge, the SS *Hemorrhoid,* as we call it — give him the gray plastic submarine with the baking soda propulsion chamber. You know, the kind that used to come in Rice Krispies.

Team 4 — Vivian (Vivvy) Muldar and her twin, Maureen (Moe)(lot 12). They get the open book.

Team 5 — And the Jacksons (lot 1). Now that's a tough one. Give them the die.

Team 6 — There's also Sky and Happy, the vegans, and their kid, Aphrodite Dylannia (the aphid, Ruby calls her) (lot

31). They live in the yurt with a composting toilet, the "product" of which they use to fertilize their organic garden. The first year they lived on Jackson Circle, Sky and Happy brought Boo and Ruby a box of home-grown vegetables: cabbages the size of basketballs, tomatoes the size of cabbages, and zucchini as big as Wiffle Ball bats. After they left, Ruby and Boo took the box out back to the sandpits. "Batter up," Boo said to Ruby, winding up with a tomato, and giving her a se-cret signal by pulling on his ear, scratching his nose, and touching the bill of his hat. Ruby picked up the biggest zucchini and did a deep knee bend. (Sky and Happy and the aphid, they get the miniature can of Chef Boyardee ravioli for their playing piece.)

Team 7 — And last but not least on Jackson Circle: Hobie and Angeline (lot 40). Hobie, he gets the tiny silver gun.

The Tuppers live in the first house you come to on the Jackson Tract, after that long stretch down Ammunition Dump Road past the firehouse. Lot 10, a mint green prefabricated Jim Walters home. Mr. Tupper is retired from Pennsylvania Power and Light. He's had three triple bypasses. "Nine lives," he says, lighting a Doral. Mrs. Tupper's name is Gladys, and her head is on fire. Her hair is a shocking, pot-scrubber orange. Lucille Ball meets Albert Einstein . . . on a bad-hair day. Sometimes, to save time, Gladys, a retired cosmetologist, will perm and color her hair at the same time, holding her nose and mixing the chemicals in an earthenware dog bowl in the bathroom sink, her Playtex Living gloves alive with henna and ammonia-based permanent wave solution.

Ruby has rung Gladys's doorbell to deliver a package the UPS man brought next door to her. Gladys is vacuuming, her hair wound around what looks like hundreds of tiny pink and blue rods. Gladys June with her head steaming like Mount St. Helens, Gladys with her skinny freckled legs, clam diggers, white anklets, and shiny plastic jellies. Gladys in her cat-eye glasses, zooming down the hall, past the front door, singing, *". . . red roses for a blue lady . . . ,"* oblivious to Ruby and the package and the doorbell's Westminster goings-on. Comet Gladys, with the Electrolux's fiery exhaust. Shorty-Long, her dachshund, barking and chasing behind.

"Mrs. Tupper's vacuuming again," Carl, the UPS man said, and Ruby scribbled her own name on his clipboard while he blew his nose. The package is small and the return address says, as usual: *Thank you for shopping with Harriet Carter. Free gift inside chosen especially for you,* GLADYS JUNE TUPPER.

Lot 12. Vivian and Maureen Muldar are identical twins who look *a lot* like Sigourney Weaver. Strong jaws, Jane Fonda smiles. Twenty-nine and in their prime. In their brown Speedo swimsuits, they're both lean and muscular, freckled and tall. Maureen (Moe, everyone calls her) is a librarian on the mainland. She comes to visit Vivvy on nice weekends. There's an easy way to tell them apart: Vivvy has a prominent blue vein that pulses in her left temple and a gap between her front teeth.

Vivvy and Ruby are waitresses at the Pirate's Cove. All summer long, they spend the nights taking orders for catch of the day, seafood platters, and clam fritters. Then they bicycle home to their beds, their hair reeking of fried onions, French fries, fried seafood platters. In the winter, Ruby and Vivvy collect sea shells and unemployment and do their "research" and their knitting.

On the beach on sunny Saturdays, the freckled Muldar twins — Vivvy and Moe — sun themselves. Sometimes Ruby lies down between them, pale and slathered with zinc oxide, in her faded green Jantzen one-piece, looking from a small airplane like a piece of turkey breast with iceberg lettuce between two slices of rye.

Boo and Ruby live between Vivvy and the Tuppers in a kind of Swiss Family Robinson dwelling that is part tree house without a tree, two tents joined by a boardwalk and a wraparound deck, all part of a house-in-progress. The one tent's a circus tent with striped sidewalls and a center pole in which they carve their favorite words with their Swiss army knives. SFUMATO, the pole says. SYZYGY. ESTUARY. ANTIDISESTABLISHMENTARIANISM (written sideways, top to bottom). WORCESTERSHIRE. WAPITI. SQUIRREL. It's quite charming, really, Boo and Ruby's house (except when it rains). Plastic pink flamingos stuck in the sand by the hide-a-bed couch. A tightrope (only three feet off the ground) for Ruby to practice on, walking between the center pole and the door flap.

From the library on the mainland, Moe (the twin without the temple activity) brings Vivvy and Ruby books. Virago Modern Classics, resurrected feminists like Rebecca West and Charlotte Perkins Gilman. British greats like W. H. Hudson (Ruby's favorite) and George Gissing. Part of Moe's job is purging the library's limited shelves of deadwood — books the library trustees feel no longer reflect the tastes of Hyde County nor represent a significant element of its history. Ruby and Vivvy give Moe lists of books they need for their "research"; Moe does her purging.

"It's OK," Moe says to Vivvy and Ruby. "I can justify tearing up a few catalog cards to support your 'research.' I mean, like Dewey Decimal gives a damn, and who, tell me, who, appreciates George Gissing these days but you, Vivvy? And really, Ruby, *Green Mansions?* Hell-oooo!"

Moe laughs and gives Ruby a pretend shove that nearly knocks her over because Moe is so strong and Ruby's such a weakling. Moe hands over a dozen or so former library books in a brown paper Piggly-Wiggly bag. Ruby peeks in: *Green Mansions* (Hoorah!), *Our Spoons Came from Woolworths!* (Yippee!), *The Odd Women* (Wow! Thanks, Moe!).

"You're so weird," Moe says, "both of you."

In the hide-a-bed that night, Ruby removes the library's plastic dust jacket and runs her fingertips over the cover and spine of the first-edition *Green Mansions*. Copyright 1915. One of her father's favorite books and the last one he ever read to her. An etching of W. H. Hudson for the frontispiece. From the weight of other books pressing against it, a piece of frail tissue bound in the book to protect the etching now bears a ghostly imprint of W. H. Hudson, too. A pale, reversed doppelganger.

Vivvy and Moe have that twin ESP thing. One time Vivvy awoke in the middle of the night with a terrible, a *biting* pain, she described it, in her left ankle. Moe at that very moment had been bitten by a rabid pug. Other things, too. Moe will be thinking of a song, and Vivvy will start to sing it. Ruby has conducted scientific experiments with them, placing them back to back in folding chairs in Boo's and her tent, each with a waitress's guest check book. "Write down the name of a color," Ruby instructs them, "the name of a country, a letter of the alphabet, a number between one and three thousand . . ."

Vivvy is very artistic. She has built her own little house, a cedar-shake lean-to, decorated inside and out with mirrors. Vivvy collects mirrors: rearview and side mirrors from cars; mirrors from powder compacts and makeup cases, Cracker Jack boxes, toys, and periscopes; mirrors from dressers and sideboards and medicine cabinets. Inside and out, Vivvy's house presents a fractured picture of the Jackson Tract and throws it back at itself, like a kaleidoscope. When you walk up the straw path to Vivvy's house, what you see is pieces of yourself growing bigger. Walk backwards to Jackson Circle when you leave Vivvy's house, and you will see yourself, in pieces, disappearing. If you ever want to dispose of a mirror, call Vivvy: 919-555-0122.

"Aren't you afraid you'll break one?" Ruby asks.

Sometimes in the winter when the Pirate's Cove is closed for the season, Vivvy and Ruby venture across the ferry to the mainland to visit Moe at the Hyde County Library and to hit all the Goodwills and Salvation Army thrift stores. Ruby's car now is a 1971 Plymouth Belvedere named the Bluesmobile. The Bluesmobile has a big hole in the driver's seat where the previous owner, a fat man named Fleming Ball, sat, smoking cigars and driving around the eastern seaboard selling Electrolux vacuum cleaners. On the last trip Ruby and Vivvy made to the mainland, Ruby found an evening gown at Goodwill, a gown like a mermaid's, covered in gold sequins. The dress, honest to goodness, weighed eighteen pounds. Ruby brought it home and put it on.

"Pick me up, Boo!" she said. "Pick me up!"

"Jesus," Boo said, straining and swinging Ruby around like an airplane, "Virginia Woolf could have used this one!"

Boo has a part-time job now, too, in addition to the bartending at the Dolphin. He works with Hobie, the plumber, when the necessity arises. One of Boo's jobs as assistant plumber is to get everyone—animals and humans—out of the house when Hobie's adding another toilet to a house that already has one.

"Everybody out!" Hobie shouts, and Boo does the herding, directing everyone out into the street. Hobie trudges up the stairs, huffing and puffing, up to the second-floor bathroom and takes out his pistol. *Ba-boom!* At the sound of the shot, Boo herds everyone back in.

"The new toilet goes there!" Hobie shouts down through the bullet hole in the floor, next to the toilet upstairs.

Angeline, Hobie's wife, is as black as Ray Charles but claims she's really Caucasian and that her skin is discolored due to too much pigment, too much beta carotene, and too much sun. This is all Angeline talks about. What do you say to a person like that?

"You know, Angeline," Boo says, "I never told anybody this, but I'm really black. Ethiopian. Descended from Nebuchadnezzar . . ."

Angeline, she hates Boo with a passion.

On the last trip to the mainland to visit Moe, after they went to Goodwill, Ruby and Vivvy went to see a psychic named Miss Donna.

"You will marry three times," Miss Donna told Ruby, and Ruby laughed nervously, *Ha ha ha. Ha ha ha.*

"You will cross the North Atlantic with a sandy-haired gentleman who speaks a language you will never understand."

Ha ha. Ha ha ha, Ruby laughed nervously.

"You will work as a technical writer. Something to do with ashes."

Ha ha ha, Ruby laughed nervously.

"Many years from now, you'll write a book, and I'll be in it," Miss Donna said.

Ha ha ha, Ruby laughed nervously.

Sometimes when she can't sleep, Ruby gets out her ball of yellow yarn and knits in bed in the darkness, pretending that she's blind. Knit two. Purl two. Skip three. Twist. She thinks she knows the cable knit pattern by heart, but inevitably, she makes glaring, irreparable mistakes, knots as big as horse chestnuts. She falls asleep on the metallic blue aluminum needles twisted in yellow yarn, dreaming of Venezuela, dreaming of Rima, the half-bird, half-woman love of the narrator of *Green Mansions.* Ruby dreams that Rima comes and perches on the arm of the hide-a-bed, singing and calling to her like one of Ulysses' sirens on the bow of his ship. Beside Ruby in the hide-a-bed, Boo snores, paddling his own boat with Felicia Jackson naked in the bow.

"SFUMATO," Ruby says, and claps the dictionary closed. "The word is 'sfumato,' S-F-U-M-A-T-O."

The circus tent is filled with smoke — cigarette and other — and too many people: Sky and Happy, Chick and Felicia, Moe and Vivvy, Boo and Ruby. Strands of Christmas bubble lights are strung here and there haphazardly, dangerously, connected to a long extension cord that runs straight to a utility pole. A kerosene lamp on a footlocker near the door is about to catch on fire. Right now, its wick is thinking about smoldering, getting ready for the conflagration, and the rim of its chimney's turning black. In a little while, someone will smell it and call out, "Hey, the lamp's on fire!" and a great commotion will ensue. The dogs will run in, knocking things over and ending the game prematurely. People will wander outside to the barbecue pit where the mullet is cooking and nearby a keg of Stoney's beer is bobbing like a buoy in a washtub of melted ice.

Sky passes Ruby the bong filled with Scope mouthwash as everyone adjusts the record album on his or her lap and writes the word "sfumato" on a sheet of paper. Heads are spinning.

Ruby holds the Electric Light Orchestra's *Eldorado* album on her lap, a record jacket displaying a pair of bigger-than-life-size ruby slippers. Ruby looks down at them and laughs and licks the point of her pencil.

"Sfumato?" Sky asks.

"Sfumato," Ruby nods and spells the word again, very seriously, then bursts out giggling. Although Boo used to make fun of Happy and Sky and their composting toilet, Boo and Sky are now best friends. Boo discovered that Sky and Happy's greenhouse is full of primo pot plants.

Ruby collects all the papers. They're playing a game called dictionary, which Ruby has taught them all. Possibly, even, Ruby has made it up. In a few years, after Ruby's gone, Boo will introduce this game to someone who buys a lot from him on the Jackson Tract. The new Jackson Tract landowner will name the game Balderdash, sell it to Parker Brothers toys, and make a bundle off it.

"*Sfumato.*" Ruby reads from the first paper, trying not to laugh. "Definition number one. *Sfumato.* A form of Italian rugby played with tomatoes."

Laughter. Snickers.

"*Sfumato.* Definition number two:" Ruby reads again, "One tenth of a lira."

Boo laughs. Papers shuffle.

"*Sfumato.* Definition number three: A term of endearment, e.g., Oh, my little sfumato. Come with me to my sfumato. We will make zee most beautiful sfumato together."

"*Sfumato.* Definition number four: Smoke-filled. From Latin 'fuma,' i.e., this tent is pretty damn sfumato."

Actually, Ruby has cheated. She didn't just randomly pick the word *sfumato* from the dictionary. She came across it two days ago in her "research." Sfumato is a painting technique developed by Leonardo da Vinci. Essentially, it is a technique for painting what one cannot see: the air between objects. The Italian word *sfumato* means vaporous, hazy, misty. It refers to a feature of da Vinci's painting—for example, the background in the Mona Lisa

—that is difficult to put into words, although it is immediately apparent to the eye. Italian writers on art in the Renaissance used the word *sfumato* to describe an especially soft, almost imperceptible gradation of tone and shade. A sfumato effect gives the impression of all the objects in a picture being connected—the near and the far—from a single uninterrupted continuum in space, and a slight fuzziness allows objects to appear intangible and almost unreal.

"Definition number five"—which Ruby has written in paraphrase—"*Sfumato:* a painting technique involving the blurring of brush strokes to create a distant, disappearing effect. Stand back, Leo said, while I sfumato this here room."

Soon they will all vote on what each thinks is the correct paraphrase, and then someone—Boo probably—will carve the word on the center pole.

Sfumato: . . .

"Ohmygod! The lamp's on fire!" Vivvy screams, and a great commotion ensues. The dogs run in, knocking things over and ending the dictionary game prematurely.

The next day is glorious, salubrious. Carolina chickadees flutter in the cedars, a salty breeze from the bay licks Ruby's bare arms with its sea-tongue, and a thin, damp sea mist diffuses the sun's rays. Ruby is up late, a little hangover, a little headache, hanging up laundry, her clothesline flapping sheets, her wringer washer doing its belly dance on the porch behind her. Boo was up and out early. Gone fishin'.

Vivvy is next door, out in her yard, too, stirring something in a cauldron, and they see Gladys Tupper drive by in her duct-taped blue Impala, hands at two and ten, looking straight ahead. Vivvy waves with her dye-stirring stick, and Ruby smiles a clothespin smile and waves a pair of polka-dot satin boxer shorts from Goodwill, but Gladys doesn't seem to see them. She passes by—a smurf in a blue chiffon scarf at the wheel—past Ruby and Boo's house, past her own, and disappears around the curve on Jackson Circle.

And Ruby goes back to her basket, her pins, and the Lovin' Spoonful song spinning in her head.

Not a minute later, Gladys passes by again. Then again. And again. Again. Very slowly, but moving. And again! Something's wrong. Ruby walks out to Jackson Circle and stands by the utility pole in her flowered sundress and flip-flops. Vivvy's come out to the road too. Here comes Gladys. Ruby steps out into Jackson Circle and Gladys nearly runs her over.

"Gladys!" Ruby hollers, running beside the car and looking in, but Gladys doesn't look Ruby's way. Across the blue vinyl seat, Ruby sees Gladys's face, blank and tear streaked, staring straight ahead, hands at two and ten. Shorty-Long's in the back seat, standing up and looking out the window. He runs to Ruby's side and starts barking. Ruby runs alongside the car, tapping on the window, looking down and in.

"Gladys! Gladys!" Ruby hollers, but Gladys keeps going. Vivvy's caught up with them now, too.

Gladys — they will all learn later — is lost. Some cerebral tethering has come undone, and Gladys's blue Impala is orbiting Jackson Circle like Sputnik II, Shorty-Long staring out the rear window like Laika, Gladys at the controls, a terrified cosmonaut unable to pierce through reality's atmosphere and identify her own house, her own oyster-shell driveway flanked by chubby blue hydrangeas, her own front yard with the little Dutch boy and Dutch girl kissing.

Washie Howard, the dredge captain, is out in his front yard. He hears Ruby hollering and comes running out, too, in his bare feet. "Ruby!" he calls to her. "Ruby, what is it?"

Washie's trotting along the driver's side of the car now, hand on the door handle, calling to Ruby and Vivvy across the car roof. Shorty-Long's running back and forth across the back seat. Behind them now in the road comes Gladys's husband, Leviticus, running awkwardly, holding his heart. Leviticus's face is red, his gray fluffy hair floating above his head like a dust bunny.

"Gladys!" he calls hoarsely. "Gladys!" But Gladys keeps going, speeding up now.

Washie lets go of the door handle and yells out to Boo and Felicia, who are coming toward them in one of the Jacksons' dune buggies.

"Get out of the way!" Washie yells.

Ruby lets go, Vivvy too. Ruby looks back and sees Leviticus Tupper stumble. Behind him, way down around the bend in Jackson Circle, the Jacksons' Jolly Roger is pointing due east, and from Ruby's vantage point, it looks like a tiny birthday cake flag on a toothpick, stuck on the top of Leviticus Tupper's head. In sfumato, Ruby thinks. The background. *Sfumato.* Off to the left, behind the row of young cedars and nesting chickadees, Ruby's sheets are flapping. *Goodbye!* they wave like the handkerchiefs of invisible ladies sending their loved ones out to sea. *Goodbye!*

Ruby turns and looks the other way, up the road in the direction from which Boo and Felicia are approaching, their faces and bodies almost distinct.

The Blue Hat

1959—Our father was often out of town on business. He was a demolitions expert, a professional blaster for the Atlas Powder Company. In the evenings he sat at the kitchen table, drawing on graph paper. The lines on the graph paper were pale blue, and in the upper-left-hand corner was a drawing of Atlas in black ink. Atlas was a man about as big as my pinkie and bare naked, except for a bunch of animal skins tied around where his underpants should be. Above his head, Atlas held a beach ball that my father said was supposed to be the world. The Earth, my father said, was held up by Atlas.

"But then what's he standing on?" I asked my father.

My father only laughed and patted me on my head. "Good question, Ruby!" he laughed. "Those Greeks, Ruby," he said, "they were full of baloney."

One Saturday morning, my sister, Albertine, was missing. She was not in our bed next to me when I woke up. She was not in the living room watching *Circus Boy* or in the kitchen, fixing a bowl of Sugar Pops. She was not out in the yard or swinging on the porch swing, reading. Her purple J. C. Higgins bike was leaning against the garage. Our mother called and called her name. She was there the night before, I remembered, because we had played twenty questions and Name That Tune, lying in bed, and counted the cars that went by, making a xylophone on the ceiling out of the venetian blinds. I ran around the neighborhood and knocked on all the doors, and my father drove up and down the streets in his company car, calling out the window, "Albertine! Albertine!"

First the Ivkovitches, then the Rossis, then the Wagners joined in, and before we knew it, everyone in Ashport was calling, "Albertine! Albertine!" Larry Ivkovitch ran down to the Strand and the skating rink and Woolworth's Five-and-Dime. Then two policemen came to the house, and my mother gave them a description, twisting a dish towel in her hands and biting her lower lip. Eleven years old. Chubby. Blue plastic glasses with rhinestones. Black eyes. Black hair. Pigtails.

"What was she wearing?" they asked. They asked so many questions, my mother became hysterical, and all the neighbor women gathered around, patting her and saying things like, "She's someplace reading, Eva," or "Eva, you know she couldn't have gone too far." Out behind the garage where my father smoked his cigarettes, I came across him crying.

Around dusk, Albertine came trudging up Cherry Street in her Girl Scout uniform. She wanted to win the badge for being the Girl Scout who sold the most cookies in the United States. She got up before dawn and walked more than seven miles, out to the end of Elysian Avenue to the Ashport city limits and then across the suspension bridge and up the River Road to the little town of Davis, and then she worked her way back, up and down the streets and all the side roads, knocking on every door, selling Girl Scout cookies. She sold more than a thousand boxes of trefoils and vanilla creams and chocolate mint Girl Scout cookies. She had water blisters as big as gum drops on her toes. That night in bed, after all the commotion had died down and we'd had our baths, Albertine told me she walked so far she saw Atlas's fingers holding up the Earth, just as the sun was coming up over Ashport.

"He bites his nails," she told me and fell fast asleep.

Our father worked with explosives in the mines around Ashport, but then in the late fifties many of the mines closed because of floods caused by Hurricane Diane, and the Atlas Powder Company began to send our father far away to blow things up—to New York state, New Jersey, New England, even Canada. From these places, he brought us home fossils, rocks and minerals; old buried bottles—brown and green and beautiful cobalt blue; sometimes a record; and oftentimes a big box of Fannie Farmer candy, a new piece of sheet music, and a pretty teacup for our mother.

On Sundays, our father directed the choir at Riverview Lutheran Church out on the River Road, and on Thursday nights we had choir rehearsal. Now that our father was often out of town, our mother directed the choir or led the rehearsal. Both our parents had degrees in music, but they couldn't make a living from music. It was at a music conservatory where they'd met during the second week of school when they were both cast as the leads in the Gilbert and Sullivan light opera *The Pirates of Penzance.*

Our father, who was a senior, heard our mother, a freshman, sing before he ever heard her speak. "The voice of an angel," he leaned sideways and whispered to a fellow conservatory tenor during auditions, "and the countenance to go with it." In *The Pirates of Penzance,* our mother, with her long black hair and clear blue eyes, played Mabel, Major-General Stanley's beautiful youngest daughter. Our father was Frederic, the nobleman turned pirate. When they met, our father—in striped pantaloons, a real sword, and a shredded scarlet sash—was wandering among papier mâché boulders in front of a plywood, white-capped sea. On the sea rocked a mechanical frigate operated by creaky pulleys and flying the Jolly Roger. On a platform of hay bales stage right, draped in painted canvas and aspiring to be a rugged mountain pass, our mother hummed and picked straw flowers. After an eight-measure introduction, our mother espied our bedraggled, shipwrecked father below. "Poor Wand'ring One!" is the aria she sang:

Poor wand'ring one!
Though thou hast surely strayed,
Take heart of grace,
Thy steps retrace,
Poor wand'ring one!
Poor wand'ring one!

As a blaster, our father traveled to heavy construction sites like the building of the hydroelectric power plant on the Niagara River and the construction of U.S. Route 80 across the entire United States. Sometimes he went way down into a salt mine at the bottom of the Finger Lake Cayuga. As a child, I thought the Atlas powder he used was like Johnson's baby powder or Cashmere Bouquet in its slim, flowered can, or Heaven Scent in a round cardboard container with a big soft blue puff like my mother kept next to the jewelry box that played "Stardust." But the powder our father used wasn't talcum powder at all. It was nitroglycerine and ammonium nitrate. It was highly explosive, and he stored it in a building called a magazine and transported it on business trips in the trunk of his car.

One summer our father was on such a business trip in Buffalo, New York, and he sent for our mother. It was a Thursday, and I was cutting out my new June Allyson paper dolls on the living room floor. Albertine was painting her toenails pink and reading *Gone with the Wind*, and we were watching *Art Linkletter's House Party* on television. Our mother walked into the living room with a glass and a tea towel in her hand and announced, "I'm going to Buffalo, New York, to see your father. He called last night, and he said I should fly from Philadelphia."

"Fly!" I exclaimed. "You're gonna fly? When did Daddy call?" I asked. "Why didn't you let me talk to him?"

"It was late," our mother said. "You two were sound asleep. It was way after midnight."

"You could have waked me," I said. "You should have waked me. There's something I had to tell him."

"*Awakened* or *woken*," Albertine said, not looking up, "not *waked*." She was always correcting everyone's grammar.

Our mother turned and walked back into the kitchen.

This was 1959, and airplanes were shiny silver like the Blue Comet Diner, and only people with money or business got on them. A little later, I was just folding back the flaps on a variety pack box of Puffed Rice — getting ready to eat the cereal right out of the box, milk and all — when our mother came into the living room and said that Albertine and I were supposed to get dressed in our jumpers to go downtown shopping with her. She was going to buy a new outfit to wear on the airplane when she flew to Buffalo, New York, to meet our father.

While our mother stood in front of the oval mirror hiking up her black full slip, I took the Maybelline eyebrow pencil and licked it and drew a line down the back of each of her legs, from the middle of her thigh to the first heel wrinkle. The penciled lines were meant to look like she was wearing seamed nylon stockings, although she couldn't bear the feel of nylon after having grown so accustomed to silk before the war with Japan.

One of the lines was a little crooked.

Our mother put on a tight black dress and her single strand of simulated pearls. She twisted her braid around her head and into a doughnut at the nape of her neck, pinned a little black velvet hat like a burnt pancake with a veil on her head, and off we went to Sidler's. In the LADIES' BETTER DRESSES department of Sidler's, our mother tried on the most expensive dresses and suits. One dress was bright red with little tassels all over and had a black bolero jacket. That was my favorite! Albertine and I sat on white stools in the dressing room and zipped the zippers and worked the hangers. Albertine was reading her book. The sales clerk kept coming back and saying, "How does the red look?" or "Does the little polka-dot one work?" My foot developed a horrendous itch, and I had to take my sock off.

Finally, after our mother had tried on nearly all the most expensive suits and dresses in her size, she decided on a peacock blue silk suit with a tight, straight skirt that came just above the knee and a fitted jacket with a peplum and three-quarter-length sleeves. It was a Miss Schiaparelli and cost one hundred dollars.

Back then, department stores did not have charge cards like

they all have nowadays, nor did people have Visas and Master-cards. While the sales clerk folded the suit in tissue paper and fitted it in a dress box, our mother signed our father's name in a book with carbon paper, and the clerk handed her the pink copy, which our mother folded neatly, smiling, and stuck into her pocketbook. Then we went across the street to Endicott & Johnson's, where our mother bought a pair of shoes, signing our father's name again in a similar leather-covered book kept under the counter. The shoes were dark, semisweet brown spike heels with pointy toes. Alligator, I think. Our mother also bought a matching clutch bag with a shiny gold clasp shaped like a seashell.

Albertine was carrying the Sidler's dress box, and I was carrying our mother's new shoes and purse, wrapped in brown kraft paper and tied with string, and we started walking back home, up Elysian Avenue, our mother between us, whistling a popular tune. When we got to the corner of Vine and Diamond, a train was just approaching, and there in the window of Lacey's, the milliner's, I spotted a beautiful blue feather pillbox hat. The striped restraining arm of the railroad crossing was falling like a referee's final count, and the train was whistling its sad call as I tugged on our mother's sleeve, pointing at the hat. Just then, the proprietor, Lacey Marinelli, flung open the shop door.

Our mother's sister — our Aunt Frannie Linn — drove up from Philadelphia on Thursday afternoon to take our mother to the airport on Friday morning. Albertine and I were to go along and spend the weekend in Philadelphia, and then Aunt Frannie Linn would bring us all back on Sunday night, when our mother would fly back to Philadelphia after visiting our father in Buffalo, New York. I was so excited about going to an airport because I had never been to a real one before. I'd only been to the little grassy airstrip out by the Ashport fairgrounds and the pony pasture where our father's business associate, Mr. Harold Mosher, kept his little yellow plane. The previous summer, one at a time, Mr. Mosher took Albertine and me and a girl my age named

Cheryl for an airplane ride above the fairgrounds. Although I had seen planes before—in the sky and on *Sky King* and in movies—for some reason I thought a little plane like Mr. Harold Mosher's would flap its wings when you were flying in it, or at least wiggle them a little, so I was somewhat disappointed, and, frankly, I didn't care very much for looking down. I still feel that way about flying and always ask for an aisle seat, although before my initial plane ride with Mr. Mosher I had given some serious thought to being a wing walker when I grew up.

We were all ready to go to Philadelphia when Aunt Frannie Linn pulled up in front of our house in our dead grandfather's big black Plymouth. Grandpa Doc had died right after Christmas from hardening of the arteries. The summer before that, Albertine and I stayed in Philadelphia, and Grandpa Doc was certain that the house on Highland Avenue was surrounded by some sort of enemy soldiers and that Albertine and I were with the Red Cross. Other times, he called me Toolie and thought I was a jazz saxophonist who played in Tommy Dorsey's band.

"Are you sure you want to do this, Eva?" our Aunt Frannie Linn said, setting down her handbag. "Maybe you should just wait till Albert gets back."

"No," our mother said firmly, applying her lipstick in the hall mirror. "Don't tell me what to do, Frannie. I know what I'm doing," she said, pinning on her hat, "and I want you to cut my hair, too. I want one of those short little numbers with spit curls. Like Elizabeth Taylor in *Cat on a Hot Tin Roof.*"

"Me, too!" Albertine exclaimed.

"Me, too!" I echoed, twisting a braid, although I had never seen that movie and could not imagine any of us with short hair.

That night in Philadelphia, our Aunt Frannie Linn cut our mother's hair. "You're cutting off your best feature, Eva," our Aunt Frannie Linn told her. "What will Albert say?"

"I don't give a damn what Albert says," our mother said.

Albertine wanted her hair cut, too, and had torn a picture from a hairdo magazine to show Aunt Frannie Linn, who was a beautician.

"Once and for all," our mother told Albertine, "you are not cutting your hair. And that's final. And I don't want to hear another word about it."

Albertine whirled around and stomped out.

In the kitchen, Aunt Frannie Linn made our mother's hair into a ponytail and then braided the ponytail into one long braid, with rubber bands wound tightly around both ends. I held on to the braid while Aunt Frannie Linn cut it off with a giant pair of shears.

"This is a goddamn sin," she said to our mother. Our mother had not had her hair cut since she was a little girl and had almost died from rheumatic fever. Her braid was so long she could sit on it! When Aunt Frannie Linn had cut all the way through the braid, it fell to the floor at my feet while I held its tail, and I started to cry. I had never felt the braid except attached to our mother's head. Suddenly, I thought of all the times I had stood behind our mother at the piano bench when she wore two braids. I played giddy-up with her braids and she'd play a fast song on the piano, like for a runaway stagecoach in a movie.

While Aunt Frannie Linn was cutting our mother's hair, Albertine was upstairs in the bathroom, hacking off her own braids with a steak knife. She came back down and stood in the kitchen doorway and threw her braids at our mother.

"There," she said, and stuck out her tongue.

One side of Albertine's hair was sticking out above her ear, and the other side was down below her jaw, all jagged.

"You little brat," our mother jumped up and yelled, grabbing Albertine by the arm. "Wait till your father sees what you've done!"

"Wait till he sees the likes of you in that fancy-schmancy suit and stupid hat in Buffalo, New York!" Albertine snapped, and our mother slapped her across the face.

"Lord Jesus Christ on Calvary!" Aunt Frannie Linn said, and she started to cry.

Later that evening, Aunt Frannie Linn cut Albertine's hair even shorter and gave her a Toni. She gave me a French manicure, which is where you file your nails square and use the orange stick on the cuticles, then you soak your fingertips in a cereal bowl with a solution of dish detergent and Clorox, and then you color underneath your fingernails with a soft white pencil and buff your nails until they look shiny, like they've just been polished.

The next morning, we took our mother to the airport. She had slept all night in pin curls with a scarf tied *I Love Lucy*–style around her head, and in the morning when she took out the bobby pins and shook her head, she said her head felt so light she thought she could fly all the way to Buffalo, New York, without an airplane! Her head was full of bouncy black curls that felt so soft to touch, but I felt sorry for the braid, which Aunt Frannie Linn had put into a nylon stocking. Our mother's braid now lay coiled in the bottom of her overnight bag like a big dead snake, and every time I opened the lid and looked in at it there, I shuddered.

Our mother put on rhinestone earrings and bright poppy red lipstick and blotted it with Kleenex and smiled at herself this way and that in the mirror, and when she put on the blue suit and the blue feather hat, she really did look like the movie star Elizabeth Taylor!

Albertine looked like Mr. Kepler's toy poodle, Tippy.

I was so proud to walk beside our mother at the airport, holding her hand. I waved and waved when she walked out to the plane. She held on to her hat with one hand, and when she got to the top of the stairs, she turned and blew me a kiss. Albertine was in a very foul mood and insisted on staying in the car, reading her book. She didn't even say goodbye to our mother. She was reading *The Children's Hour*.

After we left the airport, Aunt Frannie Linn took Albertine and me to Rocky Springs Park, where we stayed all day, eating corn dogs and cotton candy, funnel cakes and cherry slushes, and riding the bumper cars and the Wildcat, the Ferris wheel, and the Whip. We went on the Wildcat twice, and Aunt Frannie Linn lost a genuine pearl earring.

When we got to our grandparents' house, where Aunt Frannie

Linn now lived alone, it was after dark and Mr. Kepler was standing next door on his porch, in his suspenders, leaning on his cane under the yellow bug light. He called to our Aunt Frannie Linn, waving something in his hand. Mr. Kepler had a candy store, and he had invented banana-flavored candy peanuts, those cantaloupe-colored peanuts called Kepler's Circus Peanuts that come in a cellophane bag with clowns and balloons on it. Every time we went to Philadelphia, Albertine and I ran over to Mr. Kepler's house as soon as we got out of the car, and he gave us each a bag of Kepler's Circus Peanuts, which we ate until one of us threw up.

"It's from Western Union, Frances," Mr. Kepler croaked, handing the telegram to our Aunt Frannie Linn. "It came about an hour ago." Tippy stood at the top of the porch stairs, snarling and yip-yapping like crazy. We played tug-o'-war with the strap of my plastic pocketbook while Aunt Frannie Linn opened the telegram and Albertine leaned against the railing, reading her book.

"Oh, Jesus!" Aunt Frannie Linn said, sitting down on Mr. Kepler's glider after she'd read the telegram. "Sweet Jesus on the Cross!"

"Frances, what is it?" Mr. Kepler asked.

"What is it? What is it? What's it say? What's it say?" Albertine and I said at the same time, the words all jumbled up on top of each other.

"Your father's in the hospital, girls. Albert's in the hospital. But he's OK. But his business associate, Harold Mosher, is dead. Some kind of accident. An explosion. Their car blew up."

The funeral for Mr. Harold Mosher was in Mountaintop the next Tuesday. Our mother wore the blue suit and the beautiful blue feather hat. She looked so very beautiful. She held on to our father's arm and dabbed at her eyes with an embroidered handkerchief. Beside our mother in her bright blue suit, with his dark hair and brown suit, our father looked to me to be her shadow. Albertine would not go in the funeral parlor or get out of the car at the cemetery. She sat in the car reading *Anne Frank: The Diary of a Young Girl*, and we just ignored her because she was so cranky. Our mother said that Albertine had just become a woman.

After Mr. Mosher's funeral, we were driving back over Buck Mountain—it had been drizzling all day—and the arc of the most beautiful rainbow appeared right across the blacktop road and down into Sugar Valley. Gogi Grant was singing on the radio:

> Oh the wayward wind is a restless wind
> A restless wind that yearns to wander
> And he was born the next of kin
> The next of kin to the wayward wind

I was so excited! I asked our father to stop the car so I could walk through the rainbow and maybe find the pot of gold. He pulled off on the narrow shoulder and I jumped out. Our mother got out, too. She had taken off her tight alligator shoes and was in her bare feet. We stood there for a moment on the wet pavement, holding hands, mist rising from the macadam all around us, our mother and I standing in the place where the rainbow crossed the road. We moved our free hands back and forth and waved to our father and Albertine sitting in our dead grandfather's Plymouth. Then we looked a little bit among the chicory and the Queen Anne's lace along the roadside for the pot of gold.

"Somebody must have already found it," our mother said, "one of the little people, probably."

Then our mother walked across the road and stood against the cabled guardrail, looking down into the valley full of mist and angel-hair puffs of fog. For some reason, she pulled the pearl hatpin out of her beautiful new feather hat and sent the hat sailing into Sugar Valley. The blue hat rose and dipped a few times like an indigo bunting, then sank and disappeared into the mist.

We had takeout pizza from the Neapolitan Pizza Parlor for dinner that night, but our parents went to bed without even eating any because they were so exhausted. Albertine and I ate the whole thing and burped and tooted a lot and stayed up and watched Jack Benny and Groucho Marx. When we got in bed, I was saying

Now I lay me . . . to myself, and Albertine turned to me and said, "Mr. Mosher wasn't the only one who died, you know. Somebody else got blown up, too."

"Whaddaya mean?" I said.

"There was somebody else in Daddy's car," Albertine went on, "a lady."

"What lady?" I asked. "Which lady? Who?"

"A lady named Charlotta Koplansky."

"There used to be a Cheryl Koplansky in my Brownie troop!" I said. "But she moved away."

"Charlotta Koplansky was her mother," Albertine said.

"Cheryl Koplansky's mother! How did she get there?" I leaned on one elbow and asked Albertine. "How did Mrs. Koplansky get all the way to Buffalo, New York, and get blowed up in Daddy's car?"

"*Blown,* not *blowed,*" Albertine said. "Think about it, Ruby," she said, and rolled over.

Statues

1957—Neddy is swinging me and swinging me. My guns are in their holsters, flapping against my thighs like basset hound ears. Neddy lets go and I'm hurled through the yard, heading for a bird bath, a lilac bush, a cement deer, a bench. I stumble. Twirl. Stop. Wobble, hop, then find my spot. I'm balancing on my left foot, leaning forward. My right foot's bent behind me, pulled up to my waist by my right hand. My left hand holds one of my braids out at arm's length. My tongue's sticking out. Everyone starts counting. *One . . . two . . . three . . . they're up to one hundred.*

"Wow! Ruby!" they say. "You're *really* good at this."

I don't even crack a smile. I know. I can make them stand there counting till the cows come home.

"Ruby has an exceptional sense of balance," my kindergarten teacher said. It comes in very handy.

"That's enough!" Albertine yells. "Give it to me! Give it to me, Ruby!"

We're fighting over a can of Hershey's chocolate syrup. I've already poured about half the can over my bowl of ice cream and am now licking the drips off the can. I've sneaked into the kitchen to make myself a porcupine while Grandma Bessie watches Billy Graham on television. A porcupine is three scoops of Neapolitan ice cream molded into a blob, decorated all over with pretzel sticks, wallowing in a puddle of Hershey's syrup.

"Give it to me, Ruby!"

Albertine is chasing me around the chrome dinette, shouting. Soon there will be an accident, a broken bowl, a flying can, a floor full of pretzel sticks, something almost lifelike catapulting from a spoon. An ice cream porcupine will slide across the kitchen floor, a wire-haired terrier on its heels. The terrier will gulp up the porcupine in one lap and then sit with a surprised look on his face, one ear inside out. Somebody's flannel nightgown will be ripped and splattered with chocolate. Somebody will start crying. Somebody will start hitting and pinching somebody else. Somebody's arm will get cut on the edge of a metal silverware drawer. Somebody will be bitten. Somebody will be scratched.

Grandma Bessie will appear in the doorway with a rolled up *Look* magazine and a cane. Grandma Bessie will grab us each by the wrist and whack our bottoms. She'll make me unbuckle my holster. She'll put my guns and my holster on top of the refrigerator. She'll yank off my nightgown, scrub the front of it in the kitchen sink with Joy, wring it out, and make me put it back on —a big spot like a cold, clammy hand on my chest. She'll push Go-Jeff outside with her cane, and eat the remaining bowl of ice cream, the very last scoop of tasty Dolly Madison Neapolitan ice cream, all by herself, with a serving spoon.

Like Rocky Marciano and Archie Moore, Albertine and I will return to our corners at opposite ends of the davenport. We'll stick our bare feet under the middle cushion where our feet will continue the never-ending Chinese Toe War . . . until it's time. Today, our Aunt Frannie Linn has cut us bangs and given us Tonies. Our heads stink like ammonia. Albertine's bangs are a ball of black curls, and mine are a ball of yellow curls, soft like a lamb. I can't stop petting my bangs.

It's time.

The television screen goes black. Velvet. Then dotted Swiss. Stars begin to twinkle. A fairy. A wand. The Milky Way.

When you wish upon a star . . . Albertine and I sing along.

Makes no difference who you are . . . we sing a little louder. I grab my blue blanket with the satin binding and stand in front of the television.

"Get outta the way, Ruby! Get outta the way!" Albertine yells. Grandma Bessie's arm reaches out and grabs the neck of my nightgown, pointing me back toward the prickly mohair davenport.

When you wish upon a star, your dreams come true! Albertine and I sing a little louder still. Albertine takes the high notes on "come true" and I sing the harmony. We snuggle into our respective corners with our blankets, me with my Revlon doll, Albertine with her book and blue pony. I wrap my head up in my blanket, lean back, and, concealed in crocheted blue cotton, pet my head and suck my thumb.

Welcome to the Walt Disney Hour, the kindest voice announces.

"I wish *we* could go there!" Albertine whines. "We never go anywhere!"

"Go where? Disneyland?" says Aunt Frannie Linn, who has just walked in the front door. "Wish in one hand; shit in the other," she says, throwing her purse on a chair and untying her chiffon scarf. Albertine and I cover our mouths with our hands and giggle.

"Frances!" Grandma Bessie snaps, and whacks Aunt Frannie Linn's ankle, as she passes, with her cane. "You watch your tongue! The mouth on you!"

1985 — Once we are on the plane and I complete the final requirement — fasten my seatbelt for the trip home — the statue is complete. I'm one hundred percent ice, except for my eyes. I don't want to be like this. I want to speak, but I can't. Owen — Albertine's youngest — has the window seat, then Albertine, then me on the aisle. Mattie, Albertine's fourteen-year-old daughter, is in the row ahead, and next to her, Albertine's other son, Reese, who's twelve. I want to close my eyes. I want to lean my head back but should have thought of these things before buckling up. Albertine's chattering away, still in the black Mickey Mouse ears, pointing out the window. Owen is looking out the window, his little bald head like some kind of medicine ball. A long scar like a zipper runs from the base of his skull, between two long tendons, to just above ear level. Owen is seven years old, and he has six months to live.

Once we're in the air, a stewardess is pushing a clanging cart closer and closer to me. Albertine reaches over and pulls down Owen's tray, then mine. "What do you want, sweetheart?" she asks Owen. "Orange juice? Soda? Ginger ale?"

"I don't want anything, Mommy," he says, leaning his head against her.

"Ruby, what do you want . . . Oh, look, Owen, honey-roasted peanuts, your favorite!"

"Ma'am?" the stewardess is saying again to me. "Would you care for a drink, ma'am?"

I'm staring straight ahead. I want to shake my head, but it won't move. I blink and blink again, but she doesn't understand.

"Ruby, what do you want?" Albertine asks me. I want to look at her, but I can't turn my head.

"Give her a diet Coke with no ice," Albertine tells the stewardess, and I start to cry.

"Listen, Ruby," Albertine says, putting her hand on top of my two hands, folded like a geode in my lap. "Ruby, we're almost home. It's almost over. It's OK. We're almost home. You'll be OK. We'll all be OK."

She's crying, too. She dabs at her eyes and quickly, in a cheery voice, turns to Owen. "Sweetheart," she says to him, "look! Honey-roasted peanuts!"

"Ruby," Albertine says to me, "look at me. Can you look at me?"

I want to tell her I'm OK. I blink, hoping she'll notice.

"Oh, Ruby! Ruby!" she exclaims. "Is it the blink thing?" She sticks her face in front of me. I blink. She hugs me.

"OK, that's a relief! So, I forget, what is it? One if by land; two if by sea, right? One is yes; two is no; three: don't know or can't answer, right?"

I blink. A flood of relief washes over me but freezes quickly like the glaze on an igloo. She remembers. She remembers way back—twenty-two years ago—when our mother died. She remembers. She understands.

"Listen, sweetie," she says to Owen, "we're going to play a game with Aunt Ruby. Aunt Ruby is a statue. You can only ask her yes or no questions. If she blinks once . . ."

Owen crawls across Albertine's lap and sticks his little ashen face in front of mine. His mouth is like a small bruised rose. "Aunt Ruby, can I have your peanuts, yes or no?" he asks. I blink. He smiles, grabs the peanuts. "Thanks," he says, and plops back down in his seat by the window.

Once we're on the ground and taxiing toward the gate, we see the Make-a-Wish crew waving behind a glass window-wall. We're celebrities. We're the first ones off the plane. We've just spent a week in Disney World. Breakfast with Minnie Mouse. Lunch with Cinderella. Dinner with Huey, Dewey, and Louie. Every day.

"Put your ears on! Aunt Ruby, put your ears on!" Owen urges. Albertine plops the pink glitter Minnie Mouse ears on my head. She's never taken her black Mickey Mouse ears off since she first donned them this morning. Her hair is black and short and permed, and the ears look almost indigenous there. Owen wears the Goofy hat with the long hound dog ears, and Mattie wears a cap with wiggly eyes and a bright yellow Donald Duck bill. Reese's decked out like Davy Crockett in a faux coonskin cap. A band is playing "Zip-A-Dee-Doo-Dah," and a giant bird is dancing, kicking his legs out from side to side like they're broken. Owen smiles ear to ear as he's helped into the wheelchair. Balloons. WELCOME HOME OWEN banners. A drum roll. Greetings.

We're walking through the concourse. The tiny, sour band is marching in front of us, playing "Be Kind to Your Web-Footed Friends." The Make-a-Wish Foundation president is pushing

Owen in the wheelchair. Albertine's smiling, holding my hand.

"Ruby," she says to me, "I'm going to let the Make-a-Wish people take the kids out to their van. Come on, I'll walk you to your car. You can drive, can't you?"

[BLINK]

"Come on, say goodbye to Owen."

"Sweetheart," Albertine says to Owen, "I'm going to walk Aunt Ruby out to the parking lot. She just wants to say goodbye."

I want to say goodbye to Owen, but all I can manage is a feeble smile and tears.

"Don't cry, Aunt Ruby," Owen says cheerily. "We'll go back someday, won't we, Mom?"

I put my face down to his and kiss him. He puts his face in mine and squeezes his eyes open and closed in an emphatic blink. "My Aunt Ruby is a statue!" he turns and announces to the Make-a-Wish Foundation president.

"You don't say, buddy!" the president replies.

Albertine and I walk away.

"See ya soon, ya big baboon!" Owen calls, waving after us.

On the way out of the terminal, Albertine stops at a newsstand. "Ruby," she says, "are you sure you're going to be OK?"

[BLINK]

"Are you sure you can drive home?"

[BLINK]

"Do you want to come home with me?"

[BLINK BLINK]

"Do you have enough gas to get home?"

[BLINK]

"Do you have money?"

[BLINK]

"Ruby, listen, it's almost three o'clock now. When you get home, call me. Let the phone ring twice, and then hang up. I won't answer. You don't have to say anything. Just call. Let the phone ring twice, hang up. Then call again and do the same thing. I promise, no one will answer. That way, I'll know you're OK."

[BLINK]

"OK?"

[BLINK]

"Call me at seven?"

[BLINK]

"You promise?"

[BLINK]

"OK. Come on in here. I'm going to get you something to eat. You have to eat. Drink lots of fluids. When you get home, take a bath, call me, get your pillow and get under the bed. You'll feel better tomorrow."

[BLINK]

"You'll be OK. Remember, we're survivors, right?" She starts to cry, then snaps right out of it. She picks up a diet Coke and a Golden Delicious apple and sets them on the counter. She walks over to the section of stationery, notebooks, pocket guides, maps. "Here, Ruby," she says, "which one do you want?" picking up two tiny pocket-size notebooks like I like. One is red; one is blue. "Do you want red . . .?"

I blink twice and point to the blue one.

"OK, blue." She picks up three of the doll-size blue notebooks.

"What color pen do you want? Blue?"

[BLINK BLINK]

"Black?"

[BLINK BLINK]

"Oh! I remember! A pencil, a mechanical pencil! OK, here's one. OK?"

[BLINK]

The cashier rings up the soda, apple, notebooks, pencil. "Will there be anything else?" he asks. Albertine and I blink twice, in unison, two weary women in Mickey and Minnie Mouse ears, staring at the young cashier like giant, startled mice.

Our appearance doesn't phase him. "Will there be anything else?" he asks again.

"Dammit, Ruby," Albertine says. She laughs and bumps me with her hip, "Now you've got me doing it, too!"

Out at my car, Albertine unlocks the doors, and we both get in.

Once inside, we just sit a long time. Albertine opens up the paper sack from the newsstand and takes out one of the little blue notebooks.

"I love you," she writes and passes the book to me.

"U-2," I write and pass it back.

"Thank you, Ruby. I'm sorry," she writes.

"Me-2," I write.

She rips off the page, crumples it, sticks it in her pocket. On the next page, she draws a tic-tac-toe board with a big X in the center. I take it, draw an O in three corners.

"Cheater!" she says, drawing tic-tac-toe with X's across the middle.

She adjusts my pink Minnie Mouse ears, smoothes back my hair. "Ruby," she says, crying, "I don't know how I can live through this. I need you. I really need to know you're out there, OK? You know what I'm saying, don't you?"

[BLINK]

"I have Matthew, but he's all torn up by this, too. I don't know how we'll get through this. I know you love me. I know you love Owen. Just let me know you're there, OK? I understand you. We've always understood each other. We're different, but we're the same. We're both strong. You know that."

Tell me why the stars do shine, Albertine sings in our mother's voice.

Hurriedly, I scribble out the next line in my notebook and we both pretend I'm singing it, though Albertine sings it for me: *Tell me why the ivy twines.*

Tell me why the sky's so blue, Albertine sings.

She sings, I write: *And I will tell you why I love you.*

[BLINK]

"This is ridiculous," Albertine says. "Two middle-aged women in Mickey Mouse ears, sitting in a car, playing tic-tac-toe, blinking, singing, and . . ." She starts to cry, then stops immediately.

"OK. I'm leaving. Now call me twice at seven. Just start driving. Drive real slowly, and if you have to stop for anything, you have your little notebook and your pencil, OK?"

[BLINK]

Albertine kisses my cheek and gets out, checking to make sure the door is locked. She presses her nose against the window and blinks. In the rearview mirror, she gets smaller and smaller—a tall woman in Mickey Mouse ears and a turquoise raincoat—until she's about the size of my thumb. Then a Greyhound bus comes between us, passing its black plume as it moves on, and—poof!—Albertine's gone. On my dashboard is a digital travel clock that says it's 3:25 P.M. I want to go home. Want to lie down. Crawl under the bed. Want to die. My hand is only inches from the ignition, but it's frozen on my lap. I can't raise it to turn the key. An hour goes by. Another and another.

At seven P.M., I will my body to a pay phone just inside the terminal, call Albertine's number, hang up, call again, hang up, tiptoe to the ladies' room and back out to my car. Another hour. Another. I'm watching the travel alarm blinking its time-talk, its green, flickering life story to me. I understand and blink back. My favorite times, I decide, are 1:00, 1:01, and 1:10. Behind 1:00, 1:01, and 1:10, for sixty seconds, the outlines of all the other times are most visible, like tracings, possibilities. It's two A.M. Outside the windshield, the moon has risen and taken its place like a tiny cigarette burn in the sky; beside it a spark, a cinder, a burned-out little star.

"*Star light, star bright* . . ." I say to myself, out of habit. "*May the peace of God, which passeth all understanding* . . ." My right hand has thawed. It has a life of its own now and is moving toward the key in the ignition.

1980—Vivvy and I and a bunch of guys are playing horseshoes in the sandpits behind Boo's and my house-in-progress. The game's almost over, and Vivvy and I are way ahead. The guys hate it. We love it. We don't even aim. I think it all has to do with magnetism, but Vivvy says it's visualization. We just close our eyes and throw. I love games where you get to shoot and throw things—darts, horseshoes, quoits—but I don't like the ones like softball where things come flying at you.

"Come on, Ruby Tuesday," Nick says, pulling me away, "sing 'Someday Soon.'"

"Somebody shoot for me," I call over my shoulder.

Nick is walking toward the benches—I love the way he walks—playing the introduction on his Gibson guitar. I love the introduction, but the song is hard to sing. It reminds me of Neddy. My first love, Neddy. I made him a lariat in Brownies. We were going to join a Wild West show when we grew up. I would do a balancing sharpshooter act, galloping around a ring at high speed, dressed in a satin cowgirl outfit with long blue fringe, standing, bareback of course, on a pinto pony, a six-shooter smokin' in each hand. Neddy would snap cigarettes out of my mouth with a bull whip and throw knives at me as I spun around on a giant wooden wheel. He would rope steers and ride a bucking bronco. We would have three children, also sharpshooters: Buffalo Bill, Wild Bill, and Annie.

"Come on, Ruby," Nick says, and I look at him and melt as he plays the intro over again. I start to sing, and Nick bends his head down close to his guitar like it's his lover, closes his eyes, and smiles:

> *There's a young man that I know, His age is twenty-one*
> *Comes from down in southern Colorado*
> *Just out of the service, and he's lookin' for his fun*
> *Someday soon, I'm goin' with him, someday soon.*

Horseshoes are clanging against a stake behind the cedar trees. People are shouting. *Oooh. Ahhh.* A bonfire is blazing. We're all drinking frozen margaritas, eating roasted clams and oysters. About an hour earlier, Boo, Nick, Vivvy, and I split three tiny psilocybin mushrooms, just enough to feel good, nothing serious. We're at that place where everything twinkles. My voice has never sounded so beautiful. I think it must be my mother singing for me. An angel. Nick's hair is full of stars. My dress is the most beautiful blue the world has ever seen. It's cobalt and midnight. It's indigo and electric. The blue of old Blue Willow china. The blue of jars and bottles in windows. Of Morpho butterflies and indigo buntings. It's scarlet blue. It's the blue of my mother's glass ink pot. It shimmers in the moonlight. It glimmers. It glows. It burns and dances, flame blue. When I move, my dress feels like a silk hand passing over my body. I love my dress. I cross my hands on my shoulders, touching my blue dress, and sing:

> *My parents cannot stand him, 'cause he rides the rodeo*
> *My father says that he will leave me cryin'*

My husband, Boo, is leaning against the shed, a drink in one hand. He's so dark his white shirt looks like a searchlight. He's talking out of the corner of his mouth, like he does when he's been drinking. He's talking to a dark-haired woman in a sarong and a lime green bathing suit top. He's laughing with Vivvy, but he's looking, he's smiling, at me.

> *I would follow him right down the toughest road I know,*

I sing. Boo comes up and sits down on one of the makeshift benches. He pulls me to him and starts unbraiding my hair.

> *Someday soon, goin' with him, someday soon.*

The song is over, but my mother is still singing it. The song is spinning around Jackson Circle like it's a carousel calliope or a music box playing, floating through the cedar trees and out into the marsh. It's hanging like threads caught on the briars at the edge of the marsh, the briars sticking to the hem of the universe. My mother is standing above the water in her concert gown like Beautiful Dreamer, her palms out like Jesus, singing "Someday Soon."

"Are you having a good time?" Boo says. "You look so foxy in that dress. Where did you get that dress?"

"You know, my stepmother. Deenie. Deenie gave it to me. She bought it in nineteen forty-one. You've seen it before. I've worn it before. It was Deenie's."

"You can really wear that stuff, Ruby," he says. "You know, Nick really likes you," he adds.

"I really like him, too. I like him better than any of your friends that I've met. I feel like I've known him forever. What's Tina like? What's his fiancée like? How comes she doesn't like you?"

I had heard about Nick for years — Nick this and Nick that — but this is the first time I've met him. He's a high school English teacher in Minnesota. This is the first time he's been back east in six or seven years. It's spring break and he's been visiting us for a week. All Nick and I have done all week is sing and talk. He has a car full of books, and every night I can't wait to get home from the Pirate's Cove and talk to him. He's going back to Minnesota tomorrow.

"Tina's a bitch," Boo says.

"Why doesn't Tina like you?"

"Because she knows I know who she really is. I went out with her before Nick. That's all. Let's not talk about Tina."

"Vivvy really likes Nick. It's too bad he's engaged."

"Nick doesn't like Vivvy, though. You know who Nick likes," Boo says.

"Who? Who does Nick like?"

"You know, Ruby," he says, pulling me closer against him. "Come on, you know, Ruby. Don't pull that dumb-blonde act on me."

"No, I don't know. Who?"

He takes my hand and pulls it behind me, puts it on his crotch. "Feel this, Ruby," he says. "You know who Nick wants. Say it."

I try to pull away. "Stop it, Boo," I say. Suddenly, I feel sick. Boo has my arm in one hand, and in his other hand, he has my hair.

"Say it," he hisses in my ear and twists my arm.

"Please don't. You're hurting me," I whisper. I want to get away. I feel dizzy, and I think I might start crying.

"Say it," Boo says again.

"I won't say it!" I say.

He pushes me forward and I fall in the sand.

He grabs me again like he's helping me up. Nick is playing another song, singing an old blues song, "Cocaine Blues."

"Yes, you will say it," Boo says. "If you don't say it, Ruby, you're gonna do it. I know why you're wearing that dress. You're wearing that dress for Nick. I've seen how you walk around in front of him. I've seen how you flirt with him. Well now you're gonna get what you want, Ruby. I'm your husband, Ruby, and I'm gonna see that you get what you've been asking for."

Boo's eyes are on fire. A tiger's eyes. *Tiger, tiger burning bright, in the forests of the night.* His skin feels so hot and he's trembling all over and the tremor of his body has migrated into me like I'm a bridge over a canyon that is responding, though it doesn't want to, to some howling decibel of wind that will set it vibrating like a streamer and rip it apart molecule by molecule.

"Come on, Ruby," Boo says, "we're going inside."

"Ruby, what are you doin'? Are you playing or not?" Vivvy calls out to me, stepping out from behind the cedars. For a second, I breathe. I think I'm safe, but Boo twists my wrist.

"Ruby, you OK?" Vivvy asks, sensing something's wrong.

"I can't," I whisper. "I don't feel good. I feel sick. I feel like I'm going to faint."

"She doesn't feel good," Boo says. "She shouldn't have eaten those mushrooms. You know how she is. We're goin' inside."

"Damn you, Ruby," I hear Vivvy say as she stomps away. "Who wants to throw again for Ruby?" she calls out into the cedars.

Inside our bedroom, I'm shaking all over, looking out the window at the laundry in the moonlight. There's my gingham sundress. There's my cowboy shirt; my 1950s dungarees with the side zipper; my polka-dot silk shorts; my favorite Jantzen bathing suit. There's my linen tablecloth with the green apples. Boo has me pinned against the wall. He's stroking my neck. His hand comes down my neck and his fingers curl around the sweetheart neckline of my dress.

"I hate this dress, Ruby," he says, and rips it down the front. "You shouldn't have worn this dress, Ruby."

I'm a mannequin. A stone statue. An ice sculpture. He rips the dress off me, and bangs my head against a stud in the wall.

"Did you hear me, Ruby? Say it. Say, 'I shouldn't have worn this dress.'"

"I shouldn't have worn this dress."

"Say, 'I shouldn't have worn this dress for Nick.'"

"I shouldn't have worn this dress for Nick."

"Say it again. Keep saying it."

I hear the screen door open and slap shut. Boo reaches behind me and opens his top bureau door.

"Please not that, Boo. Please," I say. "Please don't."

The door closes. The latch. Footsteps.

He's holding my hands behind my back. I want to scream, but I have no voice. Out in the yard, I see a deer. A little deer, a fawn with spots. And another one. Two more big deer. One of them could have wings, but maybe it's just my tablecloth trying to tell me something. No, it's wings. Wings for sure.

"No, Ruby," Boo says, "you need this. I'll teach you to wear that goddamn dress for Nicky." I hear the duct tape ripping from itself and he starts wrapping it around my wrists.

1971 — "You know, Albert," my stepmother, Deenie, is saying, "she could talk if she wanted to. Anybody can talk if they want to. You just humor her. She's not a baby. She's a grown woman. She's twenty-one years old, and she's upstairs lying under the bed like a crazy person. You need to go up there and drag her out. I'll get her out. I'll vacuum her out! I won't have this nonsense. June and Guy are coming tomorrow from Miami. I spent all week cleaning, and I won't have this. Where am I supposed to put them? I'm supposed to put them in that room and say, 'Oh by the way, don't pay any attention to the woman under the bed. That's just Albert's daughter and her shadow, that damn dog.'

"Where did she get that damn dog? As soon as you close the door, he gets up on the bed. I mean, you can see that. There's dog hair all over my Martha Washington bedspread. As soon as you knock on the door, you can hear him jump down . . ."

I'm lying under the bed, my ear pressed against the gray flowered carpet. I can hear every word they're saying.

"Deenie, Deenie," my father is saying. He probably has his hands on her shoulders. Now he is probably patting her back. "Calm down, Deenie. It's OK. She'll come out. Just leave her alone. She'll come out. She'll go back to school tomorrow. She'll let me take her back."

"She'll come out, all right," Deenie says, "because I'll call Shady Point and they'll come with a straitjacket and take her out."

"Deenie, Deenie," my father is saying, "don't say that. You're making a mountain out of a molehill. She's under the bed, so what?"

"I just can't believe she'd come here and act like this."

"She can't help it, Deenie. Don't be mad at her. She's upset. Deenie, a friend of hers was just killed. You saw the obituary Frannie sent. He was only a year older than her; she's known him almost her whole life. They spent every summer together in Philadelphia when they were kids. Think of all the boys her age being killed in Vietnam. You remember the war, Deenie. You remember what it was like. She'll come out. Her mother used to do the same thing. Get under the bed. I know it's peculiar . . ."

"What! Your wife? Eva used to get under the bed? You mean as a child or as a grown woman? Get under the bed? A grown woman? Why? Why on earth would she get under the bed?"

"Just to think. When she was depressed. Just to get away from it all."

"Albert, that's crazy! Of course, Eva was . . . I'm sorry. I didn't mean it, Al. I know she was special. I just can't take these kids . . . between Ruby and Mason . . . Jesus, they're a buncha crackpots, if you ask me."

"One day I came home from work . . ." my father continues, "and I couldn't find anybody. It was the day their dog Go-Jeff was run over on Elysian Avenue. All four of them were under the brass bed in the attic. Eva and Mason and both the girls. All four of them under the bed, crying."

"What did you do?"

"What I'm going to do now," my father says. In a few minutes he comes upstairs and knocks on the door of the guest room. Roo jumps down off the bed and comes and lies beside it.

My father comes in and sits down on the chair by the bed. He has on argyle socks, gray slacks, and brown leather slippers. He blows into his pitch pipe. A B-flat. He's a choir director and always has a pitch pipe in his shirt pocket.

"MMMM," he hums in B-flat. My father sometimes calls me Jeanie, after my middle name, Jean. I know by the B-flat "MMMM" what he's going to sing. I squeeze my eyes tight and cry. He pulls a chair over by the bed and sings,

> *I dream of Jeanie, With the light brown hair*
> *Borne like a vapor on the summer air . . .*

I reach my left hand out from under the bed and place my fingertips on the toe of my father's slipper. Roo gets back up on the bed. My father clears his throat and blows in the pitch pipe.

"MMMM," he hums in B-flat again and begins my mother's and my favorite song, the song he sang first to us when we were crying under the bed after Go-Jeff died:

> *Thee I love,*
> *More than the meadows so green and still*
> *More than the mulberries on the hill*
> *More than the buds on the mayapple trees*
> *I love thee. . . .*

His voice is breaking, but he sings and sings and sings: "The Green-Eyed Dragon," "My Mother Bids Me Bind My Hair," "Danny Boy," "Old Dog Tray," "Between the Devil and the Deep Blue Sea," "Stardust," "Deep Purple." After a while, I crawl out and get up on the bed with Roo.

"I'm sorry about Neddy," my father says, stroking my forehead. "He was a nice boy. War is a terrible thing. It's a terrible, terrible thing, Ruby. Go take a shower, sweetheart, and then come downstairs and we'll have some tea and we'll talk. I have some good Earl Grey tea like you like. And Deenie made some quince jam. You remember those two little quince trees in town, don't you? The ones we used to tie the badminton net to? Come on down, Ruby. Life goes on. You know that, Ruby. You know that. We endure. We abideth. That's why we're here. To carry on for those who have passed on. To carry on."

He walks over to the window. "So many people I know are

gone now," he says. "It breaks my heart. That's the way it is when you grow up. Your heart will just break and break and break till you think it can't break into any smaller pieces. But it keeps ticking. Breaking and ticking. Every year, you lose somebody, but every year you carry on. You carry on for your mother, you carry on for Neddy, you carry on for those who are gone. Listen to me, Ruby, you will prevail."

Through the sheers, the worn-smooth ridges of the Allegheny foothills are rolling like blue whales toward the horizon.

"I will lift up mine eyes unto the hills," my father says to the landscape.

He comes and sits down on the bed and takes me in his arms and pats my back. I cry and cry and sob and sob. He pats and pats. I get the hiccups. He runs his hand along Roo's back. "That's a good dog, you have, Ruby. He's a really good dog, aren't you, buddy?"

Roo yawns. I hiccup.

Roo circles the bathroom rug, then plops down, and I take a long, hot shower without turning on the exhaust fan. When I step out, I can't even see Roo. Deenie will be mad that I took my dog into the bathroom. She wanted him to stay in the basement, but my father brought him upstairs. I gather up the chenille rug, full of dog hair, to put it in the washer. I put on my robe and step outside. A burst of steam, like the depiction of the Passover in Cecil B. DeMille's *The Ten Commandments*, follows me. There's Deenie in the hall, by the doorway of my father's and her bedroom.

"Ruby," she says, "come here a minute."

I walk to her door and see that she has a pile of clothes on the bed. Something a beautiful, electric blue. Something long and dark.

"Ruby," Deenie says, walking to the bed, "these are some outfits I had when I was in college. They were my favorite clothes. I've saved them all these years, but I'll never wear them again. I thought you might want them. Come on in and try them on."

I go in the guest room and pull on some underwear under my bathrobe. I don't own a bra.

"Look at this," Deenie says, holding up the most beautiful 1940s dress I've ever seen. It's electric blue silk with a sweetheart neckline; shoulder pads; petal sleeves; a peplum; a mid-calf-length gored skirt that flares at the bottom.

"Try it on. Believe it or not, I used to be just about your size," Deenie says. She's a small, plump but shapely woman with steel gray curly hair like Persian lamb. I turn around and take off my robe, step into the dress. It's as cool and soft as a breeze, a breath. I've never felt anything so luxurious. I hold up my hair, and Deenie zips me up and runs her hands over my hips, smoothing the gathers. On the bed is a gray gabardine suit; a long dark blue coat with wide cuffs, like Salvation Army ladies wore; a peach-colored satin nightgown with a matching blue quilted bed jacket; a beaded cardigan sweater. I'm turning around, admiring myself in the full-length mirror on the door, and then in the mirror I see Deenie and notice she's crying. She's sitting on the bed behind me, next to the pile of clothes. The kettle's whistling in the kitchen below.

"Deenie," I say, sitting down beside her. "Deenie, what is it? Deenie, thank you so much. I've never seen such beautiful things. Are you sure you want to give them to me?" I put my arm around her. "Deenie, what's the matter? I'm sorry I stayed under the bed. Deenie, I'm so sorry. I'm sorry I let my dog get up on the bed. Deenie, what is it?"

"I had a friend, too," Deenie sobs. She gets up and opens a drawer in the bureau, takes out a small gray box, and comes and sits back down beside me. Roo comes and puts his chin on my lap.

Deenie opens the box. Inside are old postcards and pale blue airmail letters tied together with a satin ribbon. "His name was Billy Maupin," she says. "He was a midshipman. He was at Annapolis the same time your Uncle Wilkie was there. He would have been a captain someday, but he was killed at Pearl Harbor."

She hands me a hand-tinted photograph in a gray cardstock frame with a scroll foil-stamped around the edges. A boy in a dark sailor's shirt and white sailor's hat, a boy with dimples, smiles up at us. "Look," she says, handing me a stack of postcards, "these are from New Zealand. He was stationed in the South Pacific. I went all the way to San Diego to see him before he shipped out. We danced at a fancy club for enlisted men, and Benny Goodman played. I wore this blue dress."

"Deenie, I'm so sorry," I say. "I'm so sorry." I put my arms around her.

"It was December twelfth," she says, "nineteen forty-one . . . a Friday afternoon." Deenie wipes her eyes with a pink tissue from the nightstand. "We were all waiting outside the courthouse to read the list of those in our district who had been killed. My friend Gloria Pfeiffer was secretary for the draft board, and she was supposed to type up the list. Her boss had the names on carbon copies of letters sent from President Roosevelt to the families. Gloria was supposed to type up the list of the boys from our district. Her boss started reading off the names. Gloria typed three names and fell off the chair. He picked her up and went and got Shirley Hawkins from the assessor's office to finish typing the list. Shirley typed a couple names he read off, and she fainted, too. Finally, he sat down and typed the list himself. We were all waiting outside for the list to be posted in the glass case on the stone wall. We were all standing in the snow, waiting. So quiet. Mostly women. Blowing in our gloved hands. Clapping our hands together to keep warm. I had a muff, though. A little brown mink muff, and a little round mink hat. Inside the muff, I had Billy's picture. I kept my hand on Billy's picture. I told myself if I kept my hand on Billy's picture, he'd be spared."

"It's OK, Deenie," I say. "It's OK. You just go ahead and cry." We sit there and hold each other and cry for Billy Maupin and Neddy Turner and Uncle Wilkie and all the boys and men, dead and alive, in dress blues and camouflage, gabardine and denim, in body bags and bars and living rooms, hospitals and office buildings, cemeteries and jungles and classrooms, tears splashing all over the electric blue silk dress.

"Deenie!" my father calls up from the bottom of the stairs. "Ruby! Come on down, girls, and have some tea while it's still nice and hot! Come on, Roo! There's something down here for Roo, too!" my father calls up from the bottom of the stairs.

Isotopes

1. Water

1990—Under a table an old dog is dreaming. In his doggie dream, something is bobbing in the water, and he must swim far out and retrieve it, but this is the dog's dilemma: he's afraid of water. He can't swim. Under the table, the dog's legs twitch, his paws do the doggie paddle, his heart races, he whimpers. The dog's a retriever, a water dog equipped with webbed paws for swimming and a thick, oily undercoat to insulate his pale skin from cold water and to repel the water off his back with one glorious shake. But the dog's afraid of water. Nope, the dog absolutely cannot swim . . . but . . . the dog *must* swim.

When the dog was a puppy and wouldn't listen and had never seen a big body of water before, he ran lickety-split—although someone called his name over and over from a VW microbus—across a burning hot place right into a deep, churning wet place. Suddenly a big, cold fist grabbed him, pulled him out and down into a frightful dark place full of slippery, formless things with eyes, held him there and shook him like a die, then rolled him back out onto a foamy, hard place called a beach. There, a woman in a bathing suit and a long, flapping skirt slapped him and pushed on his chest until he vomited up brine, and the sun shone so brightly in his eyes.

Now the same woman gets out of bed and crawls under the table and takes the dog's paw. "Hey, Phinny," she whispers in the dreaming dog's ear, "where ya goin', buddy?" The dog jerks his head. Blinks. Moans. He's back, safely now, on his green corduroy dog bed. So the woman and the dog sit there under the table a while, the woman with the big dog paw in her hand, as the sun rehearses another run-of-the-mill Monday and a forsythia gives it a run for its money on the lawn.

It's dawn, and the water dream, the dream of drowning, has had its little say in the dream of the dog, but the water dream isn't satisfied, and so it walks over to the man who's sleeping next to the empty space in the bed, the space still warm with the troubled dreams of the woman sitting under the table with the dog. The man sleeping next to the empty space is dreaming about birch trees in the water-filled country where he was born. The country is far north, across the Atlantic Ocean, and full of fresh water and fishes, lakes with the secret imprint of rocks and trees and bones on their floors, lakes bulldozed by errant glaciers creeping south.

White snow, paper birches, bodies of water parfaited with ice and snow: these the man dreams of. In winter, the landscape is an intricate scrimshaw of branch and bark, bark and birch, scribbled against a sky so vast it comes right down to your *gummistövlar*. The wind writes in the snow, in pictures, in curlicues and cuneiforms known only to animals and children and to those who live the old way, herding reindeer. The wind gets in your ears and sings its dolce windsongs. The wind bends and plays the birches like strings. And it is this song, in its doleful key, moving through the birches, that scores the man's dreams.

But because today it's spring and outside this American window a forsythia has been belting out its yellow song, in the man's dream it's suddenly spring, too, and the man is a little boy again in a house with an orange tile roof and yellow stucco walls, and a heavy, bright blue door with an iron handle, and a bright yellow *ölandstok* bush is singing, too, only here it sings in Swedish.

Soon there will be heather in the windowboxes and the lavender shadow of scarlet tulips cast upon the wall.

In this spring dream, the Swedish man is a little boy, and his mother brings an armful of birch branches into the house and arranges them in a stone crock so big you could hide inside it. The children of the house decorate the branches with colorful paper birds, and as the buds on the birch tree unfurl, the birds fly away, and the days grow longer and longer.

But the water dream is not content with this sweet dream of seasons and *ölandstok* and paper birds. The water dream is getting restless, impatient, so the water dream lies down beside the man. He lies on his back—the water dream—fingers laced behind his head, legs crossed, knees bent, kicking his foot, and whistling *"Frère Jacques"* softly through his teeth. The water dream wiggles his toes, rolls over, snuggles up against the man, and whispers in his ear. And so the man dreams again, this time a dream of spring and rushing water. In this dream the man is a little boy and he is standing by his father who died so suddenly. They have been fishing, the young father in an oiled yellow jacket and the little boy, and they climb up a steep bank to their house, where the father sits down on a wooden bench that looks down on the lake sparkling through a picket of birches. The father leans over to pull off his black *gummistövlar,* a flash of silver water behind his yellow back, another flash like fireworks in his head, and his heart stops so suddenly. A heavy blue door slams shut by a gust of wind, and the little boy is left standing there, alone, holding a fish.

"Fäder!" the man calls out in his sleep and awakens, startled, heart pounding, short of breath. He can almost feel his father there beside him, but it's just the water dream, not his father at all. Now, now the water dream is satisfied, done; he gets up, brushes the dog hair off his trousers, and leaves.

2. Isotopes

A long time ago—many years before the water dream—the woman under the table taught a freshman English class in a building called Armstrong Hall. The woman was young then, a graduate teaching assistant. She was supposed to be writing a thesis, a scholarly, critical study about the work of an obscure southern writer, but the young woman teaching the class hadn't written anything at all. She had bought hundreds—no, wait, she had bought *thousands*—of blue-lined index cards on which to take notes about the obscure southern writer. She had numbered the note cards very neatly in the upper-right-hand corner, sharpening and resharpening pencils, but she had written no words at all. The young woman had never wanted to be a teacher. She hated to stand in front of a class. She hated to speak in front of people. She spent a lot of time with her back turned to the class, taking little sips of Pepto-Bismol from a tiny silver flask and writing on the blackboard, because she was afraid to turn around. Fortunately, there were two students in her class who really liked to argue with each other. Every Monday, Wednesday, and Friday, the young teacher turned the floor over to these two bullshit artists, and as they blathered on, she stared out the window to where a lot of construction was going on below on a monorail that would be called a personal rapid transit system and would connect the two campuses of the university, which sat on either side of the city like ears.

One day, a few days into the semester, one of the workers from the personal rapid transit system came and sat in the woman's class. He was a teenager in a blue work shirt with the name "Etienne" embroidered in a red oval like a watchful eye above his shirt pocket. The boy had chestnut brown hair that hung down over his collar. He sat in a corner and stared at his brown, scuffed shoes. The young English teacher tried not to look at him. Every Monday, Wednesday, and Friday, the boy named Etienne came to the young woman's class and sat in the same corner, never speaking, just staring at his shoes. When the young woman came to the door to teach the class, the boy was always there in the corner looking at the door, and for a split second their eyes met in the door's tiny window, and the young woman's heart did a fantastic leap like Rudolf Nureyev, hanging in her throat an impossibly long time, defying gravity, before it settled in her chest again like a stunned bird, and she walked through the door.

The last class before Christmas break, however, the boy named Etienne was not sitting in the corner of the classroom opposite the door. The young woman stood outside the door, and through the door's tiny window, the empty space in the corner grew. The young woman's heart sank like a boulder that had broken off a steep cliff and tumbled into the sea. As she waded through the space between the doorway and the metal table in front of the room, the young woman thought about dismissing the English class, but that was something graduate teaching assistants were never supposed to do. She could say she didn't feel well. It was snowing. She thought she might faint. She walked to the table. Behind the lectern on the table was a small envelope with the woman's first name printed in pencil: RUBY. Ruby put her hand on the envelope and closed her eyes. She did what she was not supposed to do, and everyone filed out the door.

Ruby sat alone in the room and opened the envelope while outside the snow came down in big heavy flakes, such a steady, even falling of snow, the building itself seemed to be rising. Inside the envelope was a sheet of folded, blue-lined notebook paper. On the paper, in pencil, was a letter. Ruby's hands shook as she unfolded the paper and read the letter, and her eyes filled with tears. In the letter, Etienne said he had fallen in love with a face in a second-story window. He felt, he said, like a person who had ridden around and around, up and down, on a carousel pony his entire life, and suddenly, his fingers finally grasped the coveted brass ring that promised another ride. In another line, Etienne said that since he saw Ruby's face in the window, he was nothing but an electron that had met with some bitter charge, whipped to a higher, more energized ring, an electric blue isotope of himself. He said what he felt between himself and Ruby was something like a welder's arc that he could not look at without risking blindness. In another line, the last line, he said goodbye.

Ruby never saw Etienne again, but she kept the letter for many years, folded in a maroon leather jewelry box that played "Stardust" by her bed. A few months after Etienne left, Ruby took up with a man who quoted Andrew Marvell, and she went with him to the Outer Banks of North Carolina and married him one mid-summer day, standing half in the ocean, half on the beach, continental plates shifting underneath their bare feet. Every night, though, she took the letter out of the jewelry box and read it to herself, even though she knew it by heart. It was a secret thing she did faithfully, even after she was married. She read the letter with the same regularity as a nun saying her prayers: without fail. Night after night, year after year, after all the blue lines had faded, and the penciled words, too, were gone, and there was nothing at all left except two tiny incisions forming a cross in the centerfold where the letter had been folded and unfolded thousands of times, even then, Ruby read the letter.

One long, troubled night, however, Ruby decides she has nothing left to live for. She puts the wordless letter in her pocket, walks to the edge of Jackson Circle, and keeps walking through the dunes along Highway 12, to the ocean, where she closes her eyes, spreads out her arms, and in an exquisite balancing act, steps off the end of a long jetty into a gray, chilly sea, just as the sun is blossoming out of it. On the beach, in frail pink light, a black Labrador retriever who nearly drowned as a puppy runs back and forth on the sand, barking, whining, whimpering. He runs into the water, then back out. In and out. In and out. In and out. Finally, the dog who is afraid of water starts swimming.

"Go back! Go back! Bad dog, Phinny! Phinny, go home!" Ruby, treading water, screams. But Phineas T. Gooddog will not go back. He runs and runs in the water, swimming, disappearing in troughs of waves and reappearing now and then as a black speck on their white crests. Whimpering, choking, he paddles up to Ruby, a terrified look on his sweet, soaked face.

Ruby and Phinny survive. The wordless letter is lost.

Now, many years after that, poor Phinny has died of old age, and Ruby is standing in a checkout line at Giant Eagle supermarket, where she recognizes the cashier as a chunky and balding, middle-aged version of one of the full-of-himself students from many years ago in her English I class. She's seen him working here many times before but has always managed to avoid his aisle and has never made eye contact with him. When she first saw him, he looked vaguely familiar, and then when she figured out who he was, it surprised her to see him working there in Giant Eagle. She thought he would have become a successful lawyer or at least a politician. But now, here he comes, smiling and holding his cash register tray, as the cashiers change guard. No-nonsense Pat — who looks like Whoopie Goldberg and is fast and super-efficient — Ruby's favorite cashier, is done for the day, and Ruby's now trapped in line in this guy's aisle; there's someone with a whole cartload of diapers and beer behind her, invading her space. Ruby can almost remember the clerk's name, but she's praying he won't recognize her. So many years have passed. She puts on her sunglasses, touches her hat, and with her back bent over the front of her cart, her head practically in it, begins furiously to upload her groceries onto the conveyor belt.

Bartlett pears and Philadelphia cream cheese and Newman's Own salad dressing are inching their way down the belt, and the cashier says, "You're Ruby Reese, aren't you? I was in your English I class a long time ago. Like a *really* long time ago . . . Man! That was a *helluva* long time ago!"

Ruby thumbs through her Rolodex of voice prints, locates the voice of surprise, and looks up: "Oh! I thought you looked familiar!" she says, so faux enthusiastically, staring at his name badge.

WELCOME TO GIANT EAGLE, the badge proclaims, MY NAME IS DANNY.

"Danny, isn't it? Danny . . . umm . . ." Ruby says.

"Very good, Miss Reese! Danny Kelly!"

"Danny Kelly! Why yes, Danny Kelly! Well . . . small world . . . gee! Golly!" Ruby says, turning to grab a fistful of Necco wafers from the candy counter and then very busily going back to unloading her cart.

Paper towels. Bow-tie noodles. Quaker Puffed Rice. Seltzer water.

"Miss Reese, do you have a Giant Eagle card?" Danny asks, and

Ruby fumbles with one hand through her coat pockets for her keys, which sport a fan of small barcoded plastic cards like garish tail feathers.

"Listen . . . if I may be so bold . . ." Danny says while Ruby is still rooting, "there's something I always wondered," he says, passing a can of Carnation evaporated milk again and again over the green, knowing eye and leaning across the counter. "Were you . . . you know . . . like . . . *seeing* that guy Etienne Morales who used to sit in the back of the room?"

"Well . . . no . . . oh no . . . um . . . you knew him?" Ruby says, her bird-heart pounding.

"Well, yeah, I went to high school with him. Morgantown High," Danny Kelly says.

"You're kidding! Well . . . what happened to him? Where is he?"

"Oh . . . geez . . ." Danny Kelly says, "I don't know for sure . . . I think I heard that he drowned. Jumped off a bridge, I think . . . Yep. A long time ago . . . in New Jersey . . . someplace in New Jersey, I think. Or New York. He was a crackpot!" Danny says, laughing. "So was his sister . . . Gabriella, that was her name . . . Gabriella . . . Yep . . . Gabby, we called her. You know, I just always wondered . . ."—he sort of snorts—"if you were, you know, like . . ."

His voice trails off as he flips through a sheaf of laminated plastic pages on a shiny ring, searching for the price of a blue-green box of dog cookies with a picture of Lassie smiling on the front.

From a malfunctioning automated checkout aisle behind Ruby, a strangely inflected voice is calling, "*Weigh your snow peas. Move your snow peas snow peas snow peas . . .*"

"Price check on five!" Danny Kelly hollers into the jittering fluorescence. All kinds of things are moving down the conveyor belt in front of Ruby: cans, vegetables, cat litter, fruit, razor blades, all kinds of things piling up in a painful heap at the bottom of the counter. Ruby can't stay there any longer. She abandons her cart, her carefully chosen, would-be groceries, and as if responding to a hypnotist's command, wades out into the sea of red shopping carts.

The glass doors sense her coming, and part.

A bell rings.

"Hey, Miss Reese! Miss Reese!" Danny Kelly calls after her. He's still standing like the Statue of Liberty, a box with a collie his torch.

"Thank you for shopping at Giant Eagle!" the sliding doors proclaim politely as they slice through Ruby's shadow. "Have a nice—"

Snow peas snow peas snow—

3. Fringe Benefits

Now we must go backwards, back to where we started, and line everything up: a woman, a dog, a table, a nightmare of drowning, a camel-skinned dream filled with water. Do we know this place? How many years have passed? It's hard to say, because counting is very difficult for Ruby, whose mind starts to wander around seven and by eight has forgotten all about counting and is considering, instead, the promenade of shadows along a wall. And then there's the problem of dog years, which requires a mastery of multiplication tables and perhaps paper and pencil for ciphering. What *is* seven times fourteen? The dog must be very, very old now, you must think, or not the same dog at all. And dreams . . . dreams, you know, can be contagious.

Someone asked, who is the Swedish man, the man who dreamed about the singing *ölandstok* bush, the blue door, his father? What is *he* doing here? Ruby would like to answer, but unfortunately this question comes too late, because the Swedish man—her second husband, Oskar—is gone. He's gone back to Sweden, perhaps because he and the woman under the table are no longer in love. And that's another story. Maybe they never were in love but only lost in the concept, the tarnished, brass-ring/second-chance promise. And then there was the matter of the green card, too. But they both loved the dog who could not swim, and even though the woman under the table and the Swedish man Oskar lived together in a very tiny, very sturdy, three-little-pigs kind of house, they had grown so far apart that the plaster walls and the four tight corners could not keep them together. There was no wolf outside to gobble them up, only a great and silent sadness nibbling away from within.

And this is not unusual.

Now Ruby spends a lot of time alone with her old dog Phinny and a cat so fat he cannot speak. The cat opens his mouth — such a tiny pink mouth, ribbed like a scallop shell inside — and says "tuna fish," but no sound comes out. One must either know the cat or have studied catmouth reading to know what the cat has just said. If you scratch a certain part of the cat's spine near his tail, the cat lifts his head like a baby bird and opens and closes his pink mouth in total silence. Ruby puts on a *Pavarotti's Greatest Hits* CD and places the cat on the table. Scratch, scratch, scratch. *Nessun dorma . . .* , the cat stretches his neck and sings, *Nessun dorma . . .* , and Puccini's belly laugh bounces up and down the hallways of some afterlife. This is a kind of ritual. Every night the cat sings Puccini for his supper and receives a heaping table-spoon of tasty Starkist solid white albacore tuna on a Fiestaware saucer. Every night Puccini's ghost laughs its hearty laugh. (Any life can be, you know, so pleasant, so inane, so glum.)

Many years before . . . when Ruby was a little girl in red cowboy boots . . . she fancied herself a poet. Moved by the moroseness of Walt Disney, she spent two years writing an elegy to Bambi's mother. Many times throughout that somber, illuminated elegy, Ruby referred to Bambi's mother as a stag. One day, Ruby set her parents' house on fire, trying to destroy the Bambi manuscript in a closet after her fourth-grade teacher pointed out that a stag is a male deer. Many fire trucks arrived on the scene and smoke poured out from under the house roof. All this because of some unfortunate word choices.

Perhaps because of this incident — fire and humiliation —

Ruby became obsessed with words and developed a compulsion for looking up words in the dictionary and keeping track of them in tiny memo pads. She carries a pocket dictionary in her purse, another under the seat of her car. There's another dictionary by her bed, yet another one on her kitchen table, another in the living room, and a big blue one for thumbing through on her desk.

You can never be too sure about words.

Ruby grows up and somehow ends up living back in the town where she went to graduate school, and as you've probably already guessed, she never did become a poet. She's just a middle-aged, once-divorced, unhappily remarried, childless woman who lives with her Swedish efficiency-expert husband, her old black Lab, Phinny, and the cat who never learned how to meow—a woman with a job as a technical writer at a coal fly ash research center at a university where classified staff can take classes for free and receive release time from work to attend classes, in order to better themselves. After Ruby works at the university for some years, she realizes that many of her coworkers aren't there half the time.

"Where is everybody?" she looks up from her *American Heritage* dictionary one day and asks.

The answer: THEY ARE IN CLASS!

"Hmmmmm," Ruby says to herself. "Hmmmm. I shall take a class for free, too. I shall leave work piled on my desk and walk out the glass revolving doors, my spiral notebook and my dictionary in my bag, and I shall ride the personal rapid transit system and sit in a classroom and let my head fill up with poetry like a bathtub with Calgon bath oil beads, while these boring coal fly ash reports wait for me, moldering in my dark, windowless office, growing tendrils, sprouting eyes."

Ruby registers for a poetry class. The class, funny thing, is in Armstrong Hall, the same building in which Ruby taught an English I class many years earlier and where a boy named Etienne sat in a corner in the back and broke her heart into a million pieces with a handful of ephemeral words penciled on blue-lined notebook paper. The back is a good place to sit, Ruby thinks. She's so sad now, remembering so long ago and the boy named Etienne whom she loved so much, and so she takes a seat in the back in the corner of a room in Armstrong Hall, against the window-wall, a seat among very big young men in baggy black pants and big black shoes, guys with headphones and knitted watch caps and dirty black backpacks at their feet like old, obedient cocker spaniels. Poetry is a good elective, a cake class, people say. Not much reading, compared to, say, The Novel.

So much time has passed, Ruby muses, petting her velvet purse.

The classroom has just hosted an advanced math class, and three green blackboard walls are covered with white, lacy equations. Numbers are introduced to each other. They curtsy, blush, pair off, waltz around the room. They are aroused, taken to higher powers. Then, common denominators bring them back to Earth and turn them loose again to trip across the green walls in their crocheted dresses and silly, ruffled blouses.

In walks the poetry professor in a buttery brown leather jacket. There is something peculiar in the way the teacher walks, a kind of syncopated bobbing that reminds the woman of a plastic wiener dog in the rear package tray of a car pounding over speed bumps, or of a morning's robin out worming in the dew, a bird that, for one reason or another, doesn't want to get his feet wet. Quite peculiar. There is a fear the professor might fall into the dancing equations, fall completely over, crash. But he doesn't. He moves, he speaks, and the words he says draw Ruby out like excited numerals, waiting to, wanting to, dance like light, like shadows, like spinning electrons, like lace on a runaway bobbin, unraveling around the green blackboards of the room.

Ruby's in the back, stroking her velvet purse, listening, looking. The professor is talking. Sometimes his voice takes a fantastic leap like a hare, then settles down again into its briar patch. The professor's voice, like his walk, is somehow anchored in this crazy up-and-down motion, in erratic modulation, in . . . bobbing. Ruby is lost, too, bobbing on some green, peregrine sea.

Now the professor is writing with his fingertip, writing so lightly on top of this polonaise of leftover equations. He's not writing words, but drawing shapes, boxes, and ovals that represent patterns and structures and words framing words, words wrapped around words, words embracing words, words Ruby loves, and this sweet pentimento is forming in the room, another layer, another dimension, wrapped in word-lace and quadratic equations like a Pythagorean valentine, an orange pierced with whole cloves and tied with ribbon, and Ruby is totally captivated, totally lost, and she opens up the tattered pocket dictionary she's holding clandestinely on her lap, and on page 264, she reads: love (luv) 1. a deep, tender, ineffable feeling of affection and solicitude toward a person, such as that arising from kinship, recognition of attractive qualities, or a sense of underlying oneness. 2. a feeling of intense desire and attraction toward a person with whom one is disposed to make a pair . . .

Postcards from Portland

One

1990—For more than a year now, Ruby has been writing love letters to a married man in Portland, Oregon, whom she is not in love with. Ruby is married, too, and the fact that she is not in love with her husband nor this married man who is married to someone else is immaterial. She cannot relinquish the luxurious feeling of unrequited love. The pain. The longing. The heartache. Ruby is married to a Swedish efficiency expert and works as a technical writer for a coal fly ash research center. Swedish men do an average of eighteen hours of housework per week, more than men of any other nationality.

To tell the truth, though, up until a few months ago, Ruby really thought she was maybe in love with the man in Portland, Oregon: deeply, madly, truly. She couldn't look at a weather map of the United States without crying. She sent this poor man long prose poems about love and prevailing winds and separation, a cross between John Donne's "A Valediction Forbidding Mourning" and the weather channel. Instead of a compass, Ruby used a Doppler radar screen as a conceit. She was sick. She was lovesick.

Then something happened.

The man who moved to Portland, Oregon, sends Ruby postcards and pinecones, sea rocks from the Pacific, and slim volumes of poetry by dead, exiled Russians. Then, a few months ago, he wrote that he and his young wife were buying a doublewide trailer. He described the doublewide in almost glowing terms: its model number, sunken living room, champagne shag carpet, bay window, chandelier, bath and a half. Ruby was insanely jealous.

Ruby had met this man about fourteen months before at a memorial service for a retired professor she once worked with. This man who now lives in the doublewide trailer with the side-by-side refrigerator/freezer in Portland, Oregon, and Ruby were the only two people wearing hats. It was June, and they stood among a small congregation of mourners gathered on a knoll around a freshly planted dogwood tree, lavishly mulched and displaying a bronze plaque. Ruby looked up from under the brim of her black straw hat and saw a man on the fringes of the group, the bill of his black Greek fisherman's hat pointing in her direction. They both quickly looked away. The minister stretched out her arms, palms up, and said, "Would everyone step in a little closer, please?"

A slight shift, like a tilted kaleidoscope, and the group reconfigured. Suddenly, Ruby was standing next to the man in the Greek fisherman's hat: two side-by-side black shards in this new, more pleasing pattern.

Standing next to him felt very familiar to Ruby. *He* felt very familiar. Silently, Ruby admired his faded, ironed jeans and worn corduroy sports jacket with suede elbow patches, a jacket tailored for a slimmer physique. Did she know him? There was something extremely sexy about him in a faded, stocky, Harvey Keitel kind of way that only a middle-aged woman like Ruby could appreciate.

"Gee, you look familiar," the man in the Greek fisherman's hat said to Ruby.

"Me, too, I mean . . . you, too."

The two black-hatted mourners tried for a minute or two to unearth some common ground: home, work, school, politics.

"Did you ever live in Jerome Park?" the man whispered.

"Why, no," Ruby replied.

"Do you belong to the Socialist Workers Party of America?"

"No, but have you ever taken a dog to obedience school?"

"Yes, but . . ."

The service concluded.

"Well, nice to meet you," they said to each other and moved apart, walking in opposite directions to the same pavilion.

At the memorial reception, people stood around in clusters, talking quietly and eating crudités and deviled eggs. Every few minutes the man who now lives in the doublewide trailer with the forced-air heat in Portland, Oregon, stepped up to Ruby and said something like, "Did you ever work at Dunkin' Donuts?"

"No," Ruby would reply, or she would tap him on the shoulder and ask, "Did you ever play a steel drum?"

"No."

"Were you ever in a circus?"

"No."

"Did you ever take ballroom dancing?"

This tapping and asking went on and on like some weird perpetual motion gadget. Then . . . Ruby had just taken a big bite of a deviled egg, when the man who is probably now watching *Jeopardy* in a doublewide trailer in Portland, Oregon, tapped her on the shoulder and exclaimed, "Hey, I know who you remind me of! You won't believe this. You remind me of this piano teacher I had when I was a kid. I only had a couple lessons, but I was in love with her. At the end of every lesson, she used to hold me on her lap or let me sit on the edge of the piano bench between her legs and place my hands on top of hers while she played. Her hands were white and cool, and I leaned back against her bosom and closed my eyes while my hands moved up and down the keyboard on top of hers. It was like heaven. She smelled like vanilla and played something really beautiful. Then one day, my mother came early to get me—"

"Schumann," Ruby interrupted. *"Kinderszenen,"* she said. "Scenes from Childhood." Ruby inhaled and began to whistle a few bars, but nothing came out.

The man in the Greek fisherman's hat opened his eyes wider. Underneath their black hats, series upon series of synapses begin to snap, crackle, and pop like boxes of Chinese fireworks tossed into a bonfire, and Ruby was beginning to choke.

"Wait a minute," the man in the Greek fisherman's hat said, pushing back his cap, "wait . . . one . . . minute . . . you're that little brat with the pigtails and the red cowboy hat. You're that little girl with the whip and the vicious little dog. You're the piano teacher's kid who set the house on . . ." but before he could say the word "fire," he realized that Ruby was choking.

Two

After Tony Fellini saved Ruby's life by administering the Heimlich maneuver to her at the memorial service for the dead professor emeritus, she was totally in love with him. How could she not be? He had taken piano lessons from her mother, he had ridden the roller coaster at Angela Park, he had been bitten by Go-Jeff. Ruby forgave Tony Fellini the comment about Go-Jeff being vicious because she knew Tony was in love with her, too. How could he *not* be? Ruby reasoned. After all, he'd had a crush on her mother!

The next time Ruby saw Tony Fellini was three days after the Heimlich maneuver, when he stopped by her office at the university's coal fly ash research center to see if she was OK. After a bit of small talk, Tony handed Ruby a small gift box and a card. "Open the box first," he said.

Ruby unwrapped it and folded back the tissue paper. Inside was a big metal button with a picture of a roller coaster. ANGELA PARK, the button said in white letters. The original roller coaster at Angela Park was destroyed by a fire in 1958. It was rebuilt and then destroyed again in a flood six years later.

"It's my prized possession," Tony Fellini said of the pin. "I want you to have it, Ruby."

The pin itself was rusty, but Ruby pinned it on her beaded sweater anyway.

Ruby gave Tony Fellini the beautiful love poem about the Angel of Death and the Deviled Egg, which she had written over the past three days at work and at home in the bathroom so her husband wouldn't see it. It was handwritten neatly on lavender paper and folded in a lavender envelope.

"Don't read it now," Ruby said.

Tony put it in the breast pocket of his corduroy sports jacket. A little bit of it stuck out.

"Open the envelope," he said. It was heavy and creamy white. Ruby opened the envelope carefully and slipped out the card. It looked like a wedding invitation. It said,

> *The honor of your presence is requested at the wedding of*
> *Françesca Carmen Maria Garcia . . .*

Blah blah blah. Ruby skipped down a line.

> *and Anthony Joseph Fellini.*

Ruby's jaw dropped like that of a ventriloquist's dummy whose string had been cut.

"She's very young," Tony explained. "There are thirteen kids in her family . . . She was going to school in the U.S. . . . Her father was killed by the Sandanistas . . . Her visa is up . . . She would have to return to El Salvador . . . The unemployment rate in El Salvador is over thirty percent . . ."

Ruby stared at the rectangle of lavender sticking out of Tony Fellini's jacket pocket like a florid handkerchief.

"A stag is a MALE deer," she muttered. "Only chickens lay."

"Excuse me?" Tony said bending toward Ruby. "Are you OK?" he asked. "Chickens? . . . What? . . . What chickens? . . . Deer?"

He smiled a crooked little smile and laughed a charming little laugh.

Three

Ruby has not written to Tony Fellini in more than three months. She's punishing him for the acquisition of that doublewide for his little señora. Now his letters come more frequently, security lined, business size. A canceled yellow rose blooms behind an unfurling American flag. No return address. Some envelopes are thick, some carry postcards. Under the stove light, behind the blue security swirls, words and pictures emerge. Ruby holds them, unopened, unflinching as G. Gordon Liddy, to the gas flame, even though one, she's certain, is a prayer card: a portrait of a saint.

Lord have mercy upon us. Christ have mercy upon us.

There are things Ruby cannot tell you: the way her mother died or the bird's nest Mason showed her made of mud and long black hair.

Now Ruby's married to a nice Swedish man.

He pats her on the head and serves her nippon soppa.

They sit at the table and talk about El Niño.

At six and twelve a train goes by.

Lately, Ruby notices, though, he's burning things, too.

He waits till Ruby's in the shower, her hair dripping suds, then pokes his head inside the curtain: "Ruby, I think I'll run on out to Wal-Mart for a little while now, dear."

Four

When Ruby was little, there was this Saturday morning television show called *Circus Boy,* brought to you by Quaker Oats, Quaker Puffed Rice, and Quaker Puffed Wheat. At the end of every show, in a circus ring with clowns, a guy dressed in striped pants like Uncle Sam climbed up a high, steep ladder to a platform at the center of the big top and lowered himself, feet first, into a giant cannon.

That's who Ruby wanted to be when she grew up.

Five

Ruby sits at her kitchen table with her tea and fortune cookies.

(Her magic eight ball has been stuck on *Better Not Tell You Now.*)

She's trying to write, but her aproned husband is trying to distract her, running a stockinged foot up and down her calf.

Ruby's old black dog, Phineas, sits beside her, trying to get her attention by staring intently at her nose.

One pile of fortunes for Ruby (to the left); another for Phinny (here, on Ruby's right). Only two fortunes in Ruby's pile, but Phineas T. Gooddog, he has seven!

Ruby breaks open the next crispy half-moon. Pulls out the fortune, ever . . . so . . . carefully:

There is a prospect of a thrilling time ahead for you, Ruby reads out loud.

Phinny smiles sweetly, drooling, and raises his big, black paw . . .

Six

Ruby has one dream. A varnished door. A narrow staircase. Ivy twines and dogwood blossoms on the wall. At the top, to the left, another varnished door. A glass doorknob. The door, slightly ajar. Ruby touches it, and it swings open. On the wall, a framed print of *The Annunciation*. Ruby recognizes it. Is it da Vinci? Botticelli? Simone Martini? Underneath the startled virgin, a shelf with tea lights, old postcards from Italy and Spain. Straight ahead, a small window opens out. Ruby stands on her tiptoes and pushes the window open farther. A tulip tree: a yellow poplar! A constellation she cannot name. You come and stand behind her.

Seven

So Tony Fellini gets on a bus. He should have taken a plane, but he has a fear of flying so he gets on a bus. He's going to be married. He's wearing a U.S. Navy pea jacket and a Greek fisherman's cap. He will travel west for four days, across nearly the entire United States, to Portland, Oregon, where he will marry a woman from El Salvador, less than half his age, whom he has never met. First, though, he will walk along the Willamette River feeding Ritz crackers to seagulls and think about ending his life. In his vest pocket, he carries a photocopy of his bride-to-be's passport photo and their wedding invitation. The paper with the picture of the woman has been folded and unfolded so many times, a tiny tear like a cross appears in the center, vertically from the tip of the woman's nose to the hollow in her throat, and horizontally across her lips. If the man bends the paper back and forth, the woman's mouth will open and close like the mouth of a fish, like a kiss.

Behind large round glasses, the young woman's black eyes betray a smile her lips are determined to conceal. Her black hair disappears in stern waves from her smooth forehead. The young woman's hair, the man imagines, will be oiled and will feel like the coat of the little black cocker spaniel, Flo, he had as a child. The woman's hair will smell like vanilla, perhaps, and the scent will stay on his palm. Her name is Françesca Carmen Maria Garcia Santiago Sevilla, and her green card is about to expire. She is known in the organization as Carmen, but in time he will call her, affectionately, Flo.

Tony Fellini has few belongings. An old footlocker plastered with peeling stamps and decals; a knapsack with new socks and underwear, old books, some black and white photos with serrated edges, a box of Cuban cigars; a paper shopping bag with twine handles, oranges, salami, Kipper Snacks, Ritz crackers, mustard, Good & Plentys, Chiclets. On his lap he holds a leather portfolio with a broken zipper, bursting its contents like an overstuffed pita. Inside the portfolio are tattered notebooks full of poems, observations, and instructions, and wrapped in tissue paper a collection of postcards from around the world. Many of the cards are reproductions of frescoes, prayer cards, or faded, tinted lithographs from Italy and Spain.

"It-ly," Tony says. "When I was in It-ly . . ." he will sometimes begin a sentence, and that was how Ruby developed a feel for the superfluidity of vowels.

Eight

A woman named Ruby is sitting in a car at a Trailways bus station. A few years ago, she sat in a parking lot of an airport in the same city for eleven hours, staring at a digital travel alarm. Her favorite times, she decided then, were 1:00, 1:01, and 1:10.

Ruby appears to be crying, but we're not sure. Her head is bowed and she is wearing a hat that hides her face. Ruby suffers from something like the inverse of Tourette's syndrome. She's always blurting out endearments, often to strangers. "I think I love you," Ruby has said to this man Tony Fellini as he boarded the bus. She's only known him for two weeks, the only physical contact having been when he administered the Heimlich maneuver to her during a memorial service for a dead professor emeritus. Ruby wears a black coat with exaggerated shoulders. Pinned crookedly on the left lapel is a rusty tin button with a picture of a roller coaster. The button is way too big—about the size of a bus's gas cap—but serves to shield her heart, she imagines, from stray lances and bullets. Behind Ruby's heart, on a three-legged stool, sits a terrified little monkey, reading the funnies. Every now and then, the monkey gets up and whispers something in Ruby's ear. Ruby smiles, licks a pencil, and jots something down in a tiny blue notebook. She crosses and uncrosses her legs, thinking.

Then a few months pass, and Ruby, fickle Ruby, is thinking about a different man, not Tony Fellini, the man in the doublewide trailer in Portland, Oregon, and certainly not her husband, the Swedish efficiency expert. She's thinking about her poetry professor: it's spring break and he's leaving for . . . guess where? Portland, Oregon—such a coincidence! you say—boarding not a bus, but a plane. When Dr. Morrow speaks, sometimes his voice breaks, and when this happens, Ruby feels like her head is a brass lamp his voice is rubbing, and something like a novel—or maybe it's a memoir or a poem or something quite *other*—begins rising slowly from it like a djinni.

Nine

A man gets on a plane in the same city where Ruby once sat for many hours in a car, having a nervous breakdown. The plane is bound for Portland, Oregon, but this man is not about, like Tony Fellini, to take a wife; he's about to visit his brother and his nieces. Dr. Morrow wears wire-rimmed glasses and a buttery leather jacket. He doesn't need a hat, he thinks. He, too, carries books and many laser-printed papers full of words Ruby wants. Ruby barely knows this guy — he's her poetry teacher — but she has, in her illness-induced dementia, sort of proposed to him.

"Will you marry me?" she blurted out in a casual conversation, then later that evening thought about killing herself or maybe joining a traveling circus. Soon she will send him a postcard with *The Dog's Lunch* on it, blurt out on the back that she misses him, and sign the card, *Sincerely, Madam Fly Ash.*

While Dr. Morrow is fastening his seatbelt, clicking his pen, and opening his book, Ruby is walking around her house in her pajamas, banging her left fist on her forehead, saying to herself, "What's the matter with me? What the *hell* is the matter with me?" A cat is following Ruby around, making a little ducklike sound and weaving in and out of her feet like a Chinese jump rope champion. Ruby wears white socks and a glow-in-the-dark cat's flea collar around one ankle. In her right hand, she carries a book, the same book the man on the airplane is reading. The man on the plane is scribbling in the margins of the book, for future reference. Behind his heart sits a manuscript on a folding chair, obscured by the tip of a dark shadow, perhaps that of someone leaving.

Ten

"Ruby, what *is* the matter with you?" a man sitting at a kitchen table — a Swedish man in an apron — asks Ruby as she paces up and down the room in her pajamas, eating marshmallow Peeps. Ruby doesn't answer, but she pulls out a chair and sits down.

"Don't touch anything," Oskar, the man at the table tells Ruby. Oskar has been trying to fill out four Publisher's Clearinghouse Sweepstakes winning entries simultaneously all morning. He's Ruby's second husband. He has the table covered with stickers and seals, envelopes and instructions, and pages of little stamps with icons of magazines. *Reader's Digest. Good Housekeeping.*

Photography. Bon Appétit! By his side sits a cordless Dirt Devil vacuum cleaner with a Dress Stuart plaid bag. About every fifteen seconds, Oskar vacuums up a ladybug from the windowsill or tabletop. *Vrrrrroommmm. Vrrrooommmm.* The ladybugs appear endlessly from nowhere, reviving the dead theory of spontaneous generation.

"Do you want the jet black Jeep Cherokee or the white and blue Crown Victoria?" Oskar asks Ruby. *Vrrrrroooommmmm. Vrroooooom.* Ruby doesn't answer. She is staring out the window, biting her lip.

"Do you want to see *Phantom of the Opera* or *Les Misérables*?" *Vrroooommmmm. Vrrooommm.*

"*Les Misérables,*" Ruby shouts through cupped hands, above the Dirt Devil's roar. She throws on a plaid men's bathrobe, also Dress Stuart, shoves her feet into a pair of big rubber clogs by the back door, and steps outside. In the next room, a very old black dog who is sleeping on the couch rolls his eyes, displaying their bright red lining, but his eyes never quite open. One paw twitches; that's all.

Ruby walks behind the house, leans against the back wall, and eats the last marshmallow Peep from her pajama pocket, wishing she still smoked cigarettes. She closes her eyes and bangs her head against the wall, saying her favorite words over and over: RAIN-DEER. WORCESTERSHIRE. NINCOMPOOP. TAFFETA. ASPEN. SFU-MATO. SQUIRREL. It's raining. In front of her, a row of wet pine trees shimmies in the drizzle, trying to get her attention. This is Appalachia. Out in the Pacific Northwest, other, taller conifers harbor similar intentions. They awaken and stretch their long fringed limbs, shaking off the omnipresent drizzle, but the man who will soon be eating breakfast with his brother and his nieces pays them no mind. He's writing a picture postcard.

Dear Madam Fly Ash, he writes, and then a sentence, a lovely sentence about the stormy weather and another one about the view. *Dr. M,* he signs the postcard and puts it in his pocket. Along with a pen. And walks out the door. At the mailbox on the corner, the man with the pen and the postcard in his pocket quickly scratches out *Dr. M* and scribbles, *Love, Miles,* then drops the postcard in the box, sticking his hand back in the blue steel trap only after he's certain the card has already settled in the box's big blue belly, irretrievable, in motion, gone. He runs his hand through his wispy hair and sighs, and, likewise, is on his way.

The Man with the Refrigerator-Size
Hole in His Heart

1991 — A wrecking ball knocks a refrigerator-size hole in a man's wall, and the man looks out the hole at a cemetery with a pink granite stone that says *Plum* on one side and *Rude* on the other. The man looks out the refrigerator-size hole and sees his life framed differently. A rude awakening.

Or maybe the refrigerator-size hole is a hole knocked in the man's memory, and in this oval, jagged frame, his father is walking toward him. And the man with the refrigerator-size hole in his wall remembers something. Something about when he was a little boy in Portland, Oregon. Something his father said. He can barely hear it, though, what his father is saying. His father's head was full of numbers and recitations in French and Latin. Maybe it's something the father told his sons about desolation, about wind blowing through a hole in a wall in a sod house on the Dakota plains.

So the man with the refrigerator-size hole in his wall writes this all down — two or three pages — folds it in thirds, tucks it in a business-size envelope, puts the envelope in his jacket's breast pocket, and hurries off to an Indian café. There he sits in a blue vinyl booth, his leather jacket beside him, a Nubian thumb ring for good luck in his pocket, sipping sweet Masala tea and contemplating his own reflection, the size of Jiminy Cricket and upside down in a spoon.

And right then along comes a woman wearing a cloche adorned with Bing cherries, late and so apologetic, and she sits down across from this man in a booth with a view of the sidewalk, a view of the sky, and orders the same tea and a sweet rice pudding, served in a small white bowl, and in the rice pudding are cardamom seeds and a drop of rose water or maybe bergamot. The woman, it so happens, has an envelope, too, and in her envelope is a story about her mother who played the violin and couldn't sleep at night.

From the ceiling, soft music is falling. Music that sounds to the woman like someone sort of yodeling while maybe somebody's rubbing a wet balloon. Many people like black cut-paper figures, some in hats, hurry into the Café of India in fast-forward motion, eat their spicy buffet lunch, and then rewind: hurry, leave, and when everyone is gone and the restaurant is empty, the Café of India quiet save for the muffled clash of silver and china behind the kitchen's swinging doors, the man and woman with the refrigerator-size holes in their hearts place their fingertips on their envelopes and turn them on edge and guide them carefully across their table like longboats navigating around islands shaped like cups and saucers, bowls, and perilous spoons.

The Festival of Ideas

Two or three days pass. Where's Miles, the professor in the leather jacket who stared at himself in a spoon? Where's Ruby, the woman with the blurt disorder and the hat adorned with cherries?

Answer: They've gone to a poetry reading together and are sitting in the back.

The back: In the back, the world spins in opposition, as those who sit in the back well know. Those who sit in the front have no concept of ears and necks, heads, hats, postures, tattoos, and the writing on T-shirts the world has to offer. The back is the margin, the fringe, the loose ends, the exhaust; the back is the place for all forms of inappropriate behavior: for whispering, for dropping things on the floor and leaning over to pick them up, placing your hand so lightly on the thigh of the man sitting next to you—just for balance, of course, so you don't topple off your chair—your hair falling like Niagara down the man's leg, puddling on his open-toed sandal.

The back is a place for whispering *What?* into a man's ear and pretending not to hear the man's answer whispered in your ear, through the curtain of your hair. You must lean closer so his words run down your neck. *What?* you whisper. *What?* The poetry is so loud, you cannot hear the man's words soughing through the confessional curtain of your hair. He cannot hear you either, the poetry is so loud. You must lean closer. The tip of your nose touches his hair, sending a weak electrical charge down your spine. Before the night is over, your spinal cord will be all frayed and need to be replaced. Once the man had a cat named Princess who would walk with the man at night and sit beside the man on his porch and stick her slender cat tongue in the man's ear like a thermometer out of a play doctor's kit.

The poet is speaking, the poet is walking back and forth in his black beret, his black turtleneck, his Harris tweed jacket with the woven leather buttons. The poet is gesticulating. The poet is at the podium, reading from his book of poems, one hand delicately conducting the poem through the air, the other hand worrying his goatee. The people in the back are doodling; the people in the back are playing hangman, reading the student newspaper, the *Daily Athenaeum*. The people in the back are slumped in their chairs or balancing their chairs on two legs, leaning against the wall. The people in the front are leaning forward, nodding, captivated, attentive, amused. Someone in the back, someone attending the poetry reading for extra credit, is wearing a Walkman that's buzzing like a horsefly trapped between a window and a screen.

The man in the leather jacket in the back with all the extra-credit people, the man who happens to be a poet himself, pours the woman sitting next to him little sips of root beer into the cap of his soda bottle and passes these little fairy cocktails to the woman, and the woman drinks them, whispering in the man's ear, "Bottoms up, *sköl*, and here's lookin' atcha," and giggling and dribbling sweet, sticky root beer all over her pale blue dress, his khaki pants. Totally inappropriate behavior. Good thing they are sitting in the back.

Those who sit in the front are clapping. Those who sit in the back are cracking their knuckles and eating Doritos. Those who sit in the front see only what they are supposed to see, while those who sit in the back, they live, they see . . .

But wait, what's this that has arrived late for the poetry reading? What's this moving up the aisle, looking for a seat? What's this that is taking its place, that is sitting down right in front of the man and the woman sitting in the back in these two straight-backed, armless chairs?

What is it?

It is . . . A NECK!

It is a neck attached to a head and a toupee. It is a man with the biggest neck the world has ever known, the world cannot imagine. A man in a toupee with a *Ripley's Believe It or Not* neck like an enormous stump.

Absolute silence. Summer rain descends on the back of the room, on the people behind THE NECK. Awe sweeps across the back of the room like the long train of a woman's taffeta gown, a woman hurrying to get out of the rain, out of a maze, away from THE NECK, and the poetry reading comes alive, charged with the magnificent proportions of, the profundity of, the poetry of . . . this . . . this NECK.

The man and the woman steal a glance at each other, and both nod in appreciation of the moment, then stare ahead. That is SOME NECK!

The man bends toward the woman, and the woman, feeling the man's magnetic body coming closer, leans toward the man like a willing blob of metal filings. The woman is nothing but the shavings from a pencil sharpener, staring straight ahead. The man puts his mouth in the woman's hair, eating the woman's hair, and says:

"O, Neck, how like a melon under thatch!"

The marrow drains out of the woman's bones, and a little wind whistles through the hollow bone channel, dancing off the curved walls like a boy in big pants on a skateboard. The woman giggles into her palm.

"O, Neck, how big thou art!" She giggles, choking, almost spitting, into the man's ear, "What if thou shouldst contract mumps?"

The poet is speaking, the poet is walking, the poet is gesticulating, the poet is reading from his book of poems. From the back

137

of the room where the man and the woman are sitting, THE NECK totally obscures the poet, except for the poet's arms, which appear to dance like tweed-legginged antennae jutting from THE NECK's toupee, above his tiny, stewed-apricot ears. The woman is thinking of one of her favorite games as a child, a game called Cootie, a square box chock-full of plastic legs and antennae, which could be fitted to a bulbous body, depending on the roll of a large red polka-dotted die.

The woman got the game for her eighth birthday. At the birthday party, children in party hats sat in a circle and played silly games. One game involved putting an orange under your chin and passing it to the neck of the person next to you without using your hands.

The woman turns to the man and whispers, "What?" into the pale shell of his ear. She can't help it any longer: she giggles out loud. Her chin almost comes in contact with his neck. He smells like oranges. Like bergamot. He is quite fond of Earl Grey tea. It's possible there is a little can of Sterno or maybe something simmering in a Crock-Pot underneath her chair.

"O, Neck! Stout column, worthy pedestal . . . for what?" Professor Morrow's words whish through the curtain of the woman's hair. "For this sad toupee? . . ."

"How 'bout them ears!" Ruby bursts out with another giggle. She is nearly hysterical. She's dying from hysteria and something else.

"Neck so round . . ." Miles whispers, the words rushing down the long reeds of Ruby's hair, "no one knows which way you're turning . . ."

He pauses. "You're nothing but a reason to whisper in a woman's hair."

Suddenly: applause.

"Are there any questions?" the poet is asking. "Refreshments in the back of the room," the poet is saying, and those who sit in the back of the room are already there, paper plates sagging under the weight of M&M cookies, marshmallow-swirl brownies, Pecan Sandies, and blue and gold iced flying WV cookies, and Ruby and Miles are gone.

The Pleasure of Finding Things Out

1. Ruby in Bed

2002—Sometimes when she can't sleep at night, Ruby lies awake trying to name all the boys and men she's ever loved. All forty-plus years of them: Neddy Turner, with one brown eye, one green. Wally Hinchey, the little red-haired boy with eleven fingers. Darwin Gravy. Dominic Canteloupe (pronounced *Can't a Loo Pay*) with the magnificent Kafka-esque ears. Harold Moody with the Harley-Davidson, the heroin habit, and the lisp. Albino Eddie. Father Frank. Tony Fellini, the union man. Sweet Etienne Morales, the young man who seemed like a woman trapped in a man's body like a firefly in a can.

And more. Sometimes in counting Ruby even overlooks some men she'd somehow married: Boo. And Oskar the Mumbler, her Swedish husband once removed, the man she spent almost a decade with, repeating again and again: *What?* And even Miles. And the two broken engagements: Noah "Blind Gefilte Fish" Levine, the Jewish blues singer, and way back in the sixties: Mike the Hirsute.

How could that be—those significant omissions? Freudian

slips? Freudian underpants? Or because it is impossible to count, and, well, because *Counting is hard!* as Talking Barbie might say. *Linear thought is hard! Placing anything chronologically is hard!*

A lot of time has passed—that's all—and Ruby has known and loved so many, in some respect. *Some respect:* now there's the rub. What is love after all? She keeps revising the definition. A list of criteria as long and faltering as their names. And useless. *Infatuation. Lust. Admiration. Attention. Sympathy. Charity. Devotion? Desire. Wonder. Curiosity. Fear? Reciprocity? Kisses?* Or is it just a feeling? An irregular heartbeat? A fibrillation. Or some other malady; say, an eternal low-grade fever smoldering just beneath common sense like the mine fire that started in July 1962 in a garbage dump atop an exposed coal seam in Centralia, Pennsylvania, and has been smoldering, nonstop, ever since, making its way through those subterranean veins?

That would be about right.

It was all something to think about. Some listing and counting to get lost in when the moon was too bright, the quiet too noisy. A way without alcohol or sedatives to wind down: tax and tire the brain with pointless enumeration. Just saying their names, the toll of their names, like the names of the dead carved in the tombstones in Maple Grove Cemetery. Saying their names and counting them down.

Why not just get up then, Ruby? Go out in the garage in your bunny slippers, your father's old Woolrich jacket thrown over your pajamas, and your oven mitts. Get the kitchen timer, and just make something. Turn on the fluorescent light, buckle on your tool belt, plug in that old Singer sewing machine. Get your cafeteria tray and your blindfold. It's a game, you see, like Beat the Clock. You spin around three times, and then in blind staggers pick up the first six things you touch and place them on your tray. Remove the blindfold. Set your timer. You have exactly fifteen minutes, Ruby Reese, to make something useful from these items: say, a fart deflector constructed from a funnel and a vacuum cleaner hose cleverly attached to a pair of discarded Jockey briefs and with a plastic streamer tail—like those that flutter from Sears floor-model air conditioners—only this one spells out not FRIGIDAIRE or AMANA but something else: GONE BUT NOT FORGOTTEN. Or maybe something that's sort of like a hat and sort of like an astrolabe. Something heavy and uncanny that couldn't pass—now really, could it, Ruby?—as anything at all.

2. Ruby Out Walking

From a satellite, the area looks like a sixth-grade geography project, a contour map molded out of salt-and-flour paste, all mounded up on a wax-paper-covered cookie sheet, the ridges pinched in long, irregular lines, the valleys dark, shallow thumbprints. From a Cessna descending, you can make out the 1960s-era housing development, Maple Grove—the one where Ruby lives—with its split-level houses the color of Necco wafers, attached one-car garages, and flimsy redwood decks—and the two intersecting highways; the great flattening devastation of the shopping mall; the car wash, the garish Sheetz filling station and the Family Dollar, their customers coming and going like fire ants. And the small man-made lake, nestled like a powder compact's mirror in the valley's palm.

A large expanse drapes over the next ridge like an afghan thrown over the back of a couch, an afghan that has been washed, inadvertently, with a wad of Kleenex: still green but hopelessly flecked with lint. At night, the area flattens out into a dark spread bordered on two sides by the liquid red and white stripes of traffic, dark with just a glimmer like red sugar sprinkles on a chocolate sheet cake. Only from a closer perspective, that of a hot-air balloon or a bird, can you make out Maple Grove Cemetery, which spreads out along the humpback ridge, covered with thousands of tombstones, many displaying the gas torpedo-ish canisters called eternal flames, which flicker their Bic messages night and day as in Arlington two hundred miles away where President Kennedy lies buried nearly thirty-nine years now in the dirt.

It's just about a mile-and-a-half walk around the cemetery's perimeter. Ruby measured it on her pedometer nearly ten years ago, when she'd married Miles and moved in here with him. Always on the ridge, a breeze is blowing, and surprisingly, the cemetery is seldom visited, in spite of its population. The pea-gravel paths are well maintained and every quarter-mile or so a large blue trash receptacle welcomes whatever one might care to donate. All in all, it's a good place to walk a dog any time of year, in spite of a rusted metal sign on the wrought-iron gate proclaiming, NO DOGS OR BIKES. Ruby looks the other way and walks through the gates, Walter Cronkite trotting along beside her, as if St. Peter himself has waved them through.

One part of the cemetery, along the top of the ridge, facing out toward Brunners Run, is just for babies. Rows of tiny rectangular stones like pages ripped from a book, some topped with lambs no bigger than a pound of butter. Why were these babies not buried with their families but all together here? Born out of wedlock? Stillborn? Aborted? Died in an orphanage? Just first names and dates or the word INFANT. Fannie 1902, Flo 1903, Willie 1907. Lucille 1912. Grace 1903. Wilbur 1903. Serafina 1903. Fielding 1903. Hattie 1903. *Nineteen-oh-three.* There'd been an epidemic that year, Ruby knew. Diphtheria. Her Great-Aunt Izzy's little boy, Nelson, had died from diphtheria that year, and her father's siblings, Edgar Albert and Eleanor Opal, had died the same day in 1903, seven years before her father was born.

Nineteen-aught-three, Ruby's paternal grandmother, Nana Ruby, would say, shaking her head. *Back in nineteen-aught-three* . . . and in her shaky old-lady voice she would tell Ruby and her sister, Albertine, about them, about Edgar Albert and Eleanor Opal, and their little white dog, Tom Thumb. She kept the daguerreotype on the table by her bed: Edgar Albert and Eleanor Opal, both with ringlets, button shoes, and white smocks. Propped up like china baby dolls on a wicker settee draped with a Jacob's Ladder quilt. Eyes closed. Poor little Edgar Albert and Eleanor Opal. Only now, walking in the infant cemetery, nearly a hundred years later, does Ruby realize that in that old photograph Edgar Albert and Eleanor Opal most likely were already dead. A rare and expensive photograph, probably the only one ever taken of them, made, like a death mask, for remembrance.

Memento mori.

What happened to that daguerreotype? Ruby wonders.

In Maple Grove Cemetery the wind blows always from the highway—from the federal penitentiary—and because of the elevation, the wind has a gust and earnestness about it unknown to other parts of town. The wind is mischievous and bold in Maple Grove Cemetery, errant and erratic, indiscriminate and rude, snatching up wreaths and fabric-flower bouquets, dried-up potted chrysanthemums, fake poinsettias and Easter lilies, shiny cellophane bows and styrofoam hearts, and plastic banners spelling MOTHER, FATHER, SISTER, BROTHER, REST IN PEACE, BELOVED, GONE BUT NOT FORGOTTEN, EASTER—like gigantic, absurd cookie fortunes, and sweeping them into the brambles and catbriers along the south side of the cemetery's perimeter, below the baby cemetery and into the public domain, so to speak, and Ruby always carries a canvas sack along with her plastic dog-poop bag and Walter Cronkite's leash, and collects these weather-beaten, wind-discarded treasures for her late-night projects out in her other refuge, the garage.

3. Ruby Recollecting Things Boo Told Her

When he was eighteen months old, Boo's mother snatched up his identical twin Van out of their playpen and left Boo there alone in the kitchen of their house in East Orange, New Jersey—an iron set on LINEN face down on one of his father's Banlon shirts. Boo wailed when he saw his mother putting on her coat and reaching down for Van. Boo lifted up his arms like babies do. When that didn't work, Boo hollered bloody murder.

"Shut the hell up!" Boo's mother screamed at him. His mother's hair was loose and wild. Her hair was what people called salt & pepper to her face, but behind her back they said "prematurely gray." Her fingernails were painted red. Her black swing coat flared out around her legs like a wizard's cape as she flew out the door with Baby Van, a scene that stuck in a crevice in Boo's brain like a piece of gristle between two teeth. His mother's shoes had cleats on the heels and click-clacked on the linoleum floor. The kitchen faucet was dripping. *The Edge of Night* was blaring from the next room. Over their mother's shoulder, Baby Van waved bye-bye to his brother.

When the smoke started, baby Boo cried even harder, and then a voice like Don Pardo's said, "Wrap your head in your little blanket, Bub." Boo looked around. The voice sounded familiar. Baby Boo thought the voice was on television, a commercial break on *The Edge of Night*.

"Up here, Bub," the voice said. Baby Boo looked up. There was a big wooden crucifix above the archway that led from the kitchen to the living room, and from the crucifix, Jesus waved as best he could, wiggling a few bloody fingers.

"Don't worry, Bub," Jesus said, "she'll come back." That's what Jesus called him, Boo says, Jesus called him *Bub*. Boo put his head under his Huey, Dewey, and Louie blanket and sucked his thumb, and that's what saved him, people said. He was a smart little guy, people said. *Intelligenti*, neighbors said. *Naturalezza*, they said. Instinctive.

The next thing Boo remembers is his mother screaming and running toward him through the doorway, a carpet of orange flames between him and the door, orange flames running up the back of his mother's black coat like fins on a stegosaurus. Her fiery red lipstick like a rubber O-ring around the black recess of her mouth.

"She changed her mind," Boo said.

But Boo, he never forgot, he never forgave her. He hates his mother. Hates women, Ruby thinks.

What about Talking Jesus? That's what Ruby wants to know. "Boo . . . umm . . . what happened to that crucifix?" Ruby tries to ask nonchalantly.

"Never heard a peep out of Jesus again," Boo replies matter-of-factly. "No idea what happened to that crucifix, Rube."

144

4. Ruby Out Walking ... Again

There's a house in the two-hundred block of Park Street in the old section of Morgantown, not too far from Maple Grove where Ruby lives now, not a grand house, but a big, solid house Ruby has often admired and fantasized about moving into herself if one morning she should wake up and find herself in some twilight zone where birdsong is absent, traffic stopped, and all her neighbors gone missing. (A scenario she secretly considers quite appealing.) This house on Park Street is built of smooth, pale yellow bricks called butter bricks and has tasteful maroon and sea green trim. A magnificent stained-glass window graces what's probably the main stairway landing, where, Ruby imagines, the staircase splits, with a modest enclosed stairway leading down into the kitchen in the back of the house, and a wide staircase leading down into the front foyer, that staircase punctuated with a fancy newel post, one carved, perhaps, with an intricately turned, ribbon-streaming bow, a decorative motif those fussy Victorians were so fond of.

Through her tiny opera glasses, Ruby has observed the mistress of this house coming and going: a woman quite a bit younger than Ruby but about the same size, a woman with a handsome wardrobe, smart accessories including a black fedora, and a cute little BMW sports car. Often she can be seen with a curly-haired little boy who is learning to ride a bike. At night, from the street, a passerby can see clearly a grand piano with a candelabra, a large aubergine-colored couch, possibly velvet, a John W. Waterhouse print of *Ulysses and the Sirens*, and a great display of books, pottery, and stone artifacts.

Just recently, Ruby received from her old friend Vivvy, who was living at the time in an Airstream trailer at the entrance to the Cullowhee, North Carolina, city dump, a picture postcard of the house in which the late Richard Feynman, Nobel laureate in physics, was born in 1918, in Far Rockaway, on the southern hem of Manhattan, and this house on Park Street that Ruby admires so and now walks by daily with her black Labrador retriever, Walter Cronkite, looks remarkably like the Feynman birthplace, a style of house Ruby believes is called a late-Victorian four-square.

In addition to being a physicist who worked on developing the atom bomb, Feynman was also a teacher, a musician, a philatelist, an artist, and an amateur safecracker. Ruby had never heard of Richard Feynman until a night in October 1980, when her husband, Boo, had gone out gaffing for fluke (or so he said) and Ruby lay on the couch with a prescription for Darvon, one for Valium, and another one for penicillin on the end table, and a heating pad on her stomach. On that night, which Ruby remembers so well, public television aired a *Nova* interview with Feynman entitled *The Pleasure of Finding Things Out*. In this program, Feynman related an anecdote about his father, Melville Feynman — a quiet, inquisitive man. The anecdote, as Ruby remembers it, went something like this:

When he was a boy of two, Richard Feynman's father set him down on the steps of the front porch of their house in Far Rockaway and told him to stay put. His father disappeared around the side of the house. In a few moments, Melville Feynman reappeared, pulling little Richard's red wagon with one hand and carrying under his other arm a familiar blue rubber ball. Melville Feynman was a young man then, in his mid-thirties, with a copious head of dark, curly hair. He was wearing loose white trousers, brown and white saddle shoes, and a hand-knitted argyle vest. Mel Feynman placed the blue ball in the front of the red wagon and pulled the red wagon forward up the sidewalk. When he did this, the blue ball rolled backwards. He stopped and placed the blue ball once again in the front of the red wagon and when he resumed pulling the red wagon, the blue ball again rolled to the back. Mr. Feynman repeated this again and again, saying nothing, making no gestures, just repositioning the ball and pulling the wagon. Little Richard watched. Suddenly, after many repetitions, in the child's mind something wordless, something almost mathematical, clicked, something that acknowledged the strangeness of, the miracle of, the seeming preposterousness of . . . the pure *hilarity* of this blue ball–red wagon movement.

Little Richard laughed. His father laughed, too.

When this *Nova* interview was aired in 1980, Richard Feynman was sixty-two years old, his father would have been nearing one hundred, Ruby was thirty—and Richard Feynman explained that that one moment, that one image—that of his father as a young man with curly hair pulling a red wagon with a blue ball in it—had shaped his entire life. He had watched that scene, Feynman said, a thousand times since, either retrieving it from memory and bringing it fondly into play or the image coming to him of its own volition, it seemed, his father appearing, unannounced, stage left, in brown and white saddle shoes, bouncing a blue ball, emerging with a blue ball and red wagon out of the mist of dreams.

The blue ball, of course, did not move backwards; for the most part, that movement was an illusion. Like little Richard Feynman sitting on the porch steps in Far Rockaway, the blue ball stayed put. It was the back of the wagon that moved forward to meet the stationary blue ball, and the basic law that Melville Feynman was demonstrating to his son was Newton's First Law of Motion: Inertia—*A body at rest will tend to remain at rest and a body in motion will tend to remain in motion unless acted upon by an outside force.*

But imagine for a moment that the blue ball really *does* move. The woman in the blue quilted bathrobe lying on the maroon mohair couch, watching *Nova* on TV, gets up and shuffles to the bathroom, where everything is such a mess. On the way back to the couch and Richard Feynman, she detours through the kitchen, where she pours herself a big jelly jar of Dewar's from a fifth hidden underneath the sink.

Do not consume alcohol, drive, or operate machinery while taking this medication, the warning on the Darvon vial advises. With her thumb over the warning, Ruby ignores this advice and swallows. From behind a stand of cedars, a three-quarter moon floats up like a boiled pierogie in a Teflon pot and gleams across the deck and in through the living room window.

"Go away," Ruby says curtly to the potato-cheese moon as if it were a Jehovah's Witness at her door. "Please," she adds, and wipes her mouth with the back of her hand.

The moon moves over an inch or two, not to be nice, really, but just because it's bored and has nothing better to do, but Ruby doesn't notice. She's busy pulling a pilled afghan over her head and lying back down, breathing in the blanket's damp mothbally wool smell and looking out between its loose stitches at Richard Feynman, who is now describing the wild celebration at Los Alamos on August 6, 1945, the day Little Boy was dropped on Hiroshima. Richard Feynman and his Manhattan Project buddies out in the desert whooping it up, drinking martinis, and playing bongos on the bonnet of a jeep. Richard Feynman, who reportedly considered it harmful for newspapers to publish horoscopes because people might, seriously, believe them.

Seriously.

"Damn!" Ruby mumbles to herself. "Richard Feynman ... who the hell is this guy? ... And what's that out there on the porch in the moonlight?"

5. Ruby Recollecting Things Her Father Told Her

Ruby's paternal grandmother's house in Webster, Pennsylvania, was also a late-Victorian four-square, a smaller, cheaper, clapboard version of Richard Feynman's house or the house on Park Street a few blocks from where Ruby now lives in Morgantown, West Virginia. Ruby's grandmother, Nana Ruby, Ruby's father told her, was born in 1862. She was forty-eight years old when she had Ruby's father, eighty-eight years old when Ruby was born. Ruby remembers her as an old woman in a high, carved bed. A large, powdered woman in a white nightgown and quilted bed jacket and wearing a funny ruffled mobcap like the big, bad wolf masquerading as Little Red Riding Hood's grandmother. A very old woman with soft cheeks that Ruby kissed. Sometimes Ruby's grandmother called her Edgar Albert and sometimes Eleanor Opal.

In her grandmother's bedroom, Ruby often sat, rocking in a low rocker, kicking her feet and trying to whistle, or pulling the neck of her shirt up over her face and saying the nursery rhyme "Solomon Grundy" over and over as she rocked:

> *Solomon Grundy*
> *Born on a Monday*
> *Christened on Tuesday*
> *Married on Wednesday*
> *Took ill on Thursday*
> *Worse on Friday*
> *Died on Saturday*
> *Buried on Sunday*
> *That's the end of Solomon Grundy*

or winding and rewinding a jewelry box that played "Stardust," or just looking at things around the room: the lace curtains and crocheted doilies; an oval tray with a mirrored bottom and a gold filigree rim, which displayed a collection of miniature glass and china slippers; a tiny, tintype photograph in a worn brown velvet case—a photograph of a dark-haired woman with a Gibson girl hairdo and a mutton-sleeve blouse, beside her a gentleman with a gray handlebar mustache, a black floppy tie, a Buffalo Bill hat, and a cane. Although she looked at the photo a thousand times when she was little, it never occurred to Ruby that the woman in the photograph on the dresser was her Nana Ruby, the same old woman in bed. Ruby thought it was a picture of Doc and Miss Kitty from *Gunsmoke*. Now Ruby has the photograph as a screensaver on her computer at work. Her grandparents' engagement portrait: 1889.

Ruby Sayward Llewellyn emigrated from Cardiff, South Wales, in 1865, with her mother, father, and baby brother, Evan. Her father was coming to America, to Pennsylvania, to work in the deep mines around Webster, near Centralia. During the crossing, a typhoid epidemic aboard ship took the lives of 192 passengers, among them Ruby's mother and baby brother. Three men with heavy scarves wrapped around their faces came below into the immigrant quarters at night and wrapped her mother and Baby Evan in blankets. One man sewed the blankets closed with thick thread and big stitches; the men tied the blankets with ropes and took the bodies away. Nearly all of their belongings were taken, too, and then jettisoned. At dawn the next day, the bodies of those who had died the previous night were buried at sea. At the stern of the steamer *Vesta*, Ruby Llewellyn's father held her in his arms as one by one each body, tied in its rough gray blanket, was carried from a mound on one side of the deck and placed on a plank with side rails, then raised up by two men and sent shooting down, as if on a slide, into the icy sea.

> *Mae rhyw fyrdd o rhyfeddodau*
> *Yn y iachawdwriaeth rhad*
>
> *Arglwydd Iesu, arwain f'enaid*
> *Aty Graid sydd uwch na mi*
>
> *There's a wideness in God's mercy*
> *Like the wideness of the sea*
>
> *There is grace enough for thousands*
> *Of new worlds as great as this*

The living sang the Welsh hymn *In Memoriam*. Ruby Llewellyn's mother's body was easy to tell from the others, Baby Evan's body lashed to hers with rope. The sky was smeared with pink, the water black, the corpses in their blankets bobbing in the *Vesta*'s wake, small blind boats heading back home to South Wales.

It was the afternoon of April 25, 1865, when the *Vesta* docked at Ellis Island. A great solemnity was apparent to Ruby Llewellyn and her father as they descended the gang plank. Everywhere people were crying and praying, standing in windows and doorways draped in black crepe. Three-year-old Ruby Llewellyn believed this display of grief had to do with the death of her mother and Baby Evan, but she was quite wrong. It was the hour that Abraham Lincoln's body was passing through New York City, borne in a magnificent fourteen-foot hearse drawn by sixteen horses wearing long embroidered blankets. From a second-story window near Union Square, six-year-old Theodore Roosevelt was watching, too. On a train that carried Lincoln's photograph on its cowcatcher and dark garlands on its cars, Lincoln's body was retracing the route he had traveled as president-elect four years earlier. The train, the *Lincoln Special,* bore two bodies home: that of the Great Emancipator and that of his son, Willie, who had died from typhoid fever in 1862 at age eleven. Willie's body had been disinterred and was to be buried alongside his father's in Springfield, Illinois.

How strange this all seems to Ruby Reese now in 2003, sitting in front of her computer at the coal fly ash research center, staring at her screensaver: to think of all that, to think that she had sat in the bedroom and kissed the cheek of someone who was in New York City the day Abraham Lincoln's body passed down Fifth Avenue. The assassination of Abraham Lincoln — an event that seems as distant to her today as the Napoleonic Wars or the Battle of Hastings!

But she was somehow . . . through a kiss . . . connected. And then to think, whose cheek had Nana Ruby perhaps kissed? and where had that person been? and what had he or she seen? and who had they, in turn, kissed . . . all this succession and passing . . . this turning, bending, kissing . . . down through time. And in 1963, when she was thirteen, Ruby reminisces, she had sat at her school desk with her head down — as instructed by the principal's voice over the public address system — to pray for the soul of another assassinated president, but secretly Ruby cried and prayed not for John Fitzgerald Kennedy but for her mother and her lost friend Etherine's drowned little brother, Trace.

6. Ruby Driving

Before there were interstates — U.S. Route 95 shooting up from Florida and Route 80 from New York all the way to Los Angeles —

there were just the old county and state routes: the two-lane blacktops. In the fifties, on these windy roads, when two cars met, they slowed down some, making sure there was room to pass, and as they passed, the passengers in each car could look in the other car and see all the people. You waved, you and Albertine, didn't you? Or maybe you made a monster face or you held up your Revlon doll, or Albertine, her blue pony. The driver was almost always a man, and if the passing car was a DeSoto, he and your father tipped their hats. Sometimes, after the car had passed, a voice or a strain of music rushed back like someone who had just gone out a door and then darted back in, having remembered they'd forgotten to tell you something: Patsy Cline, Billy Graham, The Everly Brothers: *Bye-bye, love / Bye-bye happiness . . .*

When you went out in your family automobile in the 1950s, you dressed properly. Men and women wore hats, the women's with pearl hatpins. Women put on lipstick and powdered their noses. Children's faces were wiped clean with washcloths or, if necessary, spit on handkerchiefs, little boys' hair parted, little girls' braids redone. And before there were automobile air conditioners, you'd see cars with arms and even legs and feet dangling out the windows, convertibles the ultimate coolant. When you went anywhere, you went right down the main streets—no by-passes—and you saw people walking on sidewalks, coming out revolving doors, waiting to cross the street: men in white shirts, fedoras, and wide ties; women wearing seamed stockings, specta-tor shoes, and swing coats, and holding children's hands.

You got to know places on your route by landmarks and smells, not by exit and service signs along the freeways. You knew the smell of farms, woods, and pastures; alfalfa, corn, and cows. Factories, rain on macadam, the Susquehanna River. Lying in the back seat with your eyes closed, window down, you could iden-tify towns by their smells, like your teachers and aunts who al-ways wore the same perfume. *White Shoulders. Evening in Paris. Heaven Scent. Emeraude.*

In New York State, between Syracuse and Rochester, there's a town named Phelps where they make sauerkraut. Roll up your window, hold your nose, and holler, *Pee-U!* In Reading, Pennsylvania, a house on a hillside looks like a Japanese pagoda. Draw a picture. In another town, a Bedlington terrier always sits on a stoop, and in another place between two towns, a billy goat is staked out in a dirt yard on a dangerous hairpin curve. Beg to stop and pet him. And just outside Shickshinny, a sign your mother and father think so very funny: THE CHURCH OF GOD AND TAXIDERMY.

Driving at night you sometimes see a searchlight sweeping through the darkness, indicating a county airport or advertising a car dealership or the grand opening of a Sears and Roebuck, Robert Hall, or Endicott-Johnson shoe store.

It was these memories, this romance of driving, that made Ruby buy it — THE TERMITE-MOBILE — even though it already had 167,000 miles. It would be practical because it was cheap and the insurance would be low, but it would also be like you were in a parade or on an amusement park ride, Ruby thought. It would make driving special. A once bright yellow 1968 VW Beetle, re-painted green, with the red letters TERMINEX, INC. showing through pentimento on the doors, and an enormous black termite — big as a Doberman with wings — welded to the roof. On the back bumper, a sticker someone had tried, unsuccessfully, to remove: ESUS LOVES YOU, it proclaimed, and underneath: BUT EVERYBODY ELSE THINKS YOU'RE AN ASSHOLE.

Ruby is sick. Ruby is bleeding. Ruby is tired. Ruby's head is spinning. She sits up and lights a cigarette, the first one she's had in months. It makes her feel woozier, sicker. She's sick of everything, sick of watching Richard Feynman on *Nova*, Channel 8, the only channel they get out on the Banks. Ruby believes in stars and syzygy, the mischief of Mercury gone retrograde, the consequences of harmonic convergence, horoscopes and coincidence, serendipity, synchronicity, magic. Fig Newtons, not Isaac and his bag of tricks, certainly not Richard Feynman with his red wagon full of blue bombs.

Boo, he should have stayed home with Ruby on a night like this, not gone out fishing. Ruby's looking out the door now and she sees Boo's flounder gaff glistening in the moonlight on the porch.

"Takes a clear night, takes a full moon, takes a low tide for wading, for gaffing fluke," Ruby's thinking. Her head is doing that elevator thing. Ruby looks out. Black hole of a night. Little Chinese fortune cookie moon. Sky full of lumpy clouds like cold mashed potatoes. Late October. The full moon—the blood moon—come and gone.

"Fluke, my ass," Ruby says to herself, and starts bumping about the room, knocking over a table lamp, looking for the keys to the termite-mobile. She's going out to find him, to find Boo. He should have, he really should have, stayed home, she's going to tell him. She's really going to tell him this time.

7. Ruby Dreaming

You die and then you're in a room with two steel doors, above one a wedge-shaped sign says, ENTER ONLY, above the other, EXIT. In the room are just a metal table and a dented folding chair, three boxes, and you. In one box are blank slips of paper. Another box is full of those teenie-weenie pencils, and the last box is metal —galvanized like a milkbox—but with a slot on top, and it's chained with a padlock to the table.

Is it a suggestion box or a raffle? What should Ruby write? Should she sign her name? Her address? Maybe she should sign someone else's name. Boo's? Mrs. Buchanan Bonfili? Should she write a statement or a question? Maybe she should write something backwards or in Pig Latin . . . or Jabberwock! *'Twas brillig, and the slithy toves did gyre and gimble in the wabe . . .*

Will these slips of paper be made into bumper stickers? Cookie fortunes? Maybe there are stacks of books behind the wall: ledgers or *Famous Last Words*. Maybe she should draw a picture or attempt some origami. Once somebody tried to teach

Ruby how to make an origami crane, but it was hard, and hers looked more like an airplane with a chicken's head.

A formula!: *something*—oh what the hell is it—equals πr^2?

Hey, maybe it's *Candid Camera!*

Ruby cradles her head in her hands, bites her doll-size pencil, bites her fist, twists a strand of red hair, crosses and uncrosses her legs.

The exit sign winks.

8. *Ruby in Sweden*

One time in the late eighties, Ruby was visiting Sweden with her husband once-removed, Oskar (pronounced *Oh scar!*) the Mumbler. "Oskar the Mumbler" she began to call her husband, secretly, a few months after they were married. "Oskar the Mumbler" she called him openly for at least three years before they divorced. Oskar was an efficiency expert from Sweden who came to visit a so-called friend of a friend of Ruby's, with the ulterior motive of marrying a United States citizen and getting a permanent green card so he could stay in the United States, far away from the aunt who had raised him—a woman who was also a mumbler and an efficiency expert, although retired and living comfortably in the town where she was born. Ruby met Oskar the Mumbler on a blind date arranged by this friend of a friend. When she thinks back on it, how on earth she was ever convinced to go out on a blind date is mind-boggling, and to think that in no time she was married—again!—and Oskar was getting his green card laminated at the Kinko's downtown and a very large and gaudy plastic replica of a Viking ship was sitting on top of her television set like a headdress!

Sometimes it seems to Ruby that she's never really made any decisions in life, just bobbed with the flow, so to speak. Often at night she feels gripped with loneliness, and that's why she stayed in this relationship or that. She would lie awake and place the palm of her hand on Oskar the Mumbler's back and feel a great tenderness for his flesh, for the *fact* of him, for flesh and its sad, inevitable demise.

Mmmfblefousdflkj, Oskar would mumble in Swedish in his sleep, stir, and then fall soundly back to sleep.

This particular time more than a decade ago when they were in Sweden was the fifth and last time Ruby accompanied Oskar the Mumbler there to visit this aunt, Moster Fritjof (pronounced *Mow-stair Fdee toaf,* although Ruby secretly called her Monster Frito). Ruby didn't want to go again—she'd seen enough—and she relished the prospect of staying home alone, but at the last minute Oskar convinced her that Moster Fritjof was old and that Ruby was somehow obligated to make the long, dutiful trip across the North Atlantic as his American, wedded wife.

Every time they went to Sweden, Oskar the Mumbler and Ruby stayed the entire time with this maiden Moster Fritjof in a small town in northern Sweden, a town full of birch and fir trees and charming log buildings painted red, and not much else. Moster Fritjof the Mumbler was a big, heavyset woman with a square jaw and thin white hair pulled back in a tight little bun like a powdered mini donut. A big, square, silent woman who understood English but spoke only Swedish. For every one of these trips—which took up every single hour of Ruby's annual leave from the coal fly ash research center where she worked as a technical writer—Moster Fritjof the Mumbler planned the itinerary of their visit, down to the hour—Oskar driving the three of them here and there to visit Moster Fritjof's efficiency-expert friends in even more remote places.

Every morning, no matter how early Oskar and Ruby awoke, Moster Fritjof the Mumbler was sitting at the kitchen table in her sensible black coat and black knit hat with earflaps, holding her black pocketbook on her lap. Every morning on the scrubbed wooden table a feast was laid out for them: boiled lutefisk and boiled white potatoes, fresh twisted rolls made with white flour, a big white bowl of unsalted butter, white goat cheese, and coffee with real cream. Everything sitting on trivets and covered with embroidered white linen cozies. Getting cold. As they ate, Moster

Fritjof sat silently at the end of the table, now and then nodding and "smiling" a closed-mouth smile, looking at her wristwatch and her pocket watch and the big white-faced clock from Ikea ticking on the wall, or mumbling something to Oskar, in Swedish.

Every year after the first year's vacation in Sweden, Ruby took along a big book. *The Mists of Avalon. War and Peace. Kristen Lavransdatter.* The biggest book she could find. This year it was *The Demons,* the 1,300-page masterpiece by the Austrian World War II veteran Heimito von Doderer. Ruby hated big books, but she always picked the biggest one she could find to take to Sweden because it was a way to submerge herself in something else, like holding her nose and diving into a vat of Jell-O to block out all the mumbojibberish. The day before their flight to Stockholm, she went to the public library with a plastic ruler and scanned the fiction shelves for breadth of spine. Contenders were a number of Micheners, books like *Centennial* that began in the Paleozoic period and moved through time like a slug in catsup up into the present, describing ad nauseam things like tectonics and trilobites, flora and fauna . . . or this, something she'd never heard of: *The Demons.*

On this day in Sweden, Moster Fritjof had planned a long drive into Lapland to visit her retired mentor, Professor Bengt Bengtsson, whose village had been showered earlier that year with radioactive fallout from Chernobyl. All night, Ruby had lain awake in the hard narrow bed Moster Fritjof had made up for her, fretting about another long drive in the energy-efficient, compact Volvo, and recalling the skit from years earlier on *Saturday Night Live* in which Dan Akroyd played a custodian at Three Mile Island who spills a Pepsi on a nuclear reactor's control panel.

The next morning at the breakfast table, Ruby nibbled on a roll and feigned illness—a migraine headache—and in front of both the mumbling efficiency experts declined to make the trip. Oskar and Moster Fritjof mumbled back and forth in Swedish, and then Moster Fritjof rose from the table, glowered at Ruby, and went outside to wait in the Volvo. *Gratis po fodelsdaggen bloober slober,* Moster Fritjof seemed to mumble to Ruby as she squeaked past her in her big black practical rubber-soled clogs, heading for the door.

Oskar the Mumbler was not pleased. He glowered the same glower at Ruby—it was some family glower gene, Ruby concluded—and insisted she go, but Ruby didn't answer. In her sloppy bunny slippers, she shuffled back into the bedroom and climbed into her bed, pulling the heavy blanket over her head. She heard the door slam shut, the car start. She stuck her head out and listened for the sound of the car leaving, but in a second the door opened again, and Oskar the Mumbler came back in. Ruby ducked under the blankets. Oskar the Mumbler stuck his head into the bedroom and mumbled something about an afternoon TV show that Moster Fritjof's dog liked to watch.

The dog?

Oskar the Mumbler slammed the door, and he and Moster Fritjof headed off toward the Arctic Circle.

Ruby counted to three hundred. (Well, almost.) Then she got up and ate almost everything on the table. Six or seven rolls with butter. Three cups of coffee with heavy cream. Two platefuls of cold lutefisk and rubbery potatoes, blackened with coarsely ground pepper. All the cheese but a piece the size of a cafeteria pat of butter. After wrapping the tiny piece of cheese in cellophane, Ruby changed her mind and decided it was best to eat that, too, rather than leave an advertisement in the refrigerator that she'd eaten every bit but that. All day Ruby lay on the couch with a plaid afghan over her pajamas, drinking rose hip tea and luxuriating in the solitude, nibbling on cookies and tarts that she found stored in cans in the root cellar, and flipping through *The Demons,* reading a passage here and there at random and then, half-dozing, making up a story to go with it.

Twice Moster Fritjof's dog—a bulldog named Igor—came into the living room and stared at her, so she let him out into the back yard where he did his business, and upon his return, Ruby gave him a tart or a cookie.

At precisely two P.M., however, Igor jumped up on the ottoman in front of the television and began to bark. Ruby turned on the television set and flipped through the channels. Only four. On one channel, six men in their underpants with big needles stuck to their behinds ran around on a stage filled with balloons, trying to bust the balloons with their "stingers." A digital score card flicked above the stage with each player's name and score: Bjorn-7, Christian-6, Ulf-12, Jörgen-5 . . .

SWITCH. On another channel a surgeon was performing an inner ear operation.

SWITCH. Lutheran aerobics? A woman who looked like Liv Ullmann . . . could it really be Liv Ullmann? . . . from *Cries and Whispers* to this? . . . in a white leotard, down on her hands and knees on a blue carpet in front of a fake stone wall displaying an enormous lighted cross? The Liv Ullmann lookalike was doing a hip and thigh exercise called fire hydrants while an organ played *A Mighty Fortress Is Our God.*

On the next channel . . . woof woof woof woof woof woof woof woof woof . . . *Turbo, Salvo Hunden! (Turbo, Rescue Dog!)*

During the excitement of *Turbo, Salvo Hunden!,* Ruby gave up on *The Demons* and settled into the wonders of Swedish television. After *Turbo, Salvo Hunden!* another operation came on — a dilation and curettage of the uterus, commonly called a D&C, a term that Ruby understood by the doctor's pronunciation of the letters and by the surgical equipment and the preparation for the procedure. The actual operation lasted only about ten minutes and involved a lot of vacuuming of the uterus to remove *skräp* or debris left from a miscarriage or even an intact embryo, an unwanted one or perhaps one that had been determined through genetic testing called amniocentesis, which is conducted during the sixteenth week of pregnancy, to be chromosomally aberrant. This procedure was done by a machine that advertised its maker, ELECTROLUX, on its big stainless-steel body.

The program concluded with the patient being visited by the surgeon the day after the D&C. Although Ruby didn't understand their jibbery conversation, the patient looked happy and gorgeous, like that Swedish actress who sued the pants off of Rod Stewart when he dumped her for another Swedish actress who looked just like her, only twenty years younger. At the close of the show, the patient and doctor sat at a table with a blue-checkered tablecloth, smiling and laughing, eating enormous white bowls of vanilla ice cream with big, shiny spoons, little birds chittering at a redwood bird feeder outside the window.

That's when Ruby threw up.

9. Ruby Driving . . . Again

In 1977, when Crazy Lizzie drove her boyfriend's vintage Cadillac Eldorado into the Atlantic Ocean, she just floored it and drove right up over Ramp 52, flying across the fifty yards of beach right into the surf. It was high tide, and in no time the car had sunk down to the axle; a few months passed before the water reached the fins and then a year or so before the red roof totally disappeared.

It is long after midnight, the tide is turning, and Ruby follows Crazy Lizzie's lead. The termite-mobile hops like a flea over the sand and lands with a plop in the wash. Under the floorboards, Ruby can feel the pulse and pull of the waves, the cleansing, the gentle sucking away of sand, the tickle of foam, the ever-so-gradual shifting and sinking, the easing in and settling down.

"Continental plates," Ruby says to herself. Off to her right in an impressionist's blur, she can make out the blinking red and white lights of sea buoys trying to tell her something in Morse code about the inlet, about life on Earth maybe. The bar — the demarcation — the place where the fresh water from the Pamlico meets the salt water of the sea. "Moaning of the bar . . ." Ruby mumbles to herself. "Wine-dark sea . . . Memento mori . . ."

"Ruby, get out!" Boo is shouting, shining a flashlight in her face and banging on the driver's side window with his fist. A mess of fluke hang from his waist like silver scalps.

"Just unlock the goddamn door!" Boo is shouting. "Ruby wake up! Ruby, what the . . ."

10. Ruby in Bed . . . Again

Sometimes, instead of counting lovers, Ruby tries to remember the names of the roses in Nana Ruby's garden: *Betty Boop, Mr. Lincoln, Peace, Lowell Thomas, Queen Elizabeth, Montezuma, Europeana* (which she thought was *You're a Piano* until recently when she saw the bush in Wal-Mart's garden center) . . . or all eight of the United States that begin with the letter M: *Mississippi, Massachusetts, Missouri, Montana, Minnesota, Maine* . . . let's see, that's six . . . or the names of the nine neighbor children whose surname was Pancake and their parents named each of them after a brand of popular pancake mix, hoping for at least one advertising contract: *Sperry, National, Aunt Jemima, Nabisco, Butterworth, General Mills, Hungry Jack.* . . . Or sometimes Ruby tries naming Boo's brothers, all ten of them, all named after United States presidents, without regard for chronology or party. *Buchanan,* that's Boo. *Lincoln. Jefferson. Washington. Hoover. Harding. Taft. Truman. Eisenhower.* That's about where she gets stuck. *Oh yes, Roosevelt! Hmmm. . . . Monroe? Wilson? Dewey? Or is it Madison? Was there a Fillmore?*

When Ruby first met Boo, she thought this presidential naming prophetic, she and her sister having been named after gemstones: Ruby Jean and Albertine Pearl. If that one child had lived, Ruby would have named it Garnet, be it boy or girl. Garnet Albert or maybe Garnet Van Buren for a boy; Garnet Eva or Garnet Albertine, if a girl. Oh! Van Buren, he was the other one—Boo's identical twin who died, the one his mother chose over him.

11. Ruby Dreaming . . . Again

Some nights Ruby does not lie awake naming and counting or shuffling around out in the garage, pretending she's on *Beat the Clock.* But on the nights she sleeps, Ruby sleeps fitfully. She dreams bad dreams. Often it is the bumper car dream. The first time Ruby had the dream—a few nights after the procedure— she didn't know right away what body of water she was crossing in her dream. She thought it was the sea, the North Atlantic. She thought the forms floating below were icebergs. And then when she awoke, she knew.

But from then on, from that first time when she woke up years ago, sweating and gasping, when the dream comes to her the terror begins almost immediately, soon after her ticket is punched and she's through the turnstile and they have slip-slided across the greased sheet metal floor and picked their bumper cars, and the cars have begun their creaky, lugubrious first movements, the ceiling sprockets just starting to turn, everybody laughing and goofing, leaning over their steering wheels, grinning demonically, hands gripping steering wheels, elbows out.

They're in separate cars, usually, but sometimes Garnet is with her. Garnet's driving. He has swum up through the amnion of time, progressed to eight or ten years old. His hair's the color of marmalade or Silver Queen corn. Sometimes his hair is green, and on one hand there's an extra thumb or maybe little finger; or one eye is blue, the other green; or his cap conceals the curled auricles of enormous elfin ears. But Ruby knows it's him, her son. Ruby's there beside him, her face turned away as he gleefully turns the wheel this way and that, laughing his little-boy laugh. Ruby's face is turned because she knows their destination and he doesn't, and she can't speak it. Sometimes she has a rosary and is worrying the beads, mumbling not the mysteries but something still holy: *Thou art slave to Fate, Chance, kings, and desperate men.* . . . it goes.

Somehow, though, at some point in the dream, Garnet is no longer beside her, and Ruby ends up in her own car, a bumper car of crayon blue that shoots off an exit ramp of the bumper car pavilion and speeds along in the open air. The ramp is narrow, slick, and black, the sky above black as axle grease. Ruby's car races along, bumping against the sidewalls like a bobsled, hitting with such force that she's nearly thrown from the car with every impact. At first it seems like maybe this is part of the amusement ride. A new feature, a new thrill, wild, exhilarating even, but then it goes on too long, like tickling, and the bumping becomes more violent, the movement too fast, and the terrible fear—the terror—begins to seize her.

Where is she? Other cars enter the ramp from nowhere, but it's so dark, she can't see who's in them. She can only hear them, feel them whooshing past, sideswiping, bumping, banging. Ruby tries to let go of the wheel, but her fingers are clamped around it like a parrot's talons on a bar. Like rigor mortis. She's steering frantically, careening off the sides of the ramp; then suddenly the cars burst out into something like an enormous dock or an aircraft carrier's deck, where they skid and spin on the slippery surface. She feels the blast of icy air, the gusting wind, and hears the smack and roar of waves crashing against a wall, but everything's so black, the sky so impenetrably, so utterly black. Then someone cries out a warning: "The River Styx!"

But Ruby, oh, stupid Ruby, what does she hear? *The river stinks!*

A huge wave like a tsunami crashes over the dream's landing, and before Ruby knows what's happening, her car alone is on the crest of it, being borne up, hurled out over the black choppy waters. She's up so high now she's in the sky, she's up among the stars, she sees close up their bad complexions—their enormous pocks and craters—and she knows where she is and what's happening: her life on Earth is over.

I get it, she thinks, almost laughing, really. *I get it now! The River Styx! Damn!*

As Ruby's car hangs there for an impossible moment at the apex of its trajectory, her terror disperses, her lungs empty, the wave collapses, the bottom falls out. She hears a clip of a Beth Orton song, as of a Doppler effect floating on the wake of a car that's just whizzed by:

So much stays unknown until the time has come . . .

Ruby lets go of the wheel and relaxes into the cracked vinyl seat. Everything's out of her hands now. The past, the present, the future: vaporized.

Then begins the plummet, the free fall, rushing down to meet the black water. Behind her and far below, lights twinkle like sequins. A searchlight sweeps the sky. Dark humps appear on the water and distant voices echo all around her—familiar, faint voices, fading in and fading out and echoing back again words Ruby can't quite make out until one voice calls out above all the rest: "Goodbye, Ruby!"

"So long," Ruby whispers to the water.

When Harry Houdini Came to Dinner

It's midmorning on December 31, 1999, and a light snow is falling, a snow so light and fine it's not really falling at all. It's just an airborne, pelletized snow like the little sugar beads on chocolate nonpareils. Or maybe it's just an illusion of snow we're seeing; it's been snowing on and off now for days. Just beyond the edge of town, outside Ruby Reese's window in a swooping, bowl-like field, big, round bales of timothy lie scattered here and there like abandoned bass drums from a phantom marching band, and a rim of dead thistles along the field's rim, gathering a patina of snow, gives the impression of the white mallets used to beat such drums.

To the left of the field framed in Ruby Reese's window, Maple Grove Cemetery climbs a hill to the Methodist church, led by a weather-beaten stone angel with her right, fingerless arm raised in victory and her face turned upward. But in this snowy ghost-parade, the angel recalls a drum majorette with her baton flung high above the snow clouds, a majorette poised in an eternal pause, awaiting her silver baton's fall, the triangle's tinkle, the glockenspiel's call: *Be kind to your web-footed friends . . .*

Come closer and peep in the window. There at the table sits Ruby Reese in her frayed Beacon robe—a glorious discovery at Goodwill—her bunny slippers, and her blue cat-eye glasses with the rhinestone-studded rims. She's drinking Earl Grey tea from a chipped teacup. In the center of the table sits a flower arrangement that has just arrived, delivered by a pimply-faced boy with an obvious cold. Miniature poinsettias and red roses, pink carnations, boughs of pine and holly, sprays of baby's breath, arranged in a silver basket and bearing a tiny gift card on a stick: HAPPY NEW CENTURY, RUBY!! LOVE, ALBERTINE, ET AL. Ruby strips a few pine needles from one of the boughs, crushes them between her fingers, and holds them to her nose. One of the carnations has a broken stem; Ruby snaps off the flower head and sticks it in the uppermost buttonhole of her beautiful blue Beacon robe.

There to Ruby's left is her illustrated *American Heritage Dictionary* and next to that her laptop computer and on top of it a padded envelope plastered with canceled stamps and decorated all over with pen-and-ink drawings. Inside the envelope is a very long letter, hand printed in black ink on graph paper. The letter arrived two days ago, along with a packet of color photographs, which Ruby now looks through slowly, studying each photo before setting it aside: photos of paintings and of an old Airstream trailer camouflaged by a mural of a waterscape and a vineyard, and in one photograph a woman in faded, paint-splattered bib overalls. The woman looks to be about fifty, an attractive, boyish-looking woman who in stature and countenance resembles Sigourney Weaver; a woman with a pretty, freckled face and wild hair; a bright smile; gold hoop earrings; and twinkling black eyes. Ruby leans the snapshot of the woman against the vase of flowers, and the woman in the photo smiles up at Ruby and her cup of tea.

Across the narrow road from Ruby's house and down a steep embankment, a frozen man-made lake creaks and moans under the pressure of expanding ice. Here and there along the bank, amid the twisted rhododendrons, an old sycamore stretches its stiff white arms and yawns. At a fieldstone house across the small lake, a household busies itself with the arrangements for a New Year's Eve party to be held that evening. Outside, along a stone wall overlooking the lake, strings of tiny white lights are being strung by two teenage boys who occasionally toss a stick for an old dog named Bonnard. Bonnard takes a very long time retrieving the stick, lumbering back to the boys in his old-dog stride and wagging his tail in self-approval. Every now and then one of the boys cups his hands and calls out across the lake, "Helllooooo Echooooo," and from Ruby's side of the lake, Echo answers, *Echooooo Echooooo Echooooo.*

Tonight will be the last night of the twentieth century, the last night of the millennium, and Ruby has accepted the invitation to the lake party. "Wouldn't miss it for the world!" she heard her voice saying enthusiastically into her friend Bobbie's answering machine. But did she mean it? Ruby worries that Miles will be there, and if so, will he be alone or with his girlfriend? Surely he's been invited, too, and he has as much right to go as she; after all, they're both friends of Bobbie and Cook's.

There will be a vigil, a midnight buffet and dancing, bayberry candles burning in the windows, spiked eggnog and Bobbie's family's secret recipe Irish cream. And all the neighbors from around the lake and friends from across town will be there, as in years past, to sing "Auld Lang Syne" and watch the disco ball inch its way down to Times Square. But for now, Ruby will do what she's done every New Year's Eve day for the past eighteen years. She will write her annual letter to her friend Vivvy, her companion in spirit, whom she hasn't seen since 1981. Ruby's been working on her letter to Vivvy in bits and pieces for days now, but today is the day she'll do her cutting and pasting, put it all together, and add the finishing touches—her reverie of another year gone down the drain—seal it, decorate it with artwork from her box of old calendars, and send it off to Vivvy.

Ruby clicks open her laptop and fires it up. She refreshes her tea as Windows blares its startup song. She places her elbows on the table, her chin in her hands, takes another whiff of the sweet carnation, and begins to read out loud what she's already written, editing as she goes along.

Walter Cronkite sighs and rolls over.

December 31, 1999

Dear V —,

I've been waiting anxiously these past weeks for your annual holiday letter, and when it didn't arrive before Christmas, I must admit, I feared the worst. You know me, ol' Chicken Little, waiting for the sky to fall. We're living in an age now, though, when anything can happen, rendering my fears more justified than they were twenty-four years ago — has it really been that long since we met?

Viv, I think so wistfully of the day so many years ago when I "landed" on the Banks with Boo, and we bumped into you and Moe right off the ferry. The good ol' days when all of my belongings — and Boo's, too — fit in that Volkswagen microbus, including Phinny. Poor dear old Phinny.

So many times I wonder what would have happened if I'd not up and married Boo! What a time we had, didn't we, that summer when we were all together, sleeping on the beach and skinny-dipping in the moonlight? Drinking tequila and smoking cigarettes and marijuana. Dancing in our gypsy skirts and halter tops. Our thin arms and silver bangle bracelets. Washing out our waitress uniforms in a galvanized bucket every night and laying them out on the myrtle bushes to dry. And all the time Sandy Denny singing, "Who Knows Where the Time Goes?"

Remember the sparkling phosphorus and the night thousands of horseshoe crabs came up on the beach for their annual mating ritual? You and I had fallen asleep early — Boo was working and Moe was off somewhere.

You shook me awake: "Ruby, Ruby," you whispered frantically, "there's something dreadful outside." Your black eyes were fiery bright and your curly hair sticking out every which way! You thought we were on another planet. You had read too much Lovecraft!

Outside there was that gawd-awful clacking like false teeth, and when we opened the tent flap, those dreadful horseshoe crabs were everywhere, the males mounting the females frantically, clumsily, and falling off and landing upside down and kicking their legs like grotesque armored babies throwing temper tantrums! And we didn't know what they were! So big and prehistoric-looking and making that nerve-wracking clacking sound with their tails. (Wasn't it after they mated that their tails fell off—another wonder of Nature!—and the Bankers collected them and hung them on their Christmas trees like icicles?) Phinny, remember, had run away. We found him sitting up in the dunes, whimpering, beating his tail on the sand.

The years pass so quickly, Ruby muses, getting up to pee. And the winters have become milder, the springs more humid, rainier than when she was a child. Back when Ruby was a little girl living in north central Pennsylvania, why, you never saw such snow as they had then! Whenever she reads the beginning of *A Child's Christmas in Wales* (which her father used to read to her and Albertine on Christmas Eve), Ruby is reminded of the endless, boundless snow, the glorious blizzards of her childhood in Ashport: "*I can never remember whether it snowed for six days and six nights when I was twelve or whether it snowed for twelve days and twelve nights when I was six . . .*"

This past summer was the season of the seventeen-year cicada in northern West Virginia where Ruby lives. The cicadas were everywhere—like the horseshoe crabs Ruby was reminding Viv of, only not just for one full-moon night, for weeks and weeks on end, and during the worst heat of summer. After spending close to two decades in underground tunnels, sucking sap from tree roots, the cicadas emerge, mate, lay their eggs, and die. And what a racket they make during this resurrection! Like spring break in Ft. Lauderdale, Ruby imagines, only worse. They began their whirring and drumming every day with the rising sun, and by four o'clock in the afternoon their song had risen to a feverish jungle frenzy so that if you were outside you felt like you were on some spacecraft, winding up its jet turbines, readying itself for takeoff. It was an eternal, incessant *whrrrrrr.* Imagine the universe with a high fever, and this delirious sound as that of its ears ringing! Nearly one hundred degrees every day, and the air as thick as pudding.

In this cicada fever, Ruby began to write a story about a little boy fifty years ago, a little boy with a bent silver spoon who is digging in the dirt in the alley behind his house and uncovers a cicada pupa. There's a young British entomologist in the story who rents an attic room from the boy's mother. The entomologist is pursuing a Ph.D. at the university where the boy's father— a drinker and ne'er-do-well, a violent man—is an accountant. The mother is a black-eyed, curly-haired gypsy who rents rooms and takes in laundry, and flirts dangerously with the young entomologist.

The little boy becomes enamored with the young doctoral student and his butterfly collection—the beautiful blue Morphos and magnificent *Papilio zagreus* from the Venezuelan rain forest —and the student, whose fiancée is his childhood sweetheart in Devonshire—begins to doubt everything about his life: his profession, his engagement, his sexuality. At some point in the story, the killing of the butterflies—pinching the thorax—makes the young entomologist vomit, and he's sickened by all the specimens he has collected, their wings stretched out in mock flight and secured with steel mounting pins on black boards. The little boy is, of course, Ruby.

As Ruby was writing this, the cicadas were emerging from the ground in the graveyard across the street, clinging to the bark of the elms, the red maples, the ginkgoes, and tulip poplars. They were on the stucco, too, on the bottom half of Ruby's house, hanging off it like bag worms, struggling out of their casings like women in wet girdles. The pupae were hideous, but the adults sprouted the most glorious, fairylike wings, transparent and veined with gold threads. Ruby collected a coffee can full of wings. She's shellacked them and has them laid out to dry on a cookie sheet in her garage-workroom, where she's been making them into jewelry for Christmas presents. She plans to send her story and a pair of cicada-wing earrings to Vivvy, along with her letter.

The photos you sent are wonderful, Viv! It must be great living by the city dump, and were I shown a thousand photographs of dwellings, I would have picked without hesitation that old Airstream as yours. The trellis with the Concord grapes and thatched roof, the castor beans and Russian Giant sunflowers crowding out the door, the cleome and the cosmos, the toilet in the gravel driveway painted cerulean blue, and with the giant tomato plant climbing out its tank, a clump of pansies blooming in its hopper. The butterscotch-striped cat and all the mirrors in the lawn! And the mural!

Oh, and I loved the homemade Christmas stationery you found in the recycling bin. People make such wonderful and hideous things now with their digital cameras and scanners, their desktop publishing software, color ink-jet printers and Wal-Mart papers. Oh, I should talk! My millennium card—I went with that instead of a Christmas card this year (see enclosed)—is a photograph I scanned at work of Hale-Bopp, which a Family Dollar clerk down the road took with a 35-mm camera. It looks like a giant sperm, doesn't it, streaking across the inky sky on its blind, errant mission, dragging its star-spangled tail? I couldn't help but quote from Yeats's "Second Coming": *Surely some revelation is at hand . . .*

I'm glad to see you're still painting. From the photos, I

think my favorite painting is the impressionist one with the Banty hens, the tilled garden plot, hollyhocks, and gate. I was wondering: Do you still work on that appliqued quilt you began when you were twelve? When I met you on the Banks it was already quite detailed and you and Moe were still in your twenties. I could lie, I remember, and look at it for hours. All the embroidery! You and Moe standing by the house in the Finger Lakes, holding hands, the grapevine border. Your grandmother with the pet mockingbird perched on her finger. The sunflowers and the swimmers in their bright bathing caps behind her, and the man in the white suit and straw boater. Was that your father? I can't recall. Have you continued with that? I hope you haven't sold it or given it away.

And do you still weave baskets? Remember the bassinet we wove together for me out of sea grasses and cattails, all decorated with scallop shells and shellacked sand dollars and scotch bonnets hanging from strands of raffia? You sang that song about baby Moses and the bulrushes day after day as we worked on it, and I thought it would drive me crazy, but now I can't remember how it goes. It was some kind of round, wasn't it? *Green Grow the Rushes, O? One is one and all alone and ever more shall be so.*

Do you regret never having children? "There are mothers," my friend Moojibur says, "and then there are mothers of invention, and you, Ruby Tuesday, you're among the latter."

It's funny, Viv, that in your letter you should mention *The Underpainter.* Yes, I read it this year, too! Believe it or not, I was poking around a used bookstore here in West Virginia, and I found a copy of it signed by the author, a Canadian! I have another book of hers, *The Whirlpool,*

which is one of my favorite books. It's set in Niagara Falls, but the prologue is a beautiful short piece that appeared first somewhere else, entitled "The Death of Robert Browning." This piece takes place in Venice and the language is so luminous—like reflected, refracted light. All very haunting and essential, somber and beautiful. Like you, what I loved about *The Underpainter* is the landscape, the frozen otherworldliness of it, the looking out across the icy lake for the figure moving closer (Is that him? Is that him?) and the man in the china shop, the man painting teacups. These images now seem to be part of my life. A patina, or an undercoat, I guess.

I must tell you another thing, Viv, that the most astounding thing happened to me this year. In April, quite by coincidence (or accident, take your pick!), I began reading the letters of Helena Petrovna Blavatsky—H.P.B.—or Madam Blavatsky, the famous Russian spiritualist of the early part of this century and contemporary of Harry Houdini. I was in the university library, which is close to the coal fly ash research center, and this book of H.P.B.'s letters literally jumped off a shelf and landed on my foot! It was good I was wearing my steel-toed Doc Martens, because the book (which I have since borrowed indefinitely) is a hefty hardback, and its landing was quite painful in spite of my shoes. I was afraid I might develop another ganglion on the top of my foot, which was the outcome of a similar incident involving a restaurant-size jar of mayonnaise—I'm sure you remember. When the ganglion was removed years later—did I tell you this?—the podiatrist put it in a jar of formaldehyde—in a mayonnaise jar!—and handed it to me! It was an amazingly intricate knot, grayish-white, and resembled a monkey's paw. Do you remember the nautical knots by that name which we often marveled at along the docks?

Ah, but I digress, as they say . . . Anyway, I took the falling book as a sign and proceeded to read it cover to cover.

Remember my telling you once that before I came to the Banks with Boo I had been in love with a boy I met when I was a graduate teaching assistant? I was teaching a freshman composition class, and he came and sat in the back. His name was Etienne Morales and he wasn't registered for the class—he wasn't even enrolled in the university—but he came and sat in the class I was teaching, and he began to write to me—the most beautiful prose—and I wrote back, and we began to meet on the library steps in the evenings and walk through the alleys and up and down the steep stone steps that connect the hillside streets here and to talk long into the night like young people do.

One night we had a tremendous snowfall that lasted into the next day, and that night I stayed in his room, a small room above a noisy bar called the Bon Ton Roulette. He was a very slight boy. His mother was from the West Indies. And he was just my height, with dark, wavy hair, black eyes like yours, and a high-pitched voice like a girl.

Etienne was very interested in Harry Houdini, not the fantastic escape-artist feats Houdini had performed, but in Houdini's part in the spiritualist movement and the Theosophical Society led by Madam Blavatsky. You see, Etienne maintained that Houdini took up the case against spiritualists with such fervor because he, himself, was the real thing, and he saw right through the fakers. Houdini, according to Etienne, dematerialized—he actually left his body—when he performed his impossible feats like escaping from Scotland Yard and from inside a steel-banded packing crate at the bottom of the East River, while wearing handcuffs and leg irons.

Etienne disappeared himself in December 1974, and I never heard anything about him again until a few months ago when I ran into a former student of mine in the grocery store, someone who knew Etienne back then and recognized me, and this fella told me that he'd heard many years ago that Etienne had drowned.

"Just look him up on the Internet," my sister Albertine told me when I told her about Etienne. "If he's got a telephone, he'll be listed on the Internet. And if he's dead, you can check the U.S. Census Bureau. They have this fantastic site where you can search birth and death records. Even immigration records back to the beginning of the nineteenth century."

I admit, I did search the phone directory, but I couldn't find either an Etienne or even an "E" Morales in the whole United States, and I didn't pursue it any further.

Stories about Houdini were not unfamiliar to Ruby. In fact, her mother had eaten dinner with Harry Houdini on more than one occasion. In his youth, Ruby's mother's father — Mason Linn — or Doc as everyone called him — was a traveling magician and acrobat, a musician and circus performer. He had emigrated from Hungary as a teenager and had known Harry Houdini — whose real name was Ehrich Weiss — when Ehrich was just a child. The Linns and the Weisses were from the same part of Budapest, an area with a predominantly Jewish and gypsy population, and were in some way related. Many years later, when Ehrich Weiss was the famous Harry Houdini, he and his wife, Bess (also Ruby's maternal grandmother's name), would stop by the Linns' house — if their appearances brought them to Philadelphia. Ruby's mother, Eva Linn, who was just a little girl then, recalled Harry Houdini making a kielbasa disappear, singing "Auld Lang Syne" in a sweet falsetto, and Houdini and her father walking around the house on their hands. She also swore on the Holy Bible that Houdini climbed up on a chair on his hands and ate his dinner upside down with his stocking feet dangling over his head, but her sister, Frannie, swore on the Holy Bible that that wasn't true.

As coincidence would have it, Etienne Morales was born October 31, 1956, thirty years to the day that Harry Houdini died, and Halloween was also Ruby's mother's birthday. Eva Linn Reese recounted many times her twelfth birthday on October 31, 1926: her father sitting at the dining room table, reading the evening headline in the *Philadelphia Inquirer* about Houdini's death from a ruptured appendix, her iced birthday cake sitting pink and resplendent on the sideboard, her father folding the paper, removing his glasses, and laying his head down on the table.

The last time Etienne and Ruby saw each other — the night of the big snowstorm — they made a vow that when one of them died, he or she would come back and try to contact the other one. Rapping on walls or moving things about or sending messages through dreams and events that might seem to be merely coincidental unless examined closely. That vow and one other one: They promised each other that no matter what happened, they'd meet again on New Year's Eve 1999, on the steps of the university library where they used to meet in 1974.

"We'll be old," they'd said to each other, "that will be twenty-five years from now! Imagine! A quarter of a century! We'll be old and fat and ugly probably, but if we're alive, we'll meet here at the stroke of midnight, as the century rolls over."

"How will I know it's you?" Etienne asked Ruby.

"I'll be wearing a pink carnation," Ruby replied, laughing and quoting Oscar Wilde (or she thought).

And Etienne said to Ruby, "And I, Ruby, I'll be wearing my coonskin cap."

If Ruby closes her eyes and covers her ears with her hands, she can still hear Etienne say that. And don't think she hasn't thought about going there tonight — to the library. It's not far to the university library from Ruby's house, only two or three miles. The roads may be icy, though, and there are other things, that rumor of his death — although the source of that rumor may not be too reliable — and well, it's been so very long . . . And time itself, time is an impediment, Ruby thinks. Twenty-five years! A quarter of a century! He could be happily married. With children. He could be an Amway salesman or a Moonie. Geez! That could be what happened to him! That could explain his disappearance! Why didn't she think of that before? All these possibilities are running through Ruby's head. But still . . . a promise . . .

And as Albertine told Ruby a few weeks ago over the phone, relating the saga of her coworker who divorced her husband of thirty years to marry her old boyfriend, whom she located on the Internet and rekindled the romance via e-mail: "People always want to undo the past; they want to go back and marry that other girl or guy from high school, say, the first love they left behind. They think their life would have been better. But the thing is, if they'd spent the last twenty-five years with *that* person instead of the one they did marry—trying to manage a family and make ends meet, arguing over bills and laundry and bad habits and kids—why, they'd feel the same way about that person. It's that unrequited love thing. You see . . ."

While Albertine was talking, Ruby put her on the speaker phone and looked up *unrequited* in her dictionary, just to check its etymology: unrequited: adj. Not reciprocated or returned in kind. See requite: 1. to make repayment or return for: *requite another's love* [Middle English re- + *quiten,* to pay: see QUIT]. quit: 1. to depart from; leave. [Middle English *quiten,* to release, from Old French *quiter,* from Medieval Latin *quietare, quitare,* from Latin *quietus,* at rest. See QUIET.

These letters of Madam Blavatsky, Viv, they are the most peculiar things. She had traveled—in body or spirit—throughout America, Tibet, Egypt, and even to the North Pole, and in the letters—mostly to her sister and niece in Russia—she explains this curious phenomenon of a Voice—sometimes she calls it a Personality, or Inspiration—which envelops her at times "like a misty cloud," she says, and all at once "pushes me out of myself, and then I am not I anymore—Helena Petrovna Blavatsky — but someone else." This Personality, she says, was a Hindu who was versed in Sanskrit and was an Adept. Sometimes H.P.B. refers to him as an angel. And to make a long story short, H.P.B. became a medium through which spirits of the dead contacted the living, those inhabiting this side of the veil.

You know, Viv, I've always been interested in séances and the occult, even though my horoscope warns of Pisceans delving too deeply into such things. Do you remember the old ornate Ouija board that I found at Goodwill? It was quite beautiful really, a lacquered pecan-veneered tray with ornate letters in an arc, and a triangular planchette that glided on felt-bottomed feet. Remember when we were on that Jane Roberts kick? Reading all her books, *Seth Speaks* and *The Afterdeath Journals of William James*.

And something else: I've always wanted to believe in angels, but then it got to be such a craze. And, truthfully, I had technical issues with them ever since childhood. I wondered about practical stuff like how they got their robes on over their wings. My sister Albertine said their robes were like hospital gowns, open in the back, with just a string tie at the neck. That seemed logical, and the explanation suited me for a while, but then I started to feel embarrassed for them. Why, what if they turned around? And wouldn't it be clumsy flying, I mean trying to keep your robe together with one hand? Imagine flying in a wraparound skirt. And in paintings of angels, this never seemed to be a problem.

Seriously, though, I think the Inspiration or angel H.P.B. refers to is Imagination — what artists refer to as their muse. Who or what is your muse, Vivvy? Have you thought about it? Painted it? Mine, I think, is a mischievous Rumpelstiltskin kind of character. Female. A tinker. A little gnomish bag lady — stooped over, about as tall as a six-year-old, long brown face, one gold tooth, gnarled hands like ginseng root, wearing one of those Polish cotton babushkas, red with blue roses, soiled. She pushes her cart (it has a squeaky, spinning wheel like you get now and then at Giant Eagle) up beside my bed at night —always nights when I'm most sleepy—and whispers in my ear, and hands me little balled-up pieces of paper. Ninety-nine percent of what she gives me is poppycock, and her breath is atrocious (she's a chain smoker and a garlic eater), but now and then, oh, now and then, she's got a little gem all right. Where she got it is beyond me! I guess I don't want to know.

She's a spoiled and selfish little thing. Passive-aggressive, too. I call her Mrs. B. or sometimes just Babushka, but she wants me to address her as Angelique Aimee. You see, what she wants is to tempt me with her wares—the words in her cart—and make me get up and give her my undivided attention, just to prove my love and need. Persistent, too. And if I ignore her, why, the little witch, she'll grab my foot and give it a good twist, so I'll jump up with a horrendous cramp in my ankle or a charley horse in my thigh. And if I still ignore here, she'll leave all right, but leave angry, threatening to hawk her goods elsewhere, and to teach me a lesson, she won't come back for ages—months or years even. I thought I could fool her; I tried sleeping with a felt tip pen and legal pad next to me in bed, thinking I'd be able to serve her without getting up, but now my sheets are all ink stained, and what I wrote was just scribbles, nothing legible enough to be of any use.

Ruby is trying to be lighthearted in this letter to Viv, going on about books and art and muses and recalling the good old days when she and Vivvy were young, but really things have not been going so well for her. Her third husband, Miles, has left her. He's been gone since before last Christmas, since before she wrote last year to Vivvy, but Ruby didn't mention it then because, well, at heart she's an optimist, and she thought his leaving was temporary. But no. Miles is living on the other side of town, and Ruby's heard from Bobbie that he's been seen at the Café of India with a young Oriental woman—a graduate student at the university—about her niece Mattie's age. Imagine! An anorexic-looking young woman with stringy orange-ish hair and a small yippy dog. A Pomeranian or something. And off the wagon again, too, she's heard. Not that he was ever really on it, you know. He jogged alongside it for years, maybe hitching a ride on its running board now and then, but always dragging one foot. Never completely on it, and Ruby pretended not to notice. Maybe she didn't care.

And there's something else bothering Ruby: her heart. Her heart's been acting funny: hiding behind a hollow door in its pink chamber, listening for the slightest sound, and then jumping out at every opportunity like a little child playing Superman, with a towel tied around his shoulders for a cape. *Boo!* Ruby's heart goes every time the phone rings. *Boo! Boo!* when she nearly fell down the cellar steps with Walter Cronkite's bowl. *Boo!* when she didn't see the U-Haul and nearly pulled out in front of it on State Route 119.

She can't sleep at night because of it, and often during the day at work she hides in one of the stalls in the ladies' room, with her hand on her chest and her head against the cool metal door, whispering her favorite words over and over again—ASPEN, TAFFETA, WORCESTERSHIRE, NINCOMPOOP, RAIN-DEER, SQUIRREL—willing her heart to settle down, give up its frantic little paso doble, and leave her alone.

Sometimes at night, Ruby's heart will take a great, sudden plunge like a deep-sea diver and seem to beat from a great depth and with a resonance she can barely believe possible. BOOM-BOOM. BOOM-BOOM-BOOM her heart goes after its big dive, like the loud, reverberating bass blaring from the hot rods at the car wash across from Family Dollar. Still other times, her heart will fly up into her throat and perch on her collarbone like a frightened parakeet, trapped and fluttering, furiously beating its wings against her jugular vein, the small bones, and stringy cords of her neck. There the poor thing perches for hours, and Ruby has developed a habit of holding her throat or stroking her neck to quiet her terrified little bird-heart. "Edgar Allan" she has secretly named her heart after the pretty green and yellow parakeet Albertine had when they were little girls. "Poor Edgar Allan," Ruby coos to herself when she's alone, petting her neck or patting her chest. "Poor, poor little Edgar Allan."

Her heart, sometimes, feels so *other*, like the Hindu, she imagines, who would sometimes inhabit Madam Blavatsky, as if her heart really does live inside her like some poor creature with a secret life of its own. And why not?

Ruby can close her eyes and see so clearly the orange and black cover of the *Ripley's Believe It or Not* her mother forbade Albertine and her to read. Eva had snatched the book away from them, her face red with anger. "I never want to see either one of you with one of these again. Do you hear me? This is trash. Do you hear me? Where did you get this?" she questioned her daughters.

"Yes, Mother," Ruby and Albertine cowered and concurred. "We found it. We found it in the playground. It was nobody's."

But that was a lie. Secretly, Ruby had saved her milk money and had bought the book brand new that day for thirty-five cents at Woolworth's Five-and-Dime. And later that night, after the confiscation, she crept down the back stairway and out into the alley and found the book intact inside a bread wrapper in the trash bin and saved it, and every night after the lights were out and it was safe, she begged Albertine to read it to her under the covers with her Brownie flashlight, both of them thrilled and repulsed by the calf with two heads, the man who could blow out candles with his ear, the boy who could whistle *Dixie* through his nose, the woman who cried stones, the shrunken head that screamed.

It's not just Ruby's heart, though that's acting up. She's been having the strangest dreams. Not just the recurrent bumper car dream. The other night, she dreamed she was dancing with Etienne. She was young again, sitting in her mother's gooseneck rocker, reading *The Search for Bridey Murphy*. Suddenly, Etienne was standing beside her. "Put that down," he said, laughing and extending his hand. And then they waltzed. Her dress was blue but when she awoke she could not to save her life remember the song, but what Ruby heard was her father singing for Albertine and her,

In my sweet little Alice blue gown,
when I first wander'd down into town . . .

And a few nights later, Ruby dreamed the strangest shadow dream. She was lying on her side and a soft brownish shadow, like a weightless rabbit, lay curled against her back. In the dream, she listened to her heartbeat and to her breathing in and out, but the revelation was this: *She was the little shadow, not the body!* She lay against her own body, detached and other, and felt the strongest compassion and sadness for it. Poor old thing. The shadow-Ruby moved across the body to pet it and comfort it, but the body did not stir.

Viv, do you remember the deathplay I've mentioned to you over the years? I think of it as some kind of life work of mine, like the quilt you began embroidering as a girl in thick braids, sitting in an Adirondack chair, watching the geese on Lake Cayuga. I think that everyone should have something like that, some deathquilt or deathpoem, lifesong, lifedance—whatever—as their estate, a statement in some medium—a video, maybe—a little tune played on a kazoo!—about what this life has been. So that the survivors are not left behind, alone and grieving, bewildered, their hands rustling papers, clutching brooches, rattling teacups. Divvying things up. I doubt really, Viv, that we can come back at all. I think that this is it, and frankly, the concepts of eternal life and reincarnation I find utterly exhausting. "Will it never end?" I ask myself, but then I look out the window, at the curve and roll of these little blue mountains, the tangled purple branches of the briars and the snow-covered this-tles in winter, the majestic ironweed in late summer growing out of dung, the calico hem of sweet blue chic-ory and Queen Anne's lace along the country roads, the swooping kestrels and red-winged blackbirds, the indigo buntings, the catbird's song! and Viv, I know if it came down to it—I say I wouldn't—oh, but I'd choose to stay forever and ever. I could never say goodbye.

I've taken up the play again after a few years' hiatus. This act of it, Viv, takes place tonight, on New Year's Eve, 1999, and it's based on a dream I had about this passing of the century, this relay of Time. The scene takes place at a party, a lake house. It's snowing outside, and the guests arrive stomping their heavy boots on the porch and brushing off their coats and scarves in the amber porch light. The air is electric, and inside a fire is snapping. There are etched decanters and cut-glass goblets of sparkling wine; a peppered ham and a turkey glazed with pomegranates; a bowl of kumquats and clementines; and dainty favors of Medjool dates, dried apricots, and candied, spiced almonds, all nestled in fluted pastel pa-pers; eggnog spiked with good whiskey; and homemade Irish cream. There's a good deal of dialogue in this dreamplay about the Y2K bug, about computer viruses and all the things that could go wrong: hospitals, com-munication, banks, governments, weapons, defense and security systems, transportation—everything depend-ent so much on computers.

One of the characters is a party guest who's a survival-ist, a member of the militia really, but no one knows this. He's a project manager at the coal fly ash research center where Ruby works, and he's secretly equipped his truck with two gasoline tanks and outfitted a bunker in a nearby rural county with guns and bottled water, army blankets, and canned goods because he believes there is going to be some kind of terrorist attack tonight.

He's paranoid and on guard and always armed, but none of his friends or coworkers knows this side of him.

Another character is a doctor who's on call — a cell phone on his belt, and there's a middle-aged woman with a heart condition, and two teenage boys who have secretly planned to sneak into the basement and throw the main electrical breaker at exactly the stroke of midnight as a grand practical joke — to frighten everyone into thinking it really is the end of the world, as some suppose. There's a couple from Barcelona who are handing out handfuls of seedless grapes. There's a Spanish tradition, they explain, that in the last minute before midnight, everyone must eat one grape for each of the next twelve months to ensure good luck and prosperity throughout the coming year and an excellent vintage for wine.

As they all wait in mild, sublimated trepidation — in the back of their minds they fear some Armageddon plans — like the Oklahoma City bombing — the new year, the new millennium — it would be the perfect time for such an event. But the new year is simply passing, passing like a prestidigitator's gloved hand across the Earth, passing from the International Date Line, moving west like the setting sun, and everyone knows that, so far, this night is inconsequential. Still they all wait for midnight with some element of ripe fear because they live in America, the richest and most powerful, the most aggressive, the most heavily armed nation in the world.

The woman with the heart condition doesn't feel well. It's nearly midnight, and her estranged husband has just arrived at the party, on his arm a young woman with blue hair who sports a nose ring and a micro-miniskirt. The older woman's head is pounding, and now her heart has pulled up a chair in the percussion section, too, beating with a loud tom-tom syncopation. She shouldn't be here, she's thinking. She should have stayed home. No.

Wait. There's someplace else she's supposed to be. A rendezvous. Someone she promised long ago to meet. Why did she come out here, across the lake, on this frigid night? She's invisible, she thinks, sitting in a shadowed corner in a deep Morris chair while everyone is standing, holding glasses of champagne, counting down the seconds to midnight.

The woman rises shakily and steps through a French door, coatless and unnoticed, onto the snow-dusted deck with its redwood and fieldstone railings twinkling with tiny lights under a crisp organdy of snow. Her heart is pounding, pounding, her breath is short. Inside, everyone is counting, almost shouting the seconds to midnight, and it's in this suspended animation, in one of the spaces between seconds, that some curious revelation comes to her. She begins to think for a moment that she's not really human. She's lived her life, it seems to her now, in some not entirely human way, always on the outside, always on the rim of human emotion, the dusty rim, but never really in the hub, the core of humanness. She's lived only as an adjunct to life, to someone or something —a lover, a spouse, a fear—an auxiliary, a helping verb, being but never acting. Having chosen to remain childless, she's unbound, unentangled, unencumbered, unembraced, free falling—a broken link in the great chain of being. She's an observer only of some spiraling movement through this brief and twinkling moment of life, a person turning quickly, a person alarmed, startled by something flashing in her peripheral vision, which turns out to be nothing more than her own reflection in a shop window.

She's done the right things, it seems, but as if under glass, and now she sees her life more clearly, spread out before her, pinned and sterile and frozen like a mounted butterfly in a glass exhibit case. Or like the cicada, living blindly in the cool underground the vast span of its life, burrowing to the surface only to expire amid incredible noise and heat and confusion. The Y2K bug, the woman suddenly imagines, the Y2K bug is not within some computer, the Y2K bug is within her, inside her! Inside her heart like a worm! But that is absurd! That is some silly, absurd, sci-fi, *X-Files*, *Alien*, stupid plot twist that she can't even believe she — of all people — has imagined! What kind of crackpot would imagine such a thing! the woman thinks, but still, she's frightened, and she trembles uncontrollably at this crazy thought she cannot really fathom, leaning on the railing to steady herself, clutching her throat.

From low in the night sky the Pleiades is slowly rising. Beyond the fieldstone railing, the ice on the lake is shifting, and a large block that has been straining to do so finally breaks free.

Whhhhyyyyyyyyyyyyy? the lake roars as the ice slowly breaks away, and the wind moans through the creaky oaks and sycamores, playing them like double basses. Above the lake's low groan, a sweet, bell-like harmonic — like the eerie sound of a theremin — rings high above it through the thin air.

Whhhhhyyyyyyyyyyyyy? the lake roars again. *Whhhyyyy?* and again the celestial harmonic.

"Hello," the woman calls out weakly across the lake, "Hello Echo . . ."

Echo-echo-echo . . .

"Echo, am I dying?" she whispers to the lake as if it were a polished Ouija board. "Echo, am I living?" The woman is muttering to herself, her hands turning blue with cold, although she doesn't even notice them; she feels warm. She smells something sweet. Perfume, or is it flowers?

"What is life?" she whispers, her brain whirring, head spinning. ". . . a series of anecdotes, episodes . . . saints and sinners, crackpots, curmudgeons . . ." Toward her, gliding closer on the ice, a figure is approaching—a man, a slight man, a man in a coonskin cap, a boy leaning forward with his hands behind his back like he is skating, moving so swiftly as if he were a ludicrous carving on the prow of a ghost ship, and there's a rap-rap-rapping, but the rapping is coming from behind the wall of the woman's chest. And there's another figure—a woman—from out of nowhere—gliding along now beside the man, a woman dancing wildly in her bare feet on the ice, holding out her gay and gauzy gypsy skirt, spinning and twirling on the ice, like a toy ballerina on a magnetized mirror. Her bracelets jingle, her earrings flash.

"Etienne!" the woman calls to them. "Etienne! Viv! Etienne!"

But then the man's coonskin cap turns into a tweed cap with a bill, and the man becomes the woman's father, and the dancing woman, her mother.

Behind her now, the counting has stopped, and from inside comes a muffled commotion and then complete —utter—blackness, a raining sound of tinkling glass followed by a sharp silence. But across the lake, lights of the little community are twinkling. Suddenly the woman is a little child again, a baby, and her father is standing in a field, holding her against his chest. Her knees are bent and her diapered rump sits on her father's strong forearm. Her mother's holding the baby's sister on her hip; the toddler's legs are wrapped around the mother's waist, her arms around the mother's neck, her eyes heavy with sleep. They're standing on a hilltop of whispering, twinkling, tall grasses. It's midnight and midsummer and the field is full of fireflies. A boy is running about the field with a milk bottle, catching fireflies. At his heels, a little brown and white dog runs, too, barking, herding him, trying to keep him on the path. Beyond the field, a stand of aspens is rustling and swaying.

"You can always tell the aspens," the baby's mother has just said, adjusting the child on her hip. The mother's face is in shadow, but her gold earrings shimmer against the curtain of her long black hair. Her voice is melodic. "They sound like ladies in taffeta dresses."

Ladies in taffeta dresses. Ladies in taffeta dresses. Aspens. Dresses.

"Edrych a!" the father says, pointing, his lips brushing the baby's hot forehead, her soft, fine curls. He speaks the word in a beautiful, sing-songy language the baby understands.

"Edrych a! Look! Look, Ruby," he whispers against the baby's temple, "look at the millions of fireflies! All the world's full of fireflies for little Albertine and baby Ruby!"

The baby is looking in amazement, too, in wide-eyed wonder at the beauty of this fairy-tale apparition. She stretches out her arm and points, too, into the darkness, into the night, into the twinkling, whispering grasses — the glittering cusp of midnight — her tiny finger pointing, taut and firm. She opens her mouth, but she has no words to say it.

PERMISSIONS

ACKNOWLEDGMENTS
AND APOLOGIES

Who would have guessed that in the end these acknowledgments would be so hard? They should come first. So many people have helped me in so many ways with so many different parts and so many different aspects of writing this book and with claiming (finally), stepping into (however late and awkwardly), and zipping up (however tricky the zipper) this itchy writer's suit. How can I ever thank them or even find them all? From suggesting changes in genre, content, structure, organization, and point of view, down to reaching in with a steady hand and a pair of tweezers to pluck out a dangling modifier—and everything in between—they all have helped me, given me their precious time, their understanding, their friendship, their blessings, their gifts, their fine example. It all adds up and fits together.

There were factual and temporal blunders (at one point, a thirty-seven-year-old dog) and words pretending to be other words and missing words and words that had no business being there at all. There would be reading and rereading and *(Oh no, Mr. Bill!)* reading again—all the incarnations. It was a long winter, but then suddenly there was coltsfoot and spring peepers, ramps and forsythia, Baltimore orioles, trillium, bloodroot, bluebells, bees! And so it's been that through this quagmire of darkness and destruction, illusion and confusion: war, my charmed little life has flitted above it all like *ignis fatuus*. An amazing, unsettling grace. If there is anyone I have offended, I beg your forgiveness. I never meant to do you wrong. Thank you, all.

I am especially indebted to Gail Galloway Adams, Timothy Dow Adams, Peggy Andreas, Jo Ann Beard, Hywel Bishop, Gail Bossart, Jeanne Boury, Mark Brazaitis, Greg Carte, Jonathan W. Chaste, Ann Dacey, Harriet Emerson, Betsy Evans, Cathie Falvey, Louise Lamar Fuller, Winston Fuller, Sharon Goodman, Carolyn Hampson, Jim Harms, Sandra Grace Hartwell, Larry Ivkovitch, Andrea Rosen Lucci, Michael Lucci, Diane Meier, Alison Kerr Miller, John L. Moore, Beth Nardella, Tracy Novak, Keith Oderman, Bob Rossi, Donna Sims, Carol Houck Smith, Martha Swiss, Donna Jean Tolbert, Jane Vandenburgh, and Betty Wiley. And also to my two big fans: Worty Gide and Minkie (R.I.P., 1981–2001).

Special thanks to Ursula Hegi; the Bread Loaf Writers' Conference; faculty and students in the MFA in Creative Writing program, Department of English, West Virginia University; Canaan Valley Institute; the West Virginia Commission on the Arts; the literary journals listed on the copyright page of this book, which have published my stories; my family and many other friends too numerous to mention; and always, my husband, Kevin Oderman, with whom I am enormously pleased.

Extra credit to Corrina Lesser and Brandy Vickers at Houghton Mifflin, who envisioned this work as a novel; to my sister, Jane E. Moore, who rewrote "When Harry Houdini Came to Dinner" for me; and to those who dwell beyond this vale, for all the gifts they gave — all the stories, all the words and names.

BREAD LOAF AND
THE BAKELESS PRIZES

Since 1926 the Bread Loaf Writers' Conference has convened every August in the shadow of Bread Loaf Mountain, in Vermont's Green Mountains, where Middlebury College maintains a summer campus. The conference, founded by Robert Frost and Willa Cather—a generation before creative writing became a popular course of study—brings together established poets and prose writers, editors, and literary agents to work with writers at various stages of their careers.

While part of Bread Loaf's reputation was built on the writers associated with it—W. H. Auden, Wallace Stegner, Katherine Anne Porter, Toni Morrison, and Adrienne Rich, to name a few —it has an equally high reputation for finding and supporting writers of promise in the earliest stages of their careers. Eudora Welty, Carson McCullers, Anne Sexton, May Swenson, Russell Banks, Joan Didion, Richard Ford, Julia Alvarez, Carolyn Forché, Linda Pastan, Ellen Bryant Voigt, Andrea Barrett, and Tim O'Brien are some of the poets, novelists, and short story writers who benefited from early associations with Bread Loaf.

There are many obstacles to a successful literary career, but none is more difficult to overcome than the publication of a first book. The Katharine Bakeless Nason Literary Publication Prizes were established in 1995 to expand Bread Loaf's commitment to the support of emerging writers. Endowed by the LZ Francis Foundation, whose directors wished to commemorate Middlebury College patron Katharine Bakeless Nason and to encourage emerging writers, the Bakeless Prizes launch the publication career of a poet, fiction writer, and creative nonfiction writer annually. Winning manuscripts are chosen in an open national competition by a distinguished judge in each genre. (Past judges include Andrea Barrett, Ursula Hegi, Francine Prose, Edward Hirsch, Tomas Mallon, Louise Glück, and Yusef Komunyakaa.) The winning books are published in August to coincide with the Bread Loaf Writers' Conference, and the authors are invited to participate as Bakeless Fellows.

Since they first appeared in 1996, the winning Bakeless books have been critical successes. As a result, the Bakeless Prizes are coveted among new writers. The fact that Houghton Mifflin publishes these books is significant, for it joins together one of America's oldest and most distinguished literary presses with an equally distinguished writers' conference. The collaboration speaks to the commitment of both institutions to cultivate emerging literary artists in order to ensure a richer future for American writing.

MICHAEL COLLIER
Director, Bread Loaf Writers' Conference